MW00680013

ERASED

by

Sharon Evans-Rose

ERASED
by Sharon Evans-Rose

To order additional copies of this book or for book publishing information, or to contact the author:

Publisher Page
P.O. Box 52
Terra Alta, WV 26764

Tel/Fax: 800-570-5951
Email: mybook@headlinebooks.com
www.publisherpage.com

Publisher Page is an imprint of Headline Books

ISBN: 9780929915534

Library of Congress Control Number: 2007925801

Book Design by Travis Adkins
Cover Photo by Stephen E. Wood

PRINTED IN THE UNITED STATES OF AMERICA

Dedication

To two men in my life:

My father, John W. Evans, Jr. who was an avid reader and encouraged me to learn about life, culture, history, and the country through novels. I miss you Daddy.

My husband, Jerry L. Rose, who took me off my father's hands and continued bringing me into adulthood sanely. Growing me out of fears, quirks, shyness and lack of self-confidence into a mature, speak your mind, well adjusted adult through love, constant encouragement and—I know—many "What have I gotten myself into?" thoughts. Thank you for forming my backbone, my strength and my wonderfully happy life.

Acknowledgments

Mark Neil, assistant prosecuting attorney—
Thank you for keeping me in the correct
judicial system.

WOAY TV Weather Department for teaching
me which way the wind blows.

PROLOGUE

IT HAS BEEN said that each snowflake has its own physical characteristics, making it unique unto itself. In a sense, snowstorms are also played out in like manner.

When temperatures are extremely cold, a snowfall isn't usually severe. The flakes are small and often resemble tiny glassy slivers. In such a case, they aren't able to cling to anything, so, instead, they are blown around, unable to set up a measurable accumulation.

However, when a storm forms at the beginning or end of the winter season, or during a mild spell, it can lay a blanket two to three feet deep in a matter of hours. During these times the warm temperatures allow large snow flakes to fall heavily, grouping together in friendly accord.

The clouds gathering early on this late February morning should have warned the residents of North Carolina that the day wouldn't end as it had begun. The darkening gray skies cast a yellowish hue, suggesting that what was to follow wouldn't result in the usual cold rain.

The weather conditions were ripe for setting up a healthy nor' easter. Meteorologists watched carefully as both the north wind and the moisture from the gulf began moving toward each other. Timing was essential for determining the path of the storm.

Advanced technology and trained personnel allowed predictions to hit their target more often than not. If, however, the northeast wind picked up speed, the storm could dip into the South unexpectedly and immobilize areas.

When snow hits the North, southern Virginia and all states south thereof usually receive the residual effects in the form of rain or slush and ice. Then warmer temperatures cause a quick melting. Since snow is not common to these parts, the Department of Highways isn't prepared nor the road crews equipped to handle an accumulation. Therefore, when it does arrive with force, everyday activities are altered drastically.

Schools close and children enjoy a rarity in all manner of ways. Teens have been seen in boats being pulled around the streets by cars, little ones ride down hills on makeshift cardboard sleighs. Snowmen go up everywhere, only to be gone in a matter of days, and snowball fights are waged in fun by laughing friends of all ages. If only for a day, life is changed for the young and the old.

Adults and children alike are enthralled by the beauty that abounds. All ordinary everyday activities are ignored in the diversion from the norm. Work ceases by the hand of the Almighty and there is no class division. Everyone is at His mercy—everyone, that is, except those who drive SUV's. The four-wheel drives, although worthless on ice, have freed the snowbound almost universally.

Nevertheless, a heavy snow anywhere can wreak havoc on a population. The weight of the snow brings limbs and even whole trees to the ground, many taking power lines with them. Crews work days, sometimes weeks, to clean up after a storm.

This approaching clash of weather systems gave no warning of the shift in wind direction. It surprised everyone and those who had headed to work with umbrellas found they should have carried shovels. A normal day, many thought, but lives were about to change—some through injuries, others because of loss, and one by a stranger's hand.

CHAPTER
1

ABBY AND THE driver were sitting in the vehicle as the snow rapidly covered the windshield. Abby's companion had tried in vain to convince her to change her mind, but she refused to put herself back into a life of semi-happiness. After the morning's initial shock, the discovery had almost cast a blanket of relief over her.

"No," she said once more. Looking down into her hands resting in her lap, she shook her head slowly as she continued, "It's over. Done!"

She felt a gentle hand rest upon her head then move slowly over her crown before it grabbed a fist full of auburn locks and jerked, pulling her head back and her chin up. The pain made her eyes water. Unable to turn her head, she felt, more than saw, the face move to the side of her head. Deep angry breaths warmed her ear.

It was a whisper. Menacing, threatening and deliberate in its message. One breathy word at a time.

"No. It's. Not. Over."

A twist of the wrist caused an intense burning. She was filled with the fear that her scalp could be pulled away from her skull.

"Not yet!" the whisperer added.

She stretched her body upward in an effort to shorten the tight grip on her. Suddenly the hair was released and before she could recover, her head snapped with the blow to her left cheekbone. In stunned disbelief she gasped. Fumbling for the car's door handle, she stared into maddened eyes as the threat continued.

"You will *not* do this!" her assailant shouted as her upper arm was grabbed so tightly she winced in pain. "I won't allow it. Do you hear me?" There was another punch, this time opening a gash in her lower lip.

She pulled on the handle, oblivious to how much the weather had worsened as the vehicle had wound its way up the mountain. Her attention had been focused totally on the driver as a nagging uneasiness tugged at her.

Pulling herself free from the bruising grip on her arm, she turned toward the door. A hand grasping the back of her head pushed hard and quick, as one would crack an egg, hitting her face against the side window. The door opened and she tumbled out into a depth of five or six inches of heavy, wet snow that was continuing to fall as though it had a mission. Pushing onto her knees in an effort to rise, she turned to see a hand reaching into the glove compartment.

"I'm sorry you've brought things to this end." Spoken without feeling, the voice was now calm.

The hand holding a gun, turned to take aim. Slamming the door, she knew the only chance of surviving this ordeal would be to quickly put distance between them. Pushing herself upright and moving at as urgent a pace as the snow would allow, she headed off down the narrow road toward the woods.

Running was impossible. Frantically, she put great effort into pulling her feet from the depth of the snow, but her numbing limbs defied her futile efforts. She glanced over her shoulder to see the barrel of a gun pointed at her through the lowered window.

"No, oh God, please no!" she cried out.

"Good bye, Abigail," were the last words she heard before the deafening blast. The impact hit her in mid-stride. Her leg buckled and the force threw her face-first into a large tree trunk. She bounced to the left and went down on her side, her head above her ear connecting with a large protruding rock. Suddenly, unconsciousness ended her fight for survival.

Lowering the gun and trudging from the car toward the fallen Abby, her attacker stood watch, waiting for movement. There was none. Transfixed, the mind at first, did not register the spread of crimson in the snow.

A deep breath and a shiver aroused the senses, and with the vision of blood came the knowledge that if she were not already dead, she couldn't last long. This prompted the decision not to risk the sound of another gunshot. The temperature was dropping and the snow, already covering her limbs, showed no signs of letting up. What luck! This isolated area and weather conditions assured that the discovery of the body would be far into the future and, if good fortune continued, the animals would eliminate the possibility of her ever being found.

The gun would be disposed of in the not yet frozen lake on the way down the mountain. All evidence would disappear. This couldn't have gone better if it had been planned.

The deed done, although abrupt, but with astonishing efficiency, brought relief and security. A sense of self pride in accomplishment always followed every effort at completion. Even the difficulty of spinning the SUV into a turnaround did not dampen the elation. With the radio now offering up the expected inches of snow, the vehicle slowly left the scene.

Rafe stopped abruptly, the fishing pole in one hand while the other carried his catch. He stood rigidly erect and slowed his breathing to complete the silence. He listened. Could what he heard have simply been a small tree or branch having succumbed to the weight of ice and snow?

In the outdoors, one couldn't always tell from which direction a sound came. Waiting quietly, he heard the murmur of an automobile motor. Revving and stopping, revving and stopping. Perhaps it had backfired. Finally, securing an intuitive reading on it, he turned his head until both ears picked up the sounds.

Suddenly, headlights appeared and Rafe stood still amid the trees until the auto vanished and the engine was no longer audible. With a frown he continued his trek but curiosity altered his direction.

The few times he had known anyone to venture up this mountain had been due to a wrong turn or lovers seeking privacy. The unpaved road was not much more than a wide path and he had posted the land for no trespassing.

As dusk quickened its pace, so did Rafe. He glanced around as he moved about, seeing nothing but the beauty of the wonderland the snow was rapidly creating. The time, just between dusk and dark, cast a smoky glow with silky ribbon shadows. He loved it here. Every season clothed this mountain in its own glory, but almost never with such a heavy coat.

He had left his cabin early this morning in the hopes of making it to the lake, catching a few fish for dinner and getting back before the rain started. He had, thankfully, taken a rain cape with him. It was tied comfortably around his neck to protect his clothing from the moisture. Snow, certainly, had not entered his mind or he would have planned to open a can for his evening meal.

Counting himself fortunate to have tucked a pair of gloves in the pocket of his parka, he had put them on and pulled the hood up over his head when the precipitation first started. Had this not been the case, he would have had to abandon his catch and fishing gear long ago to allow himself to pocket his hands. He always wore his heavy boots when traversing the woods. This gave him traction in all kinds of conditions and protected him from unwanted bites of any kind. He was warm, dry, and undisturbed by the change in weather.

He paused to enjoy this phenomenon before shaking the snow from his shoulders. It was time, he decided, to head to the cabin.

Correcting his destination, he turned abruptly and almost tripped as his foot struck an object beneath the snow. A moan locked every muscle in his six-foot-two inch frame. His eyes lowered suddenly and he knelt down and laid aside his pole and intended dinner. A spreading dark area in the snow shook him into sudden anxious movements. This vision fired a sickening fear to his questioning mind. Steam was rising from the dark, bloodied, icy carpet beside him.

Brushing the snow rapidly from side to side, he quickly uncovered a form. The lack of good light prevented a clear view, but it appeared to be that of a female. Another moan spurred him into action. He removed the plastic cape and wrapped it around the injured figure. Picking up her bundled body with ease, he headed to his mountain house, pulling one foot after the other from the deep snow in a careful effort to keep himself from falling.

Reaching the cabin, he placed the body on the fur rug in front of the hearth and fading fire. Throwing more logs onto the diminishing flames, he blew into the hot embers and flipped on the lights. He moved quickly into the bedroom where a second fireplace was tended to before turning on the bedside lamp.

He had installed a generator when he bought the cabin, but kept the temperature set low so he could enjoy a glass of sherry while reading by the firelight. The sheer contentment and crackling fire often produced a peaceful sleep that transferred him right into the story line, until the dying fire and coolness would prompt him to seek the bed. Now, concerned about his injured guest and hypothermia, he turned the temperature to a higher setting.

Returning with a large towel and blanket, he lowered himself to his knees. After peeling the plastic cape back, but allowing it to remain underneath, he covered the limp form with a soft blanket and cushioned the woman's grossly injured head with folded towels.

It was disturbing to look at her. The left cheek was turning purple and her eye had become a mere slit in the swelling. The right side of her forehead was distorted by a huge, scraped hematoma-induced knot and the blood beneath the skin was forming an ugly black eye. A small chin rested below a bloody and swelling lower lip. Her head was tilted slightly in his direction, allowing the light from the fire to reveal the sticky red substance matted in her golden-flecked auburn hair above her ear. His gaze followed the thick dark fluid running down her neck.

Her lack of consciousness must be the result of a concussion. She was so deathly still he leaned his ear to her chest and reached for a wrist to feel for a pulse. Yes, she was breathing and her heart was beating, faintly.

It was then he caught sight of his blood covered arm. He had been so involved with her facial injuries he hadn't considered there could be others. Straightening onto his knees, he pulled the blanket down slowly while scanning her person until he caught sight of the clothing on her right side. It was saturated.

This little lady has big problems, Rafe thought. He stood, removed his heavy winter parka and placed it on a chair. Rolling up his shirt sleeves, he headed to the kitchen.

CHAPTER
2

SEATED FORWARD ON the sofa, with forearms resting on his knees, Tom held a glass in both hands. Nursing the Makers Mark whiskey, he stared unseeingly at the face of Fox's newscaster. Whether this perfectly groomed man was reporting on the war, the coming election or the current high profile court case didn't penetrate Tom's alcohol-dulled thoughts. He was lost in the memories of six or seven years past.

Tom Cummings and Abby Langford had met at a wedding reception. He caught the eye of this small of stature, lovely young woman and returned her persistent glances.

Without hesitation, she approached him. "I've come to see how you would look if you smiled."

Taking her suggestion, he smiled pleasantly and asked, "Is that a pickup line?"

"Absolutely!"

A whirlwind nine months of dating followed before they eloped. Two lonely people coming together for love—or was it companionship? And now, six and a half years later their marriage was disintegrating.

It had been tough going between them for almost a year now. When Abby learned about the affair she almost left him. Tom begged forgiveness with promises of never straying again. In an effort to save her marriage, Abby stayed with him. However, she was unable to forget and each time he was late or out of town, her suspicions mounted. She never made accusations but Tom knew she doubted, and that, in turn, had changed their relationship.

Tom picked up the remote and turned the television off. It was unwanted noise at this point. He leaned back and put his hand on the soft throw Abby used to cover her feet on cold evenings. They would sit together by the fire, Abby reading while he napped, totally at ease and comfortable in each other's company. Tom suffered at the thought of having had such happiness no longer available to him.

He drained the glass and set it on the side table. Adjusting his position in order to rest his head on the back of the chair, he locked his fingers over his chest, put his feet on the ottoman and gazed unseeingly through the windows.

Alice! That stupid receptionist. This is all her fault.

Once again, Tom's mind replayed the morning's events. He had been facing the windows, and with his back to his office door and the phone to his ear, he neither saw nor heard Abby enter. She waited quietly for him to finish his call.

"Listen, Mags, I told you I can't be there this time. I promised Abby I'd be home this weekend. I don't have a legitimate excuse for leaving town again." He paused, then continued, "I know it's important and I promise I'll make it up to you." Another pause and then he laughed deeply.

"You bet I—" he was saying as he turned to find Abby standing across the desk looking at him with fire blazing in her dark eyes. He blanched as he dropped the receiver into the cradle. "I didn't hear you come in."

"Obviously!" She walked behind the desk. Removing her wedding rings and slipping them into his pocket, she said, "I want you out of here." She brought her face closer to his as she added, "Right now!" She took a deep breath as she continued, "And, when you get home, start packing. You have until tomorrow night to vacate the house. I'll not come home until then. I don't want to see you and I don't want you to call or come around me again. As of this moment, you and I are over." She kept her voice strong and even, but her eyes were aglow with the anger in her heart.

Leaning over his desk, she pushed a button on his intercom and when Donald answered she said, "Don, you just got a raise and a promotion. Please be prepared to take over tomorrow. I'll be in to talk with you in a few days."

As she clicked off, Tom's hand grasped her wrist. She did not look up as she waited for him to release it.

"I love you, Abby. Don't do this." It wasn't a plea. It was a strong statement.

She neither spoke nor moved. His grip tightened slightly. Finally, twisting her arm, she slipped free, turned and walked from the office without closing the door.

"Alice, you'll be assisting Mr. Freeman as of tomorrow. He'll be taking over for Mr. Cummings," she announced to the stunned woman.

Abby turned her head to look once more into the shadowed eyes under the furrowed brow of her husband. He stood erect, a strong and handsome man, with fists clinched by his sides. *What a waste*, she thought as she wondered when she had stopped loving him. She closed her eyes, inhaled deeply, then turned and left the building. A stricken and disbelieving Tom moved to the doorway and watched her enter her car, where she sat quietly a few moments before driving off.

Tom made his way to a trembling Alice. He glared at her as he asked, "Why didn't you notify me she was coming in?"

"She asked if you were alone and I told her you were on the phone, but she walked right past me, promising to be quiet, and entered before I could do anything."

He had moved to her desk where he leaned toward her and looked menacingly into her eyes. Slamming his fist onto her desk, he said, "Then you're too damned slow!"

Tom roused himself from the memory.

How dare Abby have done that to me. All this trouble was her fault anyway. If she had stayed on at the mill, he would never have hired Maggie!

Abby's parents had perished in the crash of their private plane, leaving their entire estate to their only child. Abby was living and working in Paris at the time, so her life changed drastically overnight.

Don Freeman, who had been her father's right hand man, helped her in managing business matters until after her marriage. Tom, then, stepped into her role at the mill, allowing her to pursue an interest in publishing. With a promise to return if the magazine failed, she left the running of the mill to Tom and Don.

Yes, she should have stayed! He picked up the phone and dialed.

"Hello," the sultry voice drawled.

"It's over," he told her.

After a slight pause, she said, "I'm sorry, dear, but you'll survive."

"Were you born without feelings or was it an acquired defect?" he asked.

"Now darling, let's not be a cry baby."

"Maggie, you heartless bitch. This is what you wanted, isn't it?!"

"Bitch? That's nice! What *we* wanted, dear. Now tell me about it."

CHAPTER 3

RAFE SAT IN a chair with his right ankle propped on his left knee, his elbow on the chair arm and his jaw resting upon his fist. His eyes closed briefly as exhaustion set in, but almost instantly he jerked as they opened again to look at this small, still figure on the bed. The firelight made her look so frail.

"Who are you?" he said softly.

He put his foot on the floor, clasped his hands and stretched them over his head, then leaned back with his arms folded and continued his vigil. How had she gotten into this predicament? She hadn't come alone and whoever brought her up this mountain had done so for the sole purpose of disposing of her, and evidently assumed the deed had been accomplished.

With the exception of a pair of diamond studs in her ears and her gold watch, she wore no jewelry. The soft fabric of the beige pant suit exuded quality. Her disappearance, most certainly, would not pass unnoticed.

A physical attack had taken place on her person, but nothing, including her nose, seemed to have been broken. It appeared that some of her head injuries probably resulted from a forceful fall. This young woman had been shot, but the bullet had entered and exited her side, apparently missing all organs. She was fortunate to have received such a dangerous wound without greater damage. If no infection occurred, her side should heal nicely.

The head wounds were another matter. The superficial damage would leave no permanent scarring or disfigurement, but he didn't know what might be happening inside the head. She was still unconscious and he was unsure of the cause. His hope was that no bleeding or swelling was occurring in or on the brain. Without x-rays he could not correctly assess the damage, but the storm had made it impossible to get to a hospital.

He always kept his "house call" bag with him, especially on the mountain, as he never knew what animal might take him by surprise. This, fortunately, made it possible to work with more than boiling water.

Removing her wet clothing, he had cleaned and treated even the scratches. He then left her free of clothes. He wasn't sure if there were any internal injuries and he didn't think he should maneuver her about when she was unable to let him know if it hurt to do so. Blankets were added for warmth.

He remained seated and closed his eyes. As the trees gave way to the weight of the snow, Rafe could hear the snapping of branches and the slow cracking of trunks as they split. A whooshing sound followed as the limbs smacked and scraped against others on their descent. When a tree went down, the sound of the thump gave him an idea of its size. He was in awe, never having experienced the mighty hand of nature in such a destructive way. The fringe of a nor'easter had been bad, but to be in the grips of the full-blown storm was a great leveler of humanity.

These sounds intruded upon his dreams every time he had drifted off during the night, and each time he was thankful the house had been spared. He thought about the roadway down the mountain and hoped it wouldn't be blocked by trees and debris.

There was only a slight lightening of the sky when she stirred briefly. He picked up a bottle of antibiotic and removed the dropper. Squeezing the bulb until only a small amount of liquid remained in the stem, he put the point between her half swollen lips and emptied the tube. Then, he turned to the straw in the glass of water. Putting his finger over the opening of one end, he lifted it, placed it between her lips, released a small amount of liquid and waited until she swallowed before repeating the process twice more.

When he was certain she had calmed, he stretched his legs out in front and, again, closed his eyes.

Yes, she should have come back!

Tom had hung up the phone, but remained seated. His thoughts were still berating Abby.

She had formulated an upscale magazine in a small unused area at the mill. Her idea was to provide the public with access to areas and aspects of high fashion, jewels, design, the life of business barons, cuisine, travel and anything that the rich know and the dreamers read about.

When Tom didn't think it would go anywhere, the venture seemed to take on a life of its own and as it grew, the Langford Mill office complex added an extension for her use with the magazine's own entrance. In the beginning, *Success* published only every other month, but then developed into a more mature monthly that serviced several southeastern states and was well on its way to becoming national.

Abby needed some experienced help and she immediately thought of the one person from her past that would be perfect for the job. Her childhood cohort in mischief, Ethan Bland, who was presently employed as a literary consultant at a publishing company in Atlanta.

Ethan was born on the other side of the tracks, as the older generation would have said, but he managed to gravitate to the backyards of the wealthy. These children accepted him into their fold and so he learned how those with money lived.

Having been groomed by his friends, he developed a need and drive to become more than he otherwise would have. Academia was only a part of his education. He soon found that social skills could also be very important in the advancement of position.

When the play years ended and high school began, he studied and worked very hard to help form a basis for his future. While the others were now involved in debutante balls, sailing, clubs and other activities, Ethan often found himself alone.

Abby enjoyed his company and felt he was a friend in which she could confide. Their relationship continued until college separated them. Eventually they lost contact. She had only recently read about his position in Atlanta.

With high hopes of seeing him again, she sent him an S.O.S. He jumped ship and moved to Charlotte. Abby had been blown away with the change in his appearance.

"You look like a man of the world, Ethan," she had chided. "So elegant and prosperous! And listen to yourself—you sound like quite the executive."

Tom, on the other hand, felt he looked too primped. At any rate, Tom learned to appreciate Ethan's assistance to Abby and she, in turn, was pleased when the two men adjusted to each other and eventually became friends.

Today, Tom needed to speak with him. He called the magazine office and asked for Ethan.

"Have you two made up?" Ethan asked when he took the call.

"I haven't heard from her. Is she there?"

"No, but I told you yesterday not to worry. You got through this once—and I can't believe you did it again—but she'll come around." Ethan was consoling in his scolding.

"I'm not so sure. I've never seen her so angry, yet totally in control. She said she wouldn't come home until tonight, when she expects me to be gone. I really thought she'd show up for work. I need to talk to her."

"And what did you want to tell her this time? Do you have a new promise or were you simply going to repeat the old one?" Ethan was skeptical of Tom's wants.

"Bland, you're such an insufferable bastard! Can't you see I'm teetering here? I thought you would at least lend a sympathetic ear."

"I would be glad to do that for Abby, but I guess that will have to wait until she's ready," Ethan replied.

"No pity for the guilty? I know, I know, I don't deserve it. I really have been selfish and I want to let her know I'm so ashamed. Don't say it—too little, too late."

There was a pause in the conversation; Tom lost in his misery and Ethan questioning his lack of compassion for his friend's cheating husband.

16

"You know Abby is always the last one to arrive in the morning," Ethan reminded him. "She stops at Ground Beans for coffee and a scone. Maybe she stayed for a second cup today. Besides, the roads are a mess and the city is almost deserted. Power is off in large sections and the crews are having trouble getting around. Half the staff called to say they would get here when they could and the others can't even make it. She could be very late—if she gets here at all."

"I'm sure you're right," Tom admitted. "Well, call me if she comes in."

"You'll probably hear from her before I do. Now stop fretting and we'll talk later." Ethan dismissed him and rushed back to this month's personal biographical business section.

Ethan titled it *The Climb*. It was his baby and a successful contribution to the magazine's articles. Its focus was on the trials of a man or woman who grew from nothing into the hierarchy of business and wealth through persistence and hard work. He loved his job, and with each of his specials he thought, *One day this will be me.*

Waking abruptly, Rafe was shocked at having slept so soundly. He jumped up and stood over his charge. Pulling back the covers slightly to check for respiration, he relaxed at the rise and fall of her chest. Laying his hand gingerly on her neck and then her forehead, he was satisfied there was no fever.

With the fire dying and the room beginning to cool, he slipped into his heavy coat and boots and retrieved enough wood for several days. After stoking the fires, he washed up and redressed his patient's wounds. The swelling in her face had gone down only a fraction but he could tell that she was going to have delicate features.

Rafe busied himself about the cabin, occasionally making quick checks in the bedroom. By mid-afternoon, he had everything in its place and a pot of soup on the stove. He sat down on the blanket covered sofa and reached for the radio. He turned it on but couldn't pick up a station.

Downed lines, he figured.

The fire and solitude lulled him to sleep. A couple of hours later he awoke, he lay very still, enjoying his hideaway. No TV, no phone, no neighbors, no—

"Oh No!" he yelled, jumping from his reverie as the aroma of home cooking invaded his senses. A quick check in the kitchen proved the soup had simmered just long enough.

Sauntering back toward the fire he glanced through the bedroom door. Eyes widening, he gasped, "Oh my Lord, where's my mind?"

Abby was sleeping fretfully. He checked her once again to find her body much warmer.

This could be bad, he thought.

With a pan of tepid water and a cloth, he sat beside her, uncovered one limb at a time and sponged her off. He rolled her onto her good side and wiped the cool cloth down her back, then eased her onto her back again to cool her neck, chest and tummy. Her skin was so smooth and beautiful. Like porcelain. She must be younger than he, but until the swelling went down he wouldn't know for certain.

He covered her lightly and returned to the kitchen for a healthy bowl of nourishment. After the kitchen cleanup, he filled the pan with warm water to repeat the cooling off treatment.

As nightfall approached, she began to shake with chills. Her restlessness made it difficult for him to even get the dropper into her mouth. After watching her suffer for some time, he added wood to the fire, stripped down and stepped into the bottoms of his long underwear, then carefully slipped the top over her head. Easing her to the side slightly, to give himself room, he raised the blankets and nestled his large frame against her. Body heat, he hoped, would help. Being very careful not to touch her bandaged side he put his arm over her and pulled her closer.

He had not been with a woman for so long, actually since the death of his wife, that he had forgotten the comforting softness they exuded. Although she was small in stature, all the right curves were there and she melded firmly into his embrace.

Embrace! What the hell was he thinking? This certainly was going beyond the usual bedside manner.

"I told you not to call my house, Maggie," Tom almost shouted.

"I know dear, but it doesn't matter now. Are you doing all right?" She honey-coated her words.

"Do I sound like I am?"

"Tom, you've got to pull yourself to—"

Tom interrupted, "Excuse me, Maggie, I have a call coming in and I must answer it. We'll talk later. I'll phone *you*!"

Without waiting for a reply, he pushed the flash button. "Hello."

"Thomas," Ethan said, "is she home? I hope you bought her something nice to welcome her back. Women appreciate the little things."

"No. I've heard nothing from her. Did she come in at all today?"

"No, she didn't, but with all this ice we were only half staffed and when our power went off we called it a day. Besides, she probably wanted to get away from all distractions to clear her head and think things out. She knows everything here is in competent hands. However, I'm going to give her hell when she gets back."

"If we don't hear from her by tomorrow, I'm calling the police," Tom told him.

"Tom, you didn't just forget her birthday!"

"I know, I know." Tom paced. "It looks like she's not going to let this simply blow over."

"Well, perhaps when she's had time to cool off, she'll be back."

"Has anyone there said anything?" Tom inquired as he ceased moving about and stood staring at the floor.

"No, no one has asked why she's not been in. With half the staff out and the other half double-timing it, I don't think they even noticed her absence!" Bland assured him.

"Good. I can't help but wonder what's going on at the mill. After issuing her orders to Alice, I'm sure the rumors spread like wildfire."

"Don't let it get to you. Abby should be your only concern now. When she gets home, you two will have to work things out, and get back to business," Ethan said. "There's much riding on that!"

"I know. I'll talk to you tomorrow," Tom signed off.

The beginning of dawn brought the clearing of the skies. Rafe lay quietly looking through the window at the trees dressed in glassy white. When you're forced to put your busy life on hold, you see little things that tunnel vision had kept hidden. That was his reason for buying this cabin and its property.

Rafe's life had been completely devoted to his medical practice. As a nurse, his wife was also involved in the efforts of establishing the clinic. Then Angela became ill and he and the best specialists couldn't save her. Before she died, their short marriage had been totally consumed with work. She had not even recognized her symptoms, or was too preoccupied to get them checked and he wasn't made aware of her illness until it was too late. Blaming himself for not being observant enough, he simply had to get away and think about the order of his priorities.

Now, Rafe looked at the figure beside him. She was calm. The chills and sweating had ceased. Her breathing was slow and restful. Deep, comfortable, healing sleep had taken over.

Her hair, shirt and even the bed clothes were damp. He pushed the auburn locks back to reveal a slightly smaller face; not normal yet, perhaps in a day or two. Her eye was still quite swollen and most of the skin was discolored or beginning to scab over.

Rafe slipped from her side. He needed to get her out of her moist environment. Moving to the living room, he dressed, added logs to the fire and made up a bed on the couch. He located an old plaid bath robe he kept handy for the cool nights he chose to sit on the porch rather than sleep. Off came the damp long sleeve shirt, and with a little agility, she slipped the robe on her and loosely belted it. She reacted slightly to his handling of her. This gave Rafe cause to believe her unconscious state was giving over to a sleeping period.

After carefully settling her on the sofa and surrounding her with pillows, he changed the bed and started the coffee. Gathering the medical supplies, water and straw he returned to the living room and placed them on a table. Straightening, he was taken aback at the sight of one eye watching his every move.

He hesitated, then laughed and with hands on hips he said,

"Well, hello there." As he knelt beside her, she pulled the blanket up close under her chin, her eye never leaving his face.

"I'm not going to hurt you," he said. "I'm trying to help."

She didn't reply nor did she relax.

He sat back on his heels wondering exactly what to tell her. Finally he said, "You had an accident and your face received some superficial damage. These scrapes will heal and disappear. You took a pretty good whack to the side of your head though, and I had to cut your hair above your ear to stitch you up."

She didn't even blink. That eye just kept staring.

He wondered if she could speak or even hear. He kept talking, because if she *was* hearing him, he wanted it known what he intended to do before he touched her because her fear was evident.

"You do, however, have a more serious wound on your side that has to be treated." He spoke kindly and smiled. When she didn't respond, he added, "I need you to help me do that by cooperating."

She lay very still as tears welled up into her eyes. One spilled out of the slit in the swelling and rolled down her purple cheek but she eased the blanket down a little and released it.

Yes, she had heard him. Relieved, he straightened and pulled a chair to her side where he sat down and cleaned his hands with alcohol. As he began his task, she closed her eye and turned her head away. She lay unmoving as he carefully ministered to her injury. His large hands were soothing and moved with knowledge and care. There was no sign of infection and he was satisfied with the healing process.

"Now, I want you to turn onto your side away from me please." She did as he asked.

The exit wound had to be treated also. It was cleaned, examined and found to be in the same condition. He redressed the wound and drew the covers back up to her shoulders. Having finished, he stood, gathered his equipment and turned away from her. She grabbed his pant leg and whispered, "Wait."

He hesitated, looking surprised. "What is it?" he asked.

She spoke one word so quietly he didn't hear it. Leaning closer he said, "I'm sorry, what?'

"Bathroom," she repeated.

Yes, she can speak!

Sharon Evans-Rose

CHAPTER
4

THE PRESTONBURG POLICE Headquarters was housed in an old three story stone building. The basement contained all the old files, microfilm, a large table and chairs, and a locked room full of confiscated illegal paraphernalia.

The first floor was consumed by security, patrolmen, two meeting rooms and locker and shower rooms. Chief Robert Holloway's office was located in the back of the second floor. The four detectives in their two offices were his neighbors. The third floor was reserved for the dregs of John Q. Public with interrogation rooms and a holding area as its main focus.

An off duty gathering space containing vending machines and tables and chairs were hidden in a back corner room on this floor. This is where the workers could go for their breaks, lunch or after hours visiting, and not be interrupted. You were considered "not available" while in that room. It was the one place in the building you could become invisible.

No one really knew when or how this corner had evolved. For the current occupants, it had always been there. It was referred to as "The Rabbit Hole," in honor of James Stewart's buddy from the movie *Harvey*.

Sam was grateful to find it empty when he went up for an early lunch. He was reading the paper and eating grapes when Eric stuck his head through the door.

"Hey Boss, the chief wants us to check out this missing persons report," Eric said.

"I'm not here!" Sam replied.

Robertson, at fifty six, had been walking the beat even before Eric was born. His inquisitive mind and skills of deduction had led him straight into the detective quarters. He loved the job, but when cases kept him up at night, he envied the luxury of restful sleep.

His demeanor and attire didn't truly reveal his deductive abilities. With his lackadaisical way of dressing and laid back manner, he was slow to impress those who weren't acquainted with his deftness.

On the other hand, Eric, new to the department, was methodical in his thinking, but inexperienced and not yet on top of things. Sam knew it would take time, and he felt Eric was a good specimen for this department. However, he would observe this handsome young recruit and regret having to introduce him to the sick side of humanity.

Sam was gruff, stubborn, disheveled, and experienced but he had the patience God gave a cat. Eric, while more refined, was zealous in his efforts to find answers. He would work a problem to death to solve it and anytime Sam complained, it went right over his head. Occasionally, Eric would see the answer so obviously clear that he would want to jump right into an arrest.

That's when Robertson would remind him, "You can't get ahead of the red tape." *The Red Tape! The damn Red Tape! That's what always seems to get the perp off. That damn red tape and the perp's rights.* He was getting too old for this job and Eric, at twenty four, was tirelessly young. *What a pair*, Sam Robertson thought.

Despite their differences, the two worked well together. Eric was fully aware that Sam had a heart of gold and he respected him immensely. He felt very lucky to be partnered with Sam.

"It's important," Eric hesitantly added as he eased himself inside.

Turning to the sports section, Sam muttered, "It better be."

Eric seated himself at the table with the report in his hand and waited.

Sam scanned two pages while Eric stared at him. "Okay," the older detective breathed. He laid the paper aside, leaned back and crossed his arms, then gave Eric his full attention. He asked, "Another hooker?"

"No."

"Druggie?"

"No."

"Homeless?"

"No."

Sam unfolded his arms, straightened and put his hands on the table. He shouted, "Am I going to have to go through the whole damn phone book or are you going to tell me?!"

"Boss, you are something else, you know it?" the young man smiled.

"Eric, gimme that report," Robertson said, grabbing the paper.

Sam had not slept well for two nights. Esophageal Reflux. *They should never have started selling my prescription of antiacid across the counter*, he thought. *Now the pharmacy never calls to remind me I'm going to run out. Damn! Damn! Damn! And that's another thing. I really need to clean up my language. Control, I must learn to use some control. The doc said to cut down on stress. Maybe that would help my stomach. But if I have to force control, it would be stressful. Hell! I may as well blow off steam with a few bad words.*

Turning back to business, Sam studied the form.

"Tom Cummings made the call?" he asked, looking up at Eric.

"Yes."

"Abby Cummings has gone missing?" Still looking at Eric.

"Yes."

"Abby Langford Cummings?" Eyes on Eric.

In exasperation, Eric said, "Why did you take the report if you want me to explain it all to you?"

"*Harumph*," Sam grumped before turning back to the paper in hand.

Two officers entered the room carrying their lunches and discussing the cropped top the prostitute was barely wearing that had just been brought in. They spoke to Sam and Eric as they moved to the end of the table.

In return, they both nodded as Eric quickly picked up the report and stood. Sam gathered his lunch remains and tossed them into the trash as they exited. Taking the stairs down, they passed the other two detectives headed to "The Rabbit Hole."

"Chief Holloway said to make this a priority one," Eric said quietly.

"Of course."

"I'll call Mr. Cummings and see if we can come by. Is this afternoon all right?" Eric asked as they entered the office.

"Absolutely," Sam replied, studying the report. He mumbled, "The sooner, the better."

The Cummings home was located slightly north of Charlotte, in the quiet little suburb of Prestonburg which provided the perfect small town atmosphere while allowing the convenience of the city in less than an hour by way of I-77 S or I-40 E. This made it possible to actually get away from the office at the end of the day.

Sam brought Eric up to date on Abby Cummings' background and family history. Her parents were two of the town's most prosperous residents and all the old timers remembered the Langfords and their ascent to success. They had always been active in the community and were well-liked. It had been a number of years since the plane crash and their tragic demise had shocked and sorrowed the friendly town.

Although Abby was remembered by her childhood, Tom and Abby, the couple, weren't known personally, due to several extenuating circumstances. The residents in this small bedroom community were older and had lived there most of their lives. Consequently, they, as well as the Cummings, had no young children to create reasons for them to interact.

Many spent winter months in Florida or on an island somewhere. Abby and Tom were both heavily involved with separate businesses that depended on their supervision. After the commute and the pressures of a hard day at work, they relished and protected their privacy when home. Their solitude was not a result of a preferred antisocial existence, but was, simply, a method of surviving a hectic routine.

The home was located in a quiet upscale section with each house showcasing its own style. The houses were not built close together but were set apart by space and evergreens rather than fences. The neighborhood had character, charm, and old money. It had not sprouted from a current development but rather had grown into the countryside over many years.

Having never been in this area before, Eric viewed it with respect and awe.

"People from these kind of homes don't just vanish unless its a kidnapping or murder, do they? I mean, who would run away from this?" he asked.

"You're looking at the window dressing. The people who live here are not immune to the problems that affect us all. You never know what goes on behind closed doors," Sam replied. "I think this is it."

He turned into the drive that circled in front of the home.

Sam parked the car and they stepped out, brushing themselves off and straightening ties. Catching each other trying to tidy up, they quickly resumed their usual demeanor.

Tom had known he could wait no longer to notify the police. If he had put it off they would have questioned his decision to do so. Now they were coming to talk to him. This whole thing is going to turn into a media circus, but what was he to do, it was now or later, and later would have made the talk worse.

Waiting on the sofa and staring blindly out the windows, his mind once again took him back to Tuesday. He had relived that day a dozen times. Abby had really been hurt at learning of his affair the first time, but Tuesday she was different. There was no pain in those eyes looking back at him, just acceptance and disgust. He knew she meant what she said.

Tom had gone directly to see Ethan after watching her leave the parking lot. He related everything to Ethan, who shook his head in dismay.

"I know, Abby called me. What's the matter with you, Tom? Most men would give their eye teeth to be in your position. Abby is one of the most attractive women around. Any number of men would have married her and provided a lifetime of love and happiness. If she had left you over this before, she would be fighting them off with sticks."

"I know! You don't have to keep reminding me, Ethan," Tom almost shouted. "But now, I've got big troubles. *We've* got big troubles!"

"Settle down," Ethan encouraged. "Give her some time."

"That's not going to change things. She's different. She fired me, gave me until tomorrow night to move out of the house." Tom plopped into a chair and stared at the ceiling. "It's over. I could see it in her eyes."

Ethan stood behind his desk and leaned onto his hands to speak more directly to Tom. He stated, "I cannot believe how foolish you've been. You didn't deserve Abby. When I had become a throw away kid, she refused to let that happen. She made me understand that your origin didn't determine where or how far you could go." Ethan sat down and leaned his forearms on the desk as he continued, "I'm sure she never told you I was born dirt-poor in a broken home—no, actually it was a filthy shack. We had no running water—only a pump and an outhouse." He leaned over his arms and looked frowningly into Tom's eyes as he added, " Do you know how cold those things are in the dead of winter?"

Tom lowered his eyes. "No, Abby's not one to bring up a hurtful past."

"I would leave there each morning and at nightfall, that's where I returned, but I was fortunate in being able to establish a camaraderie with Abby and her friends and neighbors. It was a hard thing to face as we grew older and I found myself being relegated to my station as they all made other friends of class who didn't know me and failed to include me in plans." Ethan sighed as he paused, thinking of times past.

"But Abby didn't forget you," Tom reminded him.

"No, she didn't. She would have me over, teach me to play chess, lecture me about going for the gold. She instilled a hunger in me to get out of the slums and work for something. She was different from most people I knew. Always ready with an answer or suggestion, full of energy and wit, a regular little spitfire. It was contagious. We were friends in the truest sense of the word, and

28

sometimes I want to hurt you for what you've done to her." Ethan wasn't sure Tom was listening, but he kept talking anyway. "When boyfriends began to deplete our time together, we continued our companionship by phone. Neither of us had any siblings, but in our minds we were as close as brother and sister." He waited for Tom to say something.

Finally, he did. "She is exactly what you say, but my need for Maggie—that I find impossible to understand—drove me back over and over again. I don't love Maggie. She just had a wild side that I found intoxicating. I'm sorry I ever met her. She's, well, *she's* ruined my life."

With one arm folded over his ribs and the other bent to place his hand around his chin, Ethan leaned back into his chair.

Sitting silently, each lost in a mangle of thoughts, time seemed to have paused. The quiet stillness induced a dreamlike state carrying each into his own private period of his past.

The closing of a door somewhere in the building broke the spell. Ethan looked up as though surprised Tom was still there, then pushed forward, clasping his hands and once more resting his forearms on his desk. He gazed at Tom a moment before he spoke.

"Look, she'll call me. I'll talk to her. I'll make her see how important it is to keep things together. But Tom, you have to leave Maggie alone."

Tom rose heavily from his chair. "I'm going home. I'll wait there. If she doesn't call, I'll try to work it out when she comes in tomorrow night," Tom told him, moving to the door.

"Keep your head up," Ethan encouraged, "and call me when you hear from her." He put his arm around Tom's shoulders and walked him out of the office.

The doorbell rang and Tom put his thoughts away.

He opened the door quickly.

"Yes?" he said.

"Hello, Mr. Cummings. I'm Detective Robertson and this is Eric Burke. We're with the Prestonburg Police Department."

"Of course. Please, come in."

They followed Tom into the marbled entry and down three steps into the cavernous great room. It was a quiet area done in muted earth tones. A large oil canvas of contemporary art, signed by the artist, hung above the mantel. Light beige stone floors were sprinkled with fluffy rag rugs. A cream baby grand rested quietly in a bay window at the side of the room. Soft drapes covered these windows. Eric knew they were not there for effect but for a purpose. The fabric and the large oriental rug in creams, tans, and burnt umber, resting on the stone floor under the piano, were to soften the fine tuned chords emanating from the instrument when played. Eric felt in his heart that the musician in this home must be Mrs. Cummings.

The room had an immaculate but comfortable look. One wall of undraped windows revealed a large pool surrounded by a wide, tiled deck studded with canopied tables and chairs. A covered electric grill and attached chrome table stood nearby. To the left a small group of tall, old trees stood somewhat unkempt but mightily in the area otherwise groomed to perfection.

One tree, slightly separated from the others, supported a long rope swing with a wooden seat. It, too, displayed the signs of age.

Beyond that, a clearing framed by sculpted firs provided complete privacy to the residence and a perfect view of distant mountains that on days of changing temperatures become shrouded in fog. Today the lush of summer green is replaced by stark browns and blacks glistening in the sun. The tops of the mountains remained white, but here, the warming temperature had applied a shining ice coating to the brittle surface of winter.

Tom indicated one of the brushed leather sofas and seated himself in a chair facing them. The home had been built by Abby's parents, who enhanced the dwelling with a number of additions over the years. With each extension, the older rooms were sometimes enlarged and always updated melding a visual harmony of completeness. The look was not ostentatious but comfortable and inviting.

Eric, lost in his appraisal of the surroundings, was abruptly reminded, by Sam's next words, that they were at work.

"Exactly when did you last see Mrs. Cummings?" he asked.

"Let me think. Today is Thursday, so it was Tuesday morning."

30

"Two days ago?" Sam said as he glanced at Eric, who was making notes. "It was today that you called this in, right?"

"Yes, but you see, I didn't realize that she was gone until now and I'm still not sure that she's, uh, missing," Tom answered.

"How's that?"

Nervously, Tom stood and walked to the windows. With his back to them he said, "We had words that morning, Tuesday, and she walked out. I thought that she'd be back after cooling off. I kept waiting. I guess I thought that she was punishing me by staying away, but it's been too long."

"Has she ever done this before?"

He turned to face them. "No."

"Is this a habit, making you pay in some manner after you have words?"

"No, she would never do that. She also has not been in her office nor has she called. That is totally out of character. The magazine is very important to her."

"This freak storm has made the roads nearly impassable. Have you called the hospitals to see if perhaps she has had an accident?" Sam inquired.

"Someone would have notified me, wouldn't they?"

Sam shrugged then asked, "Have you had any suspicious calls?"

"What do you mean by suspicious?" Tom walked behind a chair facing them and with both hands on the back, leaned on it.

"Like a ransom demand?" Sam prodded.

"Oh God, that hadn't even entered my mind. No. No calls of that sort," Tom exclaimed, straightening.

"I don't think this is a kidnapping since you have not heard from anyone, but, as a precaution, we'll have the phone company supply us a list of all your incoming calls," Sam told him. "If a call or letter of that nature comes in, we'll, naturally, change our course of investigation. Meanwhile, we'll check all the hospitals and have the patrols keep an eye out for her car."

"Yes, I would appreciate that," Tom said.

"Okay. Suppose you give us some information, such as what she was wearing that day, the model, year and color of car and, of course, the license number. If you think there is somewhere she may have gone we'll check it out. Also, we'll need names and numbers of friends and family that may be of help. That will get the ball rolling."

Eric took the information while Sam, with Tom's permission, made a walk through of their bedroom and kitchen.

Sam found everything in order. Neat, clean and too perfect. Houses weren't usually in this spotless condition, however this was not the usual house. There must be a maid involved with both of them working. No kids! Of course, that was it. No toys, dirty clothes, snacks or any other children droppings. Ordinarily, this kind of neatness indicated a cleaning "cover up," but Sam knew this must be the normal look here.

Stepping into the master bedroom, one of his assumptions was confirmed. He caught sight of a skirted behind entering the bath area. Following the disappearing hemline, he stepped into the entry way to find a maid placing freshly laundered towels on a shelf in a closet. Upon completing her task, she turned and almost stepped into Sam. She gasped and raised her arm for attack, when Sam grabbed it and quickly identified himself. He produced his badge with the other hand.

She looked to be in her fifties, stood about 5'3, plump, and extremely neat in her gray and white uniform. She wore her hair in a bun and stomped a heavy white shoed foot as she spat out, "You could have announced yourself before sneaking up on me, sir. You scared the living daylights plumb outta this body." She laid her free hand over her heart. "Why, I could have given up the ghost right here. I thought I was going to be the next one to disappear!"

Sam released her arm, apologizing.

She walked away from him, but still talking over her shoulder. "Shame, shame on you."

Sam smiled as, putting a little distance between them, he followed her into the bedroom. She seated herself on the edge of a chair and picked up a tablet and began to fan herself. Intense blue eyes followed his movements. Her frown did not dissipate.

Sam sat down on the bed, facing her. "Again, I'm sorry. I really didn't expect you to be so close when I entered the room," he offered.

She simply looked at him. He smiled and she relaxed slightly.

"I've been a little on edge since, well, you know," she finally said.

"I understand. Mr. Cummings is downstairs with my partner. He said it would be all right for me to look around. While you're recovering, could we talk a minute?" Sam asked.

"As long as I finish my duties on time. I don't get time and a half, you know," she warned him.

"How many days do you work here?"

"Three days a week from nine to three."

"Were you here on Tuesday?"

"No, I work Monday, Wednesday and Thursday."

"Then tell me about yesterday. Was Mr. Cummings home?"

"He was here when I got to work but gone when I left."

"And what time was that?"

"I told you I start at nine and quit at three. You need to pay attention or you won't last long with the department."

Sam tried again. "What time did Mr. Cummings leave?"

"I don't know. When I'm here, I'm very busy. The vacuum, television, washer and a number of other things block out normal sounds."

"He didn't let you know when he left?"

"Never does. It doesn't make a difference to me. I've got my jobs to do and I don't need to stop to wave to everyone as they leave. He's here and then he's gone. He's not on the clock."

"Is he or Mrs. Cummings usually at home when you get to work?"

She laughed. "No. Those two are like workhorses. They run things and when you're in that position, you don't call in late or sick, you get up and beat everyone else to work and close the doors when they've all left for the day. Actually, I was surprised to find him home when I got here yesterday."

"Did he give you a reason for being here?"

"Oh, no. And I didn't ask either. He's a very private," she leaned closer at this point and lowered her voice, "and unfriendly person."

"Mean?" Sam asked.

"Well, I wouldn't know. I seldom see him. He's just not friendly. Now, Mrs. Cummings is a different bird all together. She laughs and hugs me and, well, she's real nice."

She paused briefly, then added, "Come to think of it, he was a bit edgy. Upset. More skittish than usual. After I found out that Mrs. Cummings had gone missing, I understood why he was more out-of-sorts than normally."

"Did he have any company or did you overhear any phone conversations?"

"No company and I don't eavesdrop," she said indignantly.

"Of course not." Sam pulled out his card and handed it to her. "If you do see or accidentally overhear something that might be of interest, would you call me?"

"Yes. Do you think the Mister knows something about her disappearance?" Suddenly she looked surprised and laying her hand on her cheek she asked, "You don't suppose he, I mean, he's not a suspect is he?"

"Everyone, including you, is a suspect at this point."

Now her hand moved once more to her chest as she gasped and looked at him.

"Besides," he continued, "she left on her own and could return at any moment. Mr. Cummings is simply worried about her, that's all. We're just answering his call of concern." Sam stood as he said, "Also, if something seems out of order in the house, we would like to hear from you. I suppose everything was normal yesterday?"

"Yes, yes it was." She tucked the card into her pocket.

Sam took her hand and covered it with his other one and said, "Please let me apologize once more for my stupidity. If you ever need anything, don't hesitate to call me."

"That's all right. Thank you," she smiled as a blush spread over her face.

Now we've got someone on the inside, Sam thought as he headed back down the stairs.

The kitchen was the same in appearance. He looked into the refrigerator. Other than milk, water, fruit, and a covered casserole the maid must have prepared, it was practically empty. Couples who work every day often eat out. He sighed, thinking about this situation. A beautiful house, all current appliances, expensively decorated, everything one would need, but it wasn't a home, he could sense it. Happiness, contentment, togetherness—all these things gave off an aura that was not present here. *How sad. Maybe she's on a break somewhere taking her life into account.*

Sam joined Eric who was just finishing.

Tom escorted them to the door.

"By the way," Eric asked, "Are any suitcases or her personal articles missing?"

"I don't know," Tom replied. "I'll have to check."

"Had she been home to pick up a change of clothes, toothbrush or anything on that order?" Eric prodded.

"I don't know how I would know that," Tom replied blankly.

"Look around for signs," Sam said, "and if you should notice anything to suggest she planned to be gone for a while, or on the other hand, if you hear from her, would you please notify us?"

"Absolutely!"

The detectives got into the car. "He didn't know if any of her things were missing?" Eric said.

"When you make arrangements with the phone company I want the outgoing numbers included," Sam replied.

Inside, Tom walked straight to the den and closed the door. He picked up the phone and called Maggie. "Don't call here again. All numbers calling in will be scrutinized by the police. I won't be talking to you for a while."

"But, Tom..."

"You heard me, Maggie. I'll be in touch later."

Tom seated himself with thoughts of the two women. How had he gotten involved with Maggie? She was lovely and very attracted to him. She had made that fact known the first day on the job and from there, things had moved rapidly. He hadn't stopped loving his wife, but this desire for Maggie was something that he, somehow, couldn't control. She had become obsessed with him and he often wondered if she had been Abby's source of information.

Maggie was tall, blonde and intense. Her sexual appetite was voracious and she didn't hesitate in making her needs known to Tom. Flattered and ready to be used by her hungry drive, he was more than happy to fulfill her desires. When Abby confronted him the first time she discovered what was going on, he knew he had to make the effort to give up what he considered a fling, so Tom took Maggie out of the picture—for a few months.

Tom placed his foot against the edge of the tan leather covered coffee table and shoved it over onto its side.

Sharon Evans-Rose

CHAPTER 5

RAFE BROUGHT A tray containing a bowl of soup, a banana and glass of milk and set it on the side table. Leaning close to a sleeping Abby he said, "I have—"

She jumped, waking abruptly and swinging a small fist. Sheer terror shone in her eye.

He straightened quickly, putting both hands in the air beside his head. "I'm not going to hurt you. Remember?"

Gasping, she made no reply.

He hesitated, giving her time to calm.

"I'd like you to sit up. You need to eat something," Rafe offered.

He tried again. This time she allowed him to slip his arm around her, lift and twist her into a sitting position. Her eye never left his face.

As he turned to pick up a napkin, she asked, "What's your name?"

Having just been made to feel like the Boston Strangler, he mumbled to himself, "Albert De Salvo, one would think."

"Who?" she inquired.

"Albert De Salvo," he answered as he tucked the napkin under her chin then placed the tray over her lap. "And it's nice to hear that you have a voice."

"Thank you."

He looked at that sad face and responded, "You're welcome."

Back in the kitchen, cleaning the counter, he considered how much she seemed like an injured and cornered kitten. He heard her call weakly, "Albert." Moving to the door and holding on to the jamb he leaned his head into the room.

Again came, "Albert!"

He frowned before stepping through, saying, " No, no you—"

"What?" she interrupted.

"Uh, I was just coming to see what you wanted," Rafe said to avoid confusing her further. He walked around to stand in front of the sofa.

Looking up at him, spoon in hand and chin trembling, she said, "I don't know who I am."

Removing the utensil and tray he sat down beside her and gathered her into his arms. "It's all right, it's all right. You're not alone." He pushed her away, pulled the napkin from the front of her robe and looked into that large eye. Why was its color dark brown? All the redheaded novel heroines had green eyes.

"You'll work it out. You need time, that's all," he encouraged.

He pulled her back into his arms and held her while she unsuccessfully tried to hold the tears at bay.

Later, with plastic bags of snow wrapped in cloth nestled about her face, exhaustion overtook Abby and she slept for several hours while Rafe, anxious to get news and weather reports, tried the radio again. Still nothing. The sun had played lengthy performances but temperatures remained low. On this mountain, there had been a settling of the snow, but no melting. He needed to know what the conditions were at the lower altitude. He was due back at the clinic on Monday.

If this patient, whom, it seems, had inadvertently become his responsibility, were able to be moved, what was he to do with her? Had it not been for the snow, he certainly would have delivered her to a hospital where the gunshot wound would have been re-ported, then she and this whole situation would be out of his hands and under police investigation. *If the assailant finds out she has survived, how safe will she be? When she can't even remember what happened, she can't know her enemy.* Rafe could not inten-tionally put her in harm's way. With these thoughts rattling around in his head, he, too, dozed off.

That evening he was reading by the fire when Abby interrupted him.

"I'm sorry to bother you, Albert, but could you help me, please?"

Rafe smiled and looked up. "Of course," he said, laying his book aside and rising. "Shall I carry you to the bathroom again?"

"No, I want to walk."

"That may be a little too far to try—"

She stopped him, "No, no. I only want to walk. Maybe to the chair and back, a couple of times."

"Okay, let me help you to sit first," he suggested.

Moving to an upright position, with her feet hanging over the edge, she laid her head back onto the cushions until she had adjusted and the blood resettled. She raised her head and took a look around the room from a different angle.

"Now, let's scoot you to the edge of the sofa and see how you do holding yourself in a sitting position without support."

She did so, but held tightly onto his arm. When she felt she was ready, she squeezed his arm and nodded.

He eased her up onto her feet. "Just stand here a moment. Breathe deeply. That helps with the nausea you may experience at first."

She took a deep breath. And another. "What helps the dizziness?" she asked, clinging to his hands.

He moved to encircle her shoulders, and slipping his hand under her arm, he was careful to avoid her wounds. "Now, slowly. One step at a time and lean on me."

She started moving, greatly favoring her injured side.

"Stand up straight," he encouraged.

She tried, but kept moving with a heavy lilt.

"A little straighter," he urged.

Turning her head in his direction, she said, "This is as straight as it gets! If I'm too much of a load just get me a kitchen chair and I'll push it around."

"I can handle it." He smiled inwardly. *Nothing wrong with her speech.*

They made it to the chair then back to the sofa and as she deposited herself upon it, she said, "I think I'm going to be sick."

He grabbed a waste basket as he told her, "No, you're not. Close your eyes and rest your head back. It'll pass. Remember, deep breaths."

She obeyed, asking, "What are you, a damn nurse?"

"Doctor." He kept the basket ready.

Raising her eyebrows, but with closed eyes she added, "True?"

"True."

"Oh. Well now, I guess that upgrades me from being the most unlucky to the luckiest girl around."

"Feel better?" he asked.

"A little. While I sit here trying to revive, talk to me. Do you have another life, Dr. Doolittle, or are you actually, after having spent a fortune on tuition, living your dream? Is tending to the animals and surviving on berries and fish while you wait for a real live human patient, such as myself, to drop into your lap your idea of practicing medicine? Could be your financial undoing!"

Excellent breath control, he thought.

"At this point, I can't even buy a cup of coffee," she said, then added, "Did I arrive with a purse or anything? And did I come knocking or did you pick me up? What kind of accident? A car? A hit and run, or was I just exceedingly clumsy and fell up your steps? Tell me something, anything, Albert, because if I have no past you have to provide a beginning," she pleaded.

"Rafe," he corrected, "and I must say, you certainly got your wind back."

Lifting her head and eyelid, she asked, "What?"

"It's not Albert. My name is Rafe. Raphael Andrew Musgrave Adams. How's that for a poor boy born in Rock Hill, N.C.?"

"Heavy!"

"My mother evidently read a lot of old romance novels. Anyway, my entrance into their lives must have been quite a shock as my parents are gone now and they didn't die young."

"How old are you?"

"Thirty-five. You?"

She gave him a look depicting, "Have you lost your memory too?"

40

He continued, "Yes, I have another life. I was widowed over two years ago, no children, have a partnership in a medical clinic in Winston-Salem and live alone in a quiet neighborhood. That's about it. Very boring, huh?"

"Not if that's what you want. I'm sorry about your wife," she offered.

"Thank you."

"Okay, next question. What do you know about me?" Her color was returning.

Rafe stood and stirred the fire. "Would you like a cup of coffee?"

"Do you have Ground Beans?"

They stared at each other. "Where did that come from?" she asked.

"A memory." He smiled. "The first hint of your past."

Abby paused, searching her mind. Any thread to connect a thought to a time past. Nothing. Was it important? Anything and everything was important.

Rafe waited for her to get through this thought process.

"Give me a name."

"Do what?" he asked.

"I need a name. What do you think I would be called? Am I a Linda, a Vicky, Julia? I want you to refer to me by name."

He had wondered who she was, but he hadn't even thought about her name. He had been more concerned about her response to his care.

"Albert!" she said, rousing him from thought.

"Would you remember it if I gave you a name? You can't seem to remember mine."

She shifted her position, drawing her legs up and bending them beside her, she clasped her hands in her lap.

"It's Rafe. Rafe, as in Raphael!" he chanted, standing by the fire with one hand on the mantel, the other holding the poker.

"I guess I've been concentrating on myself too much. I'm sorry," she replied with head bowed.

Rafe was sorry that he had been cross with her. She couldn't help the state of her mindlessness. It must be hard for her to concentrate. How could he expect her to remember his name when she couldn't remember her own? She was, after all, not only injured physically but in a state of amnesia.

"I shouldn't have been so short. I know you're having trouble," he told her.

"But I have to make a point to be more attentive to the things you tell me. I need to exercise my mind. I'm just so overwhelmed right now."

"It's only natural, considering your condition, but you're not going to just reach out and grab a memory. Things will come to you eventually. In pieces, at first, but you will remember in time. Now, did you want coffee?"

"You're procrastinating. I need you to tell me what happened, Albert."

He rolled his eyes. "Rafe!" he stated mildly and without another word, he waited patiently.

"Tell me," she spat. Then, "Please."

In total silence they stared at each other until Rafe finally acquiesced.

"Belle," was his reply.

"Excuse me?"

"As in Tinkerbell. She was small, feisty, spirited, and cute. So, that's your name for now. Belle."

"Why are all short people cute? One can be homely, dumpy, shapely, drop dead gorgeous, drop dead ugly, but if they're short too, they're cute. Period!" Abby stated.

Rafe sat down and leaned back in the chair crossing his arms. He looked at her. Studying her face, he said, "Right now, with bruises, swelling and funny hairdo, you *are* cute. Give yourself a few more days and maybe you'll turn ugly."

Now, *she* leaned back, crossed her arms and gave *him* an 'I'm still waiting' look.

"Okay," Rafe said, standing and going for two cups of coffee.

"It was almost blizzard conditions." He called out as he filled the cups and returned. Going back for cream and sugar he added, "It started as rain, changed quickly to sleet, then snow. I was coming back from the lake with four beautiful bass, that wound up frozen on the ground somewhere, when I heard a loud crack. After a moment or two, I caught sight of a vehicle leaving the area."

Abby sat forward, added cream to her coffee. "Thank you. Go on."

"This land belongs to me, so I was curious as to who had ventured onto the grounds and for what reason. I moved in that direction and literally stumbled into you. I exchanged the fish for you and came home."

"Who was in the car?"

"Couldn't see."

"What kind of car?"

"Not sure. I wasn't close enough. It was light in color, early evening and the snow was so heavy if it hadn't been for the headlights I might have missed it. The lights were bright and large, double, one atop the other and set high off the road so I'm pretty sure it was an SUV."

"SUV?"

"Sport utility vehicle."

"Sport utility vehicle," she repeated, thinking with knitted eyebrows. "Isn't that like a big jeep?"

Rafe pushed himself up from the chair. "Women," he said softly. Stretching first, he then returned for a second cup of coffee.

"What about my injuries?" she asked.

He stopped short of the kitchen and turned to put his cup on a table. Returning to his chair, he sat down on the front edge. With forearms resting on the top of his knees, he clasped his hands and looked kindly into her eye and a half. "You were unconscious when I found you. I'm not sure what happened to you before that. The most serious wound, as you know, is in your side and was caused by a bullet," he said.

She paused, coffee cup in hand. "Oh, but I don't understand."

"You were shot," he replied pointedly.

"Was it on purpose?" She was incredulous. Total shock was evidenced on her face.

"You were wearing an expensive pants suit and high heels. I don't think it was a hunting accident."

"But why would anyone want to do that—to shoot me?"

Watching her closely, he repeated, "Yes, why?"

"Well, I don't know," she answered in wonderment. She was

very solemn as she tightened the robe around her and stared into the fire.

He tried to imagine her shock. It must be a sobering thing to realize that someone wants you dead and the worst of it is that you don't know who wishes it so. Now, she has only a stranger to trust.

It was sometime after one O'clock when a desperate screaming from Abby's room wakened Rafe. He jumped up and ran to her.

Holding the covers up to her chin, she was searching out every corner of the room. He moved to the bed and put his hand on her shoulder. She gasped at his touch and looked up into his face with sheer fright.

"Belle, it's me, Rafe! What's wrong?"

Her eyes left him and darted once more around the room. She was pulling the covers up over her nose now.

"Belle, what is it? Look at me."

She drew her knees up to her chin where she rested her head. Without looking at him she asked, "Would you check the closet and under the bed, please?!"

Rafe, now, under the watchful eye of Belle, did as she requested, then returned to her side. He took her hands into his and sat on the edge of the bed beside her.

"Tell me what frightened you," he said soothingly.

"A bad dream, I guess. It must have been. It was so real though," she told him before glancing over her shoulder.

He tightened his grip on her and said quietly, "Belle, tell me about it. Maybe I can help you sort fact from fiction."

Looking into his concerned eyes, she said, "I was sleeping on my back when a noise awakened me. I opened my eyes and found myself looking into the barrel of a gun. I froze. It took the breath from me." She pulled her right hand from him and laid it across her heart. "Oh, my God, I could see the finger begin to tighten on the trigger." Her brow was creased and the muscles in her face were quivering.

She dropped her head back, focusing on the ceiling. Tears rolled from the outside corners of her eyes before she closed them. Her shaking voice whispered, "I was going to die. I was going to..."

Sobs began deep within her and bubbled up in agony.

Laying her head on Rafe's shoulder, she cried herself dry as he held her close and experienced a wrenching in his heart that brought tears to his own eyes. When she could cry no more and was left with little short hiccup-like intakes of air, she pulled away, with head drooping forward.

Rafe brushed her hair off her wet face, then got up and strode over to turn off the light. She remained seated and spent in the middle of the bed. When she heard his movement returning to her, she looked up.

He sat down facing her in the dark and raised his hand in front of her.

"How many fingers do you see?" he asked.

"Uh," she stuttered, while trying to read their outline.

"Am I wearing a ring?"

"I don't know, it's not light enough to tell," she replied.

"Now, you should know! Was it a dream?" he asked her.

"Oh, now I see. I can't see—couldn't see. It was too dark. It *was* a dream!"

"Correct. Feel better?"

"Relieved. Slightly. But, you see, the dream has already happened to me. Maybe not exactly as I saw it tonight, but in essence, it did happen."

Rafe stood once more and said, "Scoot."

"What?"

"Scoot," he repeated.

"I don't understand." A questioning frown appeared on her forehead.

"Over. Scoot over," he added.

She did as he asked and he slid in bed beside her.

"Now, no one can get to you without bypassing me. How's that?"

"Very satisfactory," she answered, relaxing.

"Okay. Turn over and go back to sleep."

Rafe lay very still as the morning light crept up the bedside and onto his back. In his mind, two years had vanished and he was holding his wife with his face buried in her hair. He began to feel the stirrings of arousal. Opening his eyes, he pulled her closer. As the present reared its head, he suddenly released the sleeping Abby and sprang from the bed. She sighed and rolled to her back.

With hands in the air, as proof he wasn't touching her, he stood transfixed. Staring down at this small form, he held his breath and waited for her to relax. The facial swelling had lessened and the blacks and blues of bruises were beginning to show a green tinge. He knew in a few days they would yellow out and fade. A slight smile touched her lips. This banged up face he helped to bed last night was beginning to take on a human form—one, he sensed, was going to be very nice on the eyes.

The sun-drenched, tousled, auburn hair covered part of her small high forehead with one ear clearly visible where he had cut her hair. He shook his head and looked again at her face. The thought resurfaced. *Why would anyone want to hurt her?* Yet, he really didn't know this person. What was the matter with him? He turned and moved rapidly out of the room.

"Good morning."

Rafe looked up from the table to see Abby in the large loose fitting robe. She stood, visibly bent sideways, at the door. With knuckles white, she held on to both sides of the portal. A shaky, but proud smile lit her face.

"Congratulations!" He arose to escort her to a chair opposite him. "I see you're standing straighter," he said to her lopsided back.

"I'm much stronger now, Ralph. I think I'll soon be ready to go home.

That's closer than Albert. I guess she's trying, he thought. "And where is home?"

Sliding into the chair she answered, "You tell me."

"I don't know where you live."

"Your home. You said you live alone. Don't you have more than one bedroom? I would only stay until those pieces of memory connect."

"Oh? Now why didn't I think of that? Maybe a couple of more days here would be advisable. By then we'll have removed your stitches and your recovery will be far more advanced," he suggested. "Perhaps by then, you'll remember where your home is located."

"But I'm frightened here," she said, frowning. "What if the gunman actually does return?"

"No! Belle frightened? Never!"

She smiled. "Thanks for the protection."

"It was nothing. Are you sure it was a man with the gun? Do you recall any part of the incident or what led up to it?" Rafe tried to pull something from the word *gunman*.

She looked down at her trembling fingers. "No."

Slapping the table lightly with both hands as he stood, he said, "Well, let's get you fed and take a look at that side."

After dressing her wounds and checking her head he located an old sweatsuit and a pair of socks for her to try on. She managed to pull the bottoms up and roll them over onto her hips to keep pressure off her injury. The top hung low but after the sleeves were folded, she was very comfortable. Rafe thought she looked swallowed up, which accented her "cuteness," but cautiously refrained from mentioning this.

She worked hard at building her strength by spells of walking and sitting at the table humming as she played solitaire, while Rafe performed some lightweight household chores.

He listened closely, trying to discern a familiar tune from her throaty tones but could identify nothing. The musicality was more advanced than a simple melody.

"Do you play the piano or any other instrument?" he asked.

"I wouldn't know," she replied, stopping to think it over.

"What were you humming?"

"Was I humming?"

"It wasn't me!"

"Well, I didn't hear it," she said, returning to her card game.

By late afternoon Abby felt her appetite returning. Rafe offered up a dinner of tuna steaks, baked potato and apple sauce. If they didn't leave within a few days, their dining would be strictly from cans.

After dinner, they settled themselves in front of the fire where Rafe made himself comfortable in his large chair with his feet propped upon the ottoman. He picked up his book and flipped it open. He glanced toward Abby and they exchanged smiles.

After reading a few pages, he became uncomfortable. Adjusting his position and lifting his book a little closer, he turned a page and continued.

Unable to concentrate on the dialogue, he couldn't understand what was bothering him.

He looked over his book and into the fire. He used to do that as a boy. After fishing all day, he and his friends would sit around the fire in the evening and cook their catch. When their stomachs were full, a silence would fall as the darkness surrounded them forcing their focus onto the fire. Sometimes, they would find themselves staring hypnotically into the depth of the white hot glow. Watching the logs give way to ashes, someone would throw a couple more onto the fire causing a dusting of red embers to rise with the smoke, each boy lost in thought or listening to another murmuring about a memory he had.

It was soothing. Relaxing with friends—the kind with which you didn't have to make conversation.

But he wasn't outside in the dark with friends. Slowly, he turned his head to the side and was reminded he wasn't alone. He was sitting there with... *who*?

Abby smiled once more and Rafe realized what was bothering him. This lovely stranger, with nothing to do, was observing him. *Well, I can't read under these circumstances. I feel like a lab specimen.* He laid the book aside and turned to her.

"Let's try something," he suggested.

"Like what?"

"Word association might prove helpful." He explained. First, he would say a word and then she would answer with the first thing that came to mind. He was hoping to come up with a word that would trigger a thought or that she would respond with one that would give a hint into her past.

She perked up. "Yes, let's give it a try. You start."

"All right. *Day*."

"Night."

"Black," he said.

"White."

"Marriage."

"Divorce," she replied.

He hesitated. "Are you?" he asked.

"Married? Or divorced?"

"Either?"

Hesitation. "I feel like there's someone with whom I share my time but I don't know if it's a husband, a relative, a friend or a pet."

"I doubt that you have a pet."

"Why?"

"Because you didn't reply with dog, cat, bird or snake. You simply said pet as though you had no preference."

"Snake?"

He smiled. "I had a Ball Python when I was a teenager."

She shivered and looked at him with slight disgust. He smiled as he turned back to the notes in hand.

"Work," he continued.

"Hard."

"Do you mean to work hard or that work would be hard?"

She shrugged her shoulders.

"Car."

"Small."

"Why small?" he inquired.

"I think I would be more comfortable in a small car. You know, reach the pedals. See the road better. Squeeze into parking spaces with ease."

"You must drive or you wouldn't have known the advantages of a small car."

"Perhaps." She frowned.

"Home."

"View."

"Very interesting!" he stated, then, "Happy."

She clasped her hands and laid them in her lap. After looking past him for a short time, she closed her eyes and answered, "Sometimes."

Rafe looked at her pale face and felt bad that everything was so complex for her right now.

"Snow," he continued.

"Scary," she said as her brow creased between almost translucent eyelids.

"Gun."

"No! No!"

Rafe decided it was time to change tactics. He didn't want her to go to bed with disconcerting thoughts.

"I think that produced a little insight so let's break the mood a little," he suggested.

"Yes, that sounds good."

"Turn around and lie back. I'll give you a foot massage," he said, "That's always good for what ails you."

She obeyed and soon was relaxed from head to toe. Comfortable. Like an old bedroom shoe.

"Close your eyes and let your thoughts wander." He waited, listening to the crackling fire.

"Do you see or sense any old memories?" he prodded.

"I get a feeling of being young and happy. I think there were only three of us and we liked to travel."

"Where would you go?" he inquired.

"Away. I don't know where. Part of the fun was getting ready for the trip and it was exciting to leave." She was quiet for a while before adding, "I always felt safe. They loved and protected me."

"Who?" He was working the tension all the way out the end of her toes.

"Mother and Dad, I guess," she replied.

He thought about her responses carefully. She spoke of them in the past tense. Was it because she only remembers them in the past or are they no longer living? He asked nothing more. Looking at her face, he noticed it had become very relaxed. There was no movement behind her eyelids and she was breathing slow and steady. "Belle, you've had a busy day, I know you must be tired."

"More like worn out," she answered quietly.

"Tonight, I'm going to push the sofa back so that when I settle down out here for the night, you can see me from the bed and if you become too frightened you can call to me," he said.

"I'm sure I'll go right to sleep," she replied uneasily.

Rafe walked her to the bedroom, turned on the lamp, folded the bed down and asked if he could do anything else.

"No, Doctor, you've gone way beyond the call of duty. I'll be fine now, thank you."

He pulled the door closed as he exited. The cabin was very small and provided little privacy if the doors were open. Only three rooms existed at present. Entering from a full front porch put you into a corner of the living room, with the bulk of the room on your left. About a quarter of the way back on your right was the entry to the bedroom. Passing on to the next door on the right produced the bath.

The kitchen ran across the back of the house with a small screened porch at the left. The two fireplaces he enjoyed were essential at one time, but Rafe was grateful the generator had added the modern conveniences of light and heat in this dated cabin. It was small, but he had been comfortable and enjoyed his little retreat. Extra space and other amenities had been immaterial.

He readied for bed, collected a large pillow and throw from a chair and pitched them onto the sofa.

Approaching the bedroom he said, "Belle, is it all right to open the door now?"

"Yes, thank you," she answered.

Rafe eased it open fully and flipped off all the lights. He moved back out to the fire and stirred the burning embers then added more wood.

Abby watched from the dark. She really hadn't looked closely at him before. He had been her savior and doctor. A person who had shown up at the most crucial time of her life.

She studied him now in the firelight. He wasn't mending her ailments nor caring for her needs. Simply a shirtless man sitting on the sofa staring into the fire, holding a cup in two hands, not drinking, but in deep thought. Unconsciously, setting the cup down he clasped his hands and remained there. His muscular arms rippled as he rubbed his hands together in thought. She couldn't see his dark eyes, but she knew they were not threatening nor brooding, but caring and full of life. His black hair glistened and his strong handsome features suddenly made an impact.

Who is this man? she thought. *Is he the same one who lay beside me last night?* How could he have been that close and she have been so blind to this virile, handsome male form. He was beautiful. Or maybe his kindness made him so attractive to her. No, he definitely was beautiful.

He leaned back, stretching his long legs, and lifted his bare feet onto the table, crossing his ankles. His arms came up and he laced his fingers behind his head. Closing his eyes, his breathing slowed and she watched his slightly furry chest rise and fall, rise and fall, rise and...

Sleep claimed her.

CHAPTER 6

TOM HESITATED BEFORE lifting the receiver. "Hello."

"Detective Robertson here," Sam stated.

"Yes?" Tom acknowledged.

"I needed to touch base with you on a few things. Do you mind if we do it over the phone?" the detective asked.

"Not at all," Tom answered, hoping Robertson didn't detect his relief.

"Did you find any of Mrs. Cummings' personal articles, clothing or luggage missing?" Sam inquired.

"No. I was going to report that to you in a call this afternoon."

Of course, at your convenience! Sam had no respect for this man. *His wife is missing and what is he doing to try to find her? Perhaps he really expects her to show up.*

Tom asked, "Do you have any leads?"

"Not actual leads. However, the Charlotte police located Mrs. Cummings' car."

"Where?" His voice was suddenly strong.

"At the shopping center on Sedgeway Drive. Isn't that owned by your corporation?"

"Yes, it is. This is *not* a good sign, is it?"

"No, I'm afraid it isn't."

"Were there any signs of what could have happened to her?"

There was a hint of fear in Tom's voice.

"Nothing. The car was unlocked, contained a couple of magazines, a cell phone, a briefcase full of business papers and her purse, but no car keys."

"Her purse?"

"Yes, it was on the floor and contained charge cards, money and her drivers license. There was no evidence of any kind of struggle. No robbery, obviously. It looks like she simply got out with her keys and walked away."

"Well, I know she wouldn't have done that!" Tom replied adamantly.

"Unless the decision for a quick departure was made for her as she stepped from the car," Sam suggested.

"I wonder if anyone saw anything? Did you check with the businesses?" Tom asked.

"That's what we do," Sam stated. "No one saw a thing. The staff at the coffee shop said she comes in frequently, so they couldn't remember if the last time they saw her had been on Tuesday. The manager said he noticed her car parked on the lot but hadn't been concerned because he assumed she had left it there for a personal reason."

"Which obviously is not the case. She wouldn't have left her purse. And in an unlocked car? Never!" Tom emphasized.

"That was the manager's thinking, not ours," Sam reminded him.

"I guess I need to move it off the lot."

"No, they're bringing the K9 unit in to see if the dog can pick up her scent and give a direction of her departure from the automobile. If it leads away from the car to any degree, they'll start a search."

"I see," Tom said.

"The Charlotte police will then be taking it in for a closer look. Fingerprints have already been lifted, pictures made and all the preliminary work done but they need to check for other clues. They'll let you know when they've finished. I assume you still haven't received a call from anyone wanting money for her safe return?"

"No, I haven't. So what's next?"

"Why don't you come by the station tomorrow, uh, around two o'clock and we can go over everything in detail."

"Yes, I'll be there. Thank you, Detective Robertson." Tom did not relish the idea of appearing at the police station.

He paced only a few minutes before grabbing his coat and keys and heading to the office. On the way in, he rolled the windows down and let the cold air blow over him. The adrenaline was pumping and perspiration had begun to bead up on his head and body.

He pulled into his marked parking space and got out. He looked around at the familiar, trying to establish anything that might be out of order. With the exception of the snow, which had slowly vanished where the sun was able to lift it for another time, everything was as it had been two days ago.

The building was visually impressive. The magazine quarters had added to the prosperous look and the addition of shrubbery and trees around the complex created a tailored and well kept appearance. He was proud of what had been accomplished during his reign. *Abby should have realized that I have earned a partnership here.*

The mill's business was still growing, but he knew he was creating a difficult balancing act of keeping incoming and outgoing lumber on an even keel. Not to worry, he would simply keep Donald at a distance and all would be well. Pride and an attitude carried him into the mill's office. That decree set forth from Abby was not going to be the end of it. He was back and still in charge. He felt a control that had not been available to him before. A new beginning. How refreshing!

Walking into the main business section, he passed Donald's office on the right, a couple of secretaries chatting as they left the rest room to the left and onward to Alice's desk standing sentinel for the CEO's.

She was listening to a complaint from a lumber foreman who stood at her side with a form in his hand. Suddenly, like a deadly gas, silence claimed each voice. Taking notice, Alice looked up. A look of shock veiled her face briefly before she opened her mouth to question Tom's arrival. He passed by and entered his office without as much as acknowledging her presence.

Don turned from the filing cabinet as Tom walked through the door. With a folder and some papers in his hand, Don waited, unsure about how to react.

"What are you doing in here?" Tom asked.

"I was looking for the Cumberland folder." He felt like a child who's mother had just smacked his hands. "I needed to familiarize myself with—"

"That won't be necessary, I'm handling it."

Don released the drawer upon which his free hand rested and dropped his arm to his side. "But, Mrs. Cummings said—"

Tom twisted his head to look left, right and all around. Lifting arms akimbo he asked, "Do you see Mrs. Cummings?"

"No sir."

"Did she get back with you after leaving the other day?" Tom inquired.

"No, sir, but I understand she—"

Tom's face reddened as his hands formed fists at his sides and he leaned toward Donald. "Get out of my office," he said.

Donald, sixteen years Tom's senior, had been with the company more than a decade before Tom arrived on the scene. He had worked for the Langfords and until the last few years, had known the business inside out. Lately, however, Tom had isolated him, making it difficult to stay on top of things.

Returning the papers to their proper files, Don stood his ground briefly while he announced, "I'll work out of my office until Mrs. Cummings returns and informs me of the position she wishes me to hold." He spun on his heel and headed back to his office.

"You do that," Tom said, slamming the door.

"All right, give it to me," Sam said. "And for goodness sake, sit down. Your constant moving about makes my stomach queasy." He popped a Maalox into his mouth.

Eric had entered his boss' office with a report in his hand and found Sam on the phone. He waited for him to hang up, as he had information he wanted to pass on. It might need to be followed up and in that case he wanted to get on it.

"You talking to the media?" Eric asked, having heard a portion of Sam's side of the conversation.

"Yes, they've gotten wind of Mrs. Cummings' disappearance and this phone has been ringing off the hook. Now, tell me what you've got."

He seated himself and said, "The phone company has been very helpful. And I also took steps necessary to acquire both of the Cummings' cell records."

"Of course you did. And?"

"Mrs. Cummings made two calls Tuesday morning. If the time her husband gave us as to her departure from his office is correct, the first was made before she met with her husband and the other after. They were both to the magazine office and were short in duration."

"And Mr. Cummings?" Sam asked.

"Not too much activity. Calls to and from his office, the magazine's office, the country club, the barber and The Market's Home Delivery."

"Hasn't spent too much time searching, has he?"

"If he thinks she intends to come home, I guess he doesn't want her to believe she has him excessively upset."

Sam's phone rang and he lifted the receiver, then dropped it back into its cradle without regard.

"Doesn't he have any friends?" Sam asked.

"He's received calls from an Ethan Bland who is an employee of *Success* magazine. They probably know each other well. And then there's M.A. Templeton."

"Who is M.A. Templeton?"

"To whom the bulk of the calls to and from his home, office and cell phone have been made."

"Did you get an address on this number?" Sam asked.

Eric looked at his boss and rolled his eyes. "What do you think?" he said.

Sam stood. "Let's give this Templeton a little visit."

"I've got the car warmed up," Eric told him.

Maggie had slept in again. She loved her leisurely mornings. Ever since her divorce four years ago, she lived the life of luxury. Her husband had been wealthy but he had wanted a family. She really couldn't understand how he would expect her to go through the disfiguring act of carrying a baby. Her husband had been a big man. Why, she probably would have ended up with stretch marks. She simply would not hear of it. This caused a division in their relationship. He became so unhappy that in order to dissolve the marriage, he offered her a settlement she couldn't refuse. Her life was full now and she was free to enjoy it.

She hadn't intended to get so involved with Tom. There had been many men and she found it easy to dispose of them when ready to move on, but for some reason she couldn't let Tom go. He hadn't fawned over her like the others, yet she yearned for a permanence with him. He said he loved his wife and couldn't leave her. At the same time he seemed unable to cut ties with Maggie, therefore, leaving her to wonder if it was his wife he loved or his wife's money. Now, it seems, *that* problem no longer exists. Abby should have sent him away when she first learned of the affair. Oh well, not a problem any more.

She had just finished polishing her last nail when the doorbell rang. The nails were the finishing touch to her toiletry, thus, allowing them to dry without becoming mussed.

"Oh fiddle," she said with a frown. Looking at the ends of her fingers, she added, "Now they're going to get all smudged."

At the second ring she was flowing down the winding staircase with a smile spreading across her face. She moved quickly to the door expecting to see Tom as she drew it open.

"Oh!" she exclaimed to the two men standing on the doorstep. The larger of the two was as unkempt as the other was neat. The messy one glanced toward the younger man who was looking down at his shoes before turning his attention back to her.

"I'm sorry," the big man said. "Were you expecting someone else?"

"Actually, I wasn't expecting anyone!" she emphasized.

"I'm Detective Robertson and this is Detective Burke." Sam indicated Eric. "Could we have a few minutes of your time, Ms. uh, Templeton?"

"Yes, I'm Mrs. Templeton." She had kept her married name because it got her more attention and better tables. "What is this about?"

"I'm sure you are aware that Abby Cummings has not been heard from for several days. Since you know her, we hoped you could answer a few questions."

"Actually, I didn't really know her, I just knew *of* her and I can't tell you anything about her disappearance," she said.

"Mrs. Templeton, we only have generic questions for you and we would like to do it here but if you would rather, we could go downtown," Sam stated.

Maggie stared at the older man and then the other one, both of whom glared steadily back until she responded.

"Please, come in," she said, stepping aside and pulling the door fully open.

"You have a beautiful home," Eric commented, looking around the structure with interest. Their investigative sites certainly had come up in the world. This was much nicer than looking for the drug lords in the slums.

"Thank you." She led them into the sitting room and offered them two beautiful straight back, but uncomfortable, chairs. To prevent damage to the topcoat of her nails, she carefully took her position on a luscious divan. Crossing her ankles at the end of a pair of lovely long legs and pulling them to the side, she raised her right hand to her shoulder and brushed her straight, shiny hair to the back then gently laid one hand on top of the other in her lap. Lifting thick curled lashes off her clear blue eyes, she smiled and waited.

Both detectives were so caught up in the drama of her movements that neither spoke immediately. Sam cleared his throat and gave Eric a look of discomfort.

Eric suddenly reddened and looked down as he drew his pen and pad from his pocket. Maggie continued to smile.

"When was the last time you talked with Mrs. Cummings?" Sam asked.

"Approximately a year and a half ago. I told you, I know nothing about her present circumstances."

"What about Mr. Cummings?" Sam continued.

"What *about* Mr. Cummings?" Maggie questioned.

"When did you last talk to him?" Eric pressed.

"I talk with him frequently. I have a close friendship with Tom." She smiled and glanced down at her nails.

"But not with Mrs. Cummings?" It was Sam.

"That's correct!" She lifted her chin.

"I believe you were employed at Langford Mill at one time. When was that?"

"I was with Langford for two years before my employment with them ended eighteen months ago," she offered, still smiling.

"I see," Sam noted. "Were you a friend of Mrs. Cummings while you were employed there?"

"Actually, I seldom saw her. She was always in her offices working on the magazine. I know the two businesses are housed in the same building, but they are not internally connected. There was no employment sharing at all. Two totally separate businesses owned by the same mother company."

"What was the reason for your leaving?"

"What does that have to do with your being here now?" she asked.

"I wasn't hinting there was a connection. I'm simply trying to get a little insight into the past to help me understand the present. This type of questioning is routine," Sam assured her.

"I left for personal reasons. Let's leave it at that!"

Maggie shifted slightly, moved her back foot to the front and slipped the crossed ankles to the other side. She adjusted her skirt, smiled and said, "Continue."

Another thirty minutes of questions and protected answers and the detectives departed.

Eric closed the car door, and as he buckled up said, "That was like pulling teeth. Did you get anything out of it, Boss?"

"Other than her little suggestive display after seating us, not a damn thing!"

"She sure knows how to smile," Eric added.

"Let's go nose around the magazine offices a while. Maybe we can pick up some background there."

"We can't do worse than we did this morning. That woman really knows how to keep her cool."

rased

"Her cool and her secrets, I sensed," Sam suggested.
"Yes, and she sure knew how to smile," Eric said again.

The receptionist sat at the desk looking directly at the two men seated across the room. Assuming they were two more reporters at first, she told them the magazine was behind schedule but they could make an appointment for next week. Their badges changed her mind. She had sent a message to Ethan, who was in a bull session with the staff. She informed the detectives that when he was busy on a project, he often ignored messages until he was finished. They assured her they didn't mind waiting. Each one picked up an issue of *Success* and paged through it. Sam quickly replaced his while Eric flipped the pages slowly. He stopped to read for a few minutes then turned to Sam.

"I've met this man," Eric said. "Look," he added, indicating a picture on the magazine's Personal Page, titled *The Climb*. "I was once in his store, uh, haberdashery it says here. Actually it was an accident, I meant to enter the building next door but wasn't paying attention. It was really something, and expensive." Eric whistled.

"Is that right!" Sam said, staring at nothing.

"Are you here about Mrs. Cummings?" the girl asked.

"You might say that." Sam's attention was back on her. He felt she wanted to talk—or perhaps hoped *they* would.

"Mr. Bland says she had been upset over something and that she'll be back after she cools off. I've never seen her really disturbed, but I hope that's all it is. She's so nice. I hope she's all right."

"So, she's easy to get along with?" Eric prompted.

She smiled widely. "Yes, she cares about everyone and frets over them if they're having problems, but she's demanding when it comes to the magazine. Not in a mean way. It's just important to her and everyone understands that and admires her for it," she added.

"Who's in charge when she isn't here?" Sam wanted to know.

"Mr. Bland—*Ethan* Bland—of course. He knows all about the workings around here. He'll keep it running shipshape until she returns. He loves this business as much as she."

"Do they ever butt heads?" Eric asked.

61

"No one could possibly agree on everything, but he has certain articles and duties that are his and she stays clear of them and vice versa. When they disagree, it's usually ironed out rather quickly and without any temper tantrums, or at least none I've witnessed."

The inside door opened quickly and out stepped an impeccably dressed male with a welcoming smile. "Hello, Gentlemen," he said to the men, and, "I hope you haven't chewed their ears off, Patsy," to the receptionist.

"Not at all," Sam said. "She's made us very comfortable."

"That's what I like to hear. Please, follow me," Ethan said.

They walked into a large, well lit room occupied by a few desks, several drawing tables and a bank of computers with a person seated behind each one. Ethan led them through this area to his private office where he offered coffee or flavored tea.

Each declined both as they seated themselves in leather club chairs.

Ethan positioned one hip on the top of the front of his desk and with his long left leg dangling and right foot on the floor, he folded his arms. Eric looked from the Bally shoes, up to the French cuffs and on to his razor-cut sandy hair.

"You're here about Abby, correct?" Ethan asked pleasantly.

"Have you heard from her in the last few days?" Sam asked.

"The last time I had contact with her was Tuesday morning and that was by phone. She called me twice."

"What was her demeanor then and why wasn't she at the office?"

"She was on her way in when she called the first time. She was anxious to see if we had been notified about whether the magazine was going to be distributed in the Midwest. I told her it was an affirmative. She was excited and wanted to stop by Tom's office and give him the good news. Said she would see me shortly. Her mood was happy. No, she was elated."

"What about the second call?" Sam inquired.

Ethan stood, walked around his desk and took his seat in the large brown leather tufted executive desk chair. With elbows on the chair arms, he folded his hands placing the ends of his forefingers together in front of his mouth.

"Have you interviewed Tom Cummings yet?" he inquired.

"We have."

"Did he mention there had been... Let's see, how do I put this? He and Abby had just had words."

"Words? What does that mean?" Sam asked.

"Tom didn't mention their problem?"

"He simply said there had been an argument. Most couples have disagreements but that doesn't usually send one of them running."

"I guess it depends on the content of the argument."

"Are you going to help us or not? We want to find Mrs. Cummings before the leads get cold. If you could elaborate on their *problem* we would appreciate it!" Sam stated.

Eric paused in his note taking but kept his eyes on the paper and had his pencil ready.

"I'm uncomfortable discussing the personal problems of others. If Tom—"

Sam leaned forward and stated firmly, "We didn't come here to gossip, Mr. Bland. All we need to hear from you are some facts. Now, could you tell us what transpired on Tuesday before she went missing?"

Ethan stood and poured himself a cup of tea. "Are you sure you wouldn't like a cup?" he asked again.

"Mr. Bland, please. At the risk of sounding Dragnet-ish, just the facts!"

"About a year and a half ago, Tom got himself involved with his secretary."

"Margaret Templeton!" Sam said as Eric glanced at him.

Ethan nodded. "Abby found out about it and for a while it almost destroyed her. Tom was very remorseful and after several months of indecision and heartache, Abby pulled herself together. She knew she couldn't continue living with the hurt and doubts she harbored, so she attempted to put it behind her. Tom swore he would never cause her pain like that again."

Ethan leaned forward, placing his forearms on the desk, hands clasped. He rubbed his thumbs together and frowned.

"Abby and I have been friends for a long time, so I truly hoped that he meant what he said," Ethan continued. "Actually, I didn't believe it would be possible for Tom to cause her to suffer that badly again, because, in my mind, she never felt the same about him."

"Then she didn't put it behind her," Eric stated.

"On the surface, maybe," Ethan added.

"So it was a continuation of an old argument! But why would she wait so long after the fact to leave?" Sam asked.

"A new argument over the continuation of an old affair. Abby had just caught him making plans with Maggie over the phone. She fired him. Told him to get out of the house. It was over," Ethan said with a stone face and eyes staring above their heads.

The detectives waited. They knew he had more to say.

"She called me, calmly related the whole story and said she wouldn't be in." He was looking at Sam now. "She was afraid if she came to work, Tom would call or come by and she didn't want to see him again. I really think she was almost relieved to know what she had suspected for so long was true. It was over for her and she was all right." Ethan shook his head almost unbelieving.

"Did she say what she planned to do?" Eric inquired.

"No. That was it. She said we would talk later."

"So she sounded fine?"

"Yes. As a matter of fact, I had a shoot scheduled that day and I followed through instead of offering her a shoulder."

"A shoot?" Sam said.

"Shooting, or taking, pictures for a layout. We have several photographers on staff, but I like to do the background shots for the personal page projects. I don't do the portraits however. I know our photographers are better equipped for that."

Standing, Ethan moved to one of the wooden filing cabinets where he pulled the second drawer open and removed a folder. He returned to his chair, laid the folder on his desk in front of the detectives and opened it. It contained a group of pictures which he spread out on his desk. Both men leaned forward.

An outdoor pool, a garden area, a full view of a large home from several angles, a close-up of a business entrance adorned with a canopy awning and an old picture of a very small building with the same business name imprinted on a wooden signboard, hung over the door, were included in the pictorial display. "This is the result of Tuesday's work. It took all day," Ethan said. "And that's not the end of it. One of our photographers will bring the subject in to properly light and photograph on another day. The creative process of putting it all in written form is even more involved." It delighted him to go into the makeup of his article. He knew readers had no idea how much work it entailed.

"I see. Very nice," Sam offered, then leaning back in his chair, he turned his attention to Ethan and asked, "Any idea where she might have gone?"

Picking them up one at a time, Eric continued to study each picture intently. The home was fascinating to him. He couldn't imagine having the wealth to heat a place like that.

"Abby is an exceptionally independent woman. A strong person. I imagine she's getting herself together somewhere and will return when she's ready," he said.

"Don't you think she would call you if she were all right?" Sam asked.

Ethan sat silently for a moment. He leaned back in his chair and ran his hand through his hair.

"Oh, God. I can't bring myself to think that she wouldn't be all right. Yes, I have to believe that she'll call. She won't be able to let the magazine go to press without talking it over with me first. Besides, next to Tom, I'm the closest to a family that she has."

Sam tilted his head sideways as he lifted one eyebrow and said, "You say you have known Mrs. Cummings for a long time. Just how close were you?"

Ethan looked puzzled for only a second before a smile softened his expression. He stood up and turned to face the windows before replying. With his hands clasped behind him he seemed to be reflecting on the past.

Sam and Eric looked at each other and the younger detective shrugged his shoulders.

"Abby and I came from two different worlds. She, from a happy home in the lap of luxury. I, on the other hand, lived in the shadow of her neighborhood in a fatherless disparagingly poor shack."

Ethan turned to face them and continued, "I had no siblings, so I managed to find my way to play areas of the more fortunate. Abby never asked about my background, but she knew. It made no difference to her. She welcomed me and made me a part of her circle. That was all it was. If you were asking if we had ever been lovers, the answer is no."

Ethan watched the two men who sat before him waiting to see if he had finished, and looking as if they were expecting more.

"You see, as we grew into teenagers and became interested in the opposite sex in a more sophisticated way, everyone drifted toward their own. She and I stayed friends and spoke by phone often, but when she was sent off to boarding school, our lives became too busy for old friendships. You know, you just lose contact. Isn't that the way it's supposed to be? Everyone lives about four lives before they die. You have your childhood, your young adulthood, the period of life that takes you from the dreams to your realizations and then you're old."

Ethan brightened as he continued, "True friends, however, stay connected. After many years apart, she called me to come to work and as you can see, I accepted. Yes, she'll call me soon. I have no doubt."

"Well, if she does, please let us know," Sam said as he stood.

Ethan took the card Sam offered. "I'll do that."

"Eric!" Sam said to the young man who had picked up one of the pictures.

Eric laid it down quickly. Looking at Ethan he said, "You really did a good job with those."

"Thank you," Ethan said smiling.

"That's some home," Eric added.

"Estate," Ethan corrected.

"What does this man do for a living?" Eric couldn't leave it alone.

Ethan smiled and said, "He has many investments, not the least of which are a number of home developments. Presently he's beginning construction on an apartment complex. It will be a gated community built in the form of cottages. Maybe you have heard of it, *The Green Valley Flats*?"

"No," Eric replied.

"Well, detective, when his article goes to print, perhaps you'll buy the magazine and you can learn all about this man."

"Eric," Sam tried once more. "We do have to move along."

66

"I'm coming," the young detective replied as he joined Sam. He turned once more to Bland. "By the way," he said, "Tom isn't a violent man is he?"

"He has a temper but he would never harm Abby."

"Is that so!" Sam stated. "He would hurt her but not harm her!" Sam looked down and shook his head.

They walked silently out the front door and boarded the car. Sam was almost back at the station when he glanced toward Eric who seemed to be in deep thought.

"Okay, what's in your craw, boy? I can almost hear you thinking."

"There was something wrong. I can't put my finger on it yet, but I know something's off," Eric replied.

Sam laughed. "You're dreamin', son. Studying about all that grandeur. How it must be to live like that."

"Yeah, yeah, yeah," Eric replied, staring forward with knitted brows.

CHAPTER 7

BELLE, ARE YOU okay? Can you hear me?"

Rafe stood outside the closed bathroom door listening. She had insisted on a bath but it shouldn't have taken this long.

She was definitely improving. The swelling was minimal today, but she was still quite bruised. He felt she was pushing things in her weakened condition, but he drew her bath, and put everything in order. After helping her step into the tub, she made him close his eyes while she disrobed and held onto his hand to seat herself. Then she dismissed him. He had waited for her to call for his help when she was finished, and he should have heard from her by now.

"Belle!" he called again.

He heard a mumble. This was most improper, he knew, but he turned the knob and opened the door.

She was in the robe facing the mirror but bent over the basin. Most of the blood had been scrubbed from her pant suit, which hung on the rod above the tub along with her underwear. Instantly his mind told him she had done too much and was sick.

Grabbing her by the shoulders he leaned to her side and asked, "Belle, are you ill?"

She straightened, as best she could, and he caught sight of the towel spread across the sink bowl full of auburn curls.

"What—" he started.

"I couldn't return to civilization with my hair chopped off on one side. Everybody would stare," she said, looking at his reflection in the mirror. "I had to even it out."

His eyes widened. "Oh my goodness, you've done it now."

Dropping the scissors, she whirled to face him. "What?" she asked with raised eyebrows.

"You are absolutely drop dead cute!"

She punched his chest as she smiled up at him.

He wrapped his arms around her and pulled her close. "You scared me. I thought something was wrong."

She laid her cheek against him in exhaustion, as she extended her arms around his waist, leaning her weight upon him for support. "No, nothing's wrong except it's going to take a couple of hours to recoup."

He released her, bent forward and swept her up into his arms. "You lie down and rest and I'll clean up in here."

"Sounds like an idea to me."

He carried her to the sofa, put her down and pulled the throw over her. With one hand on the seat cushion and one on the sofa back, he leaned over her and said, "Don't try doing too much again without warning me first. You could have fainted."

They were almost nose to nose and she was totally lost in those dark eyes of his. Frowning, he tilted his head, inching closer to her mouth then stopped abruptly. He felt he could see into her soul. For several seconds neither moved.

Rafe closed his eyes, took a deep breath and pushed away. "I had better get things cleaned up. We wouldn't want to clog the sink," he stated, quietly turning away. *What is the matter with me?*

Abby, in the same vein, wondered about herself. She shouldn't have this attraction to him. She could be married. There might be children. Someone could even be searching for her now. Maybe a family who misses her terribly.

On the other hand, perhaps she was a bad person, running with dangerous cohorts. She didn't know. She didn't know anything. She raised her forearm to cover her eyes and her chin trembled.

That afternoon, she was lying on the bed as Rafe carefully examined her gunshot wound. She knew he was trying not to cause her pain and was surprised at the tenderness with which his large hands worked. No infection was present and the relief was evident on his face. *All his female patients must be crazy about him,* she thought.

"What is your field of medicine?" she asked.

"Oncology. There are four of us involved in a clinic. We provide outpatient chemotherapy, radiation and most nonsurgical treatment at the clinic. Anything more invasive is done in the hospital."

That dispelled the crush idea. His patients surely had more on their minds than his good looks.

"It must get pretty emotional," she suggested.

"Any practice has its heartaches, but when you can get a patient in time it's a wonderful thing to give that life back," he answered.

"Thank you for saving mine," she offered sincerely.

"I try not to allow people to die on my property. There, all done! You're healing well. The injury in your side will bother you the longest."

He handed her a mirror. "Look at how well the swelling is going down and the discoloration is changing. Do you recognize this face?"

"Of course. It's me, Belle," she smiled. "The first thing I'm going to get when we get off this mountain is makeup."

Her smile vanished as she looked at his reflection over her shoulder. "I don't have a purse. I can't buy anything."

"You don't need makeup, but, if you insist on wearing it, I think I can afford to help with that," he offered.

"I'll make a deal with you," she suggested. "If you will grant me a loan to get a few pieces of clothing and a minimum of personal items, I'll pull myself together, get a job and pay you back over time."

Rafe considered her expensive pant suit and shoes and knew when she came out of this fog and discovered her identity that she would not be job hunting. At this point though, she needed humoring.

"Sure. What kind of job? Do you know what you're qualified to do?" he asked, hoping she might unconsciously touch on something personal.

"I can read and write. I'm not sure about cooking. Filing couldn't be too difficult. If I try, I can be personable. There are a lot of working people with less qualifications than that!" she stated.

He laughed. "You're certainly right there. Sometimes it only takes a smile." Knowing he couldn't pull anything from that, he gathered his medical instruments and left her alone.

She stayed by the window watching the remnants of the snow drip from the trees and wondered what it looked like here in the summer. "Do you have air conditioning?" she called to him.

"Only by nature," he shouted in return.

Abby thought about the spring and wondered where she would be then.

"I think I'll spend tomorrow putting things in order and Sunday we'll head to town," Rafe added.

She was almost overcome. A fear for safety had nudged her desire to leave, but now, it was a different fear that made her want to stay. She felt a creeping rise of panic. What if he took her to town and turned her over to the police? What if the person who wanted her dead found her? What if her memory never returned and she had to live the rest of her life in a world of strangers?

"What will you do with me?" she asked shakily.

He walked back into the room and over to her. Bending down and taking her hands, he asked, "What do you want me to do with you?"

"I want you to take me home to my Dad," she replied through tears. "I want to crawl up into his lap and let him hold me and tell me who I am and that he loves me and won't let anyone ever harm me." She leaned her forehead onto his shoulder and couldn't stop the overwhelming grip of loneliness.

Rafe once more felt a tugging at his heart. He put his hand on the back of her small neck, then ran his fingers through her hair to cradle her head while she worked her emotions out.

"He used to give me butterfly kisses," she said through the knot in her throat. "And now he's gone." The fact that her parents were not living had imprinted itself in her mind. She was too young to have been orphaned. It must have been a grave illness, accident or some other tragedy that had taken them.

Rafe eased her over onto his knee and wrapped his arms safely around her as he rested his chin on top of her head. "I won't let anyone hurt you. I promise, I won't let anyone hurt you," he whispered.

It was very early and Abby, still in bed, lazily rolled to her side with a smile blessing her mouth. She was fighting consciousness. In her dream state, she was in a swing hanging from a strong limb in a large backyard. Her mother was watching from a window as her father stood behind her, pushing. She laughed in glee as her stomach rose into her chest on the upswing. Leaning back, almost turning upside down, she saw her father smiling at her delight.

She blinked and the light interrupted her euphoria. The faces were so happy, the setting familiar. She wanted to go back. To see her parents again. Unconsciousness had presented their images to her, maybe she could be reminded of their times together. It wasn't to be, it was over.

Opening her eyes, she lay quietly listening for sounds. When none came, she sat up and looked into the living room. The sofa was empty. She called out, "Ralph?"

No answer. Sliding from the bed, she walked through the cabin toward the kitchen. Suddenly, the front door swung forcefully open and she spun around to face Rafe coming swiftly into the room.

"Oh Ralph!" Both hands covered her heart. "You frightened the heebeejeebees outta me."

"The what?" he laughed. "Would you spell that, and while you're at it, I would like to hear you spell my name." He continued toward the kitchen.

"Which one, Ralph or Adams?" she asked, following him.

"You remembered Adams?" He paused looking over his shoulder at her. She almost ran into him.

"I was observing your adams apple when you told me your name, so I made a mental note associating the two. Thus, *Adams!*" she said proudly, smiling up at him.

"Fine, but that's not the one I want you to spell." He turned to face her, placing the end of the object he held on the floor.

"R, A, L, P, H." She said, looking into his eyes, then waited.

He looked back at her, saying nothing.

She folded her arms and smugly watched him, and again, waited.

He didn't move or blink, simply stared.

"That's not it, is it?" she said.

"No, it isn't."

"Ray?"

He shifted his weight and rested one hand on his hip.

"Randy?"

Nothing.

"Rumplestiltskin?"

"R," he said.

"R," she answered.

"A, F."

"A, F," she copied, rolling her eyes.

"E," he continued.

"E, spells Rafe."

"Yes, Rafe! *Rafe!*" he emphasized, leaning closer with each word.

"Gosh, Rafe's a bear today."

"Look what I found," he said, ignoring her.

"Rafe's fishing rod?" she replied, noticing, for the first time, the rod in his hand.

"That's obvious. No, this." He lifted a set of keys between his thumb and forefinger and jingled them.

"Were your keys lost?" she asked.

"I decided to look around the area where I found you. I located these on the dirt road where I spotted the vehicle."

"Do you think the person who hurt me lost these keys?"

"You didn't mention common sense when you were listing your job qualifications, did you! If these keys belonged to that person, the car wouldn't have gone anywhere would it?"

With a quick intake of breath she grabbed the keys and said, "They must be mine."

"Bingo!" He started to move again, going through the cabin to the back porch where he hung the rod.

Following him again, she turned the keys over in her hands, checking them thoroughly. "They look just like yours. There's no identifying initials, no key chain, nothing but keys and a remote clicker."

"I know, but they could be an important piece of your puzzle. Put them with your things because you may need them someday."

"My things?"

He took them back. "Okay, I'll keep them for you until you have some things."

CHAPTER
8

TOM WAS SITTING in his office behind the small desk, poring over the books. This desk was used by a secretary or assistant when the work required four hands to complete. He also preferred this desk for his personal tasks and he kept this material locked inside. He didn't like to go into the office on Saturdays but it was the only time he could work uninterrupted. Today's transaction had been a good one. He missed dinner but it had paid off. Now, he wanted to finish the paperwork so he could take Sunday off.

He lifted his head. Was that a pounding he had heard? It sounded again. He walked into the front area to find Maggie standing on the other side of the entrance door.

"What are you doing here?" he asked as he let her in.

She kissed him on the cheek. "I'm missing you like crazy," she crooned.

"No, this is what's crazy. You should *not* be here."

"It's Saturday night. All those mean old detectives are home with their wives and kids or out with their girlfriends. That's what you should be doing, going out with your girlfriend!"

"Stop it, Maggie," he said, locking the door and walking back to his office.

"You're turning into such a grouch," her pouted lips complained.

She turned off the waiting room lights and followed him, closing the office door. He stepped behind the desk as she moved in beside him.

"What's all this?" she asked, picking up some of the paperwork to inspect. "Can't you finish it during working hours?"

He took it from her, slipped it into a folder and closed the books. Putting everything in the drawer and locking it, he said, "I'll wrap it up Monday. I'm tired anyway."

As he turned toward his large desk, she took his arm and walked with him. She stepped in front of him and splayed her fingertips on his chest. Looking hungrily into his eyes, she pushed him down into his chair and spun him away from her as she seated herself on his desktop.

"You're spending too much time at the office and worrying excessively," she said, maneuvering his coat down his arms. Laying her hands on his shoulders, she began massaging his taut muscles. "You're so tense. Relax."

He closed his eyes when she leaned forward and kissed the side of his neck. Her fingers worked the flesh between his spine and scapulas. The tightness was losing its grip and his mind abandoned the burdens that haunted him. The undulating hands brought on a dreamy comfort. Bringing her ministering up to the back of his neck, she lengthened the knotted muscles with lightly pressured strokes.

Just when he felt he could drop right off to sleep, she pushed her hands around his neck to loosen his tie and unbutton his shirt at the throat.

One hand took the next button as the other slid inside through the light growth of chest hair. The once muscular chest and abdomen had been neglected causing the washboard effect to be less defined. Her hand slid lower as she pressed her breasts against the back of his shoulders.

She turned her mouth toward his ear and whispered, "Feeling better?"

Her tongue touched his ear and moved along the creases as she exhaled a warm breathy "Aaaah" into his ear. She tightened her arm across his upper chest while her other hand worked its way past his belt to tease the tip of his rising desire.

"Oh, yes!" Her voice low and throaty, she added, "You *are* feeling better."

She straightened slightly, pulling her hands up to his shoulders and with a flip, she spun him back to face her. Uncrossing her legs she slid from the desk and straddled his lap. Her dress slipped upwards and he knew, before he touched her, that she wouldn't be wearing panties.

With eyes focused on her tongue that was running over her upper lip, he stretched his arm around her reaching for the lamp.

"Don't turn it off," she said. "It might look suspicious if anyone notices our cars in the lot."

"That's not why you want it left on," he growled, shifting the action to the floor. "You want to watch what I'm going to do to you!"

At eleven o'clock the jangling phone persisted until Tom answered.

"Tom," Ethan said. "Are you awake?"

"No, call me back this afternoon. Or better yet, next week."

"How did everything go yesterday?" Ethan was not to be put off.

"Don't you ever sleep in?" Tom rolled to his side and sat up with his feet resting on the floor and his head drooped forward.

"You know what they say about the early bird! How did it go yesterday?"

"I think all parties will be happy."

"Great. Have you had any news on Abby?"

"No, nothing."

"Hope is beginning to dim, isn't it? There's such a void in the office, it's like a morgue. I didn't realize how much life she brought into that place." He hesitated, then added, "I'm sorry, Tom. I'm sure it must be terrible at your place."

"Yes, it's very disturbing." Tom straightened and ran his fingers through his hair.

"Have the authorities found any clues as to where she may have gone?" Ethan asked.

"They located her car," Tom said, "or did I tell you that?"

"No, you didn't! How could you fail to get that information to me? That doesn't sound good." He paused. "Not good at all."

"No, and it's giving me nightmares. Why would she leave her car? And her purse and phone were inside," Tom told him. When Ethan didn't reply, he continued, "None of her clothes seem to be missing, there have been no withdrawals from our accounts and there's been no activity on her credit cards."

"This is sounding more and more serious," Ethan said worriedly. "Have you checked with the hospitals? Maybe she's been injured or is ill."

"The police did that. She isn't a patient and they have no Jane Does. It's strange and upsetting," Tom said.

"Upset? Really? I noticed you had company at the office last night."

"It wasn't planned. She stopped by uninvited. She was nosing around the private ledgers so I was forced to distract her."

"Am I supposed to believe that? Use your head, Tom. If you expect Abby to come back, you'd better be a little more discreet—or more importantly, how about giving The Lovely Ms. Templeton up?"

"You think I haven't tried? Every time I think I'm about to shake her, she shows up, common sense deserts me and my libido kicks in."

"Then do something about your libido!"

"I'm working on it!" Tom was almost shouting.

Ethan backed off. An uncomfortable silence followed before Ethan, more calmly, asked, "Tell me, what are the detectives saying?"

"It's not even been a week. I think until they located the car, they expected her to show up. Now they've shifted into high gear."

Another silence.

"Ethan, are you there?" Tom asked.

"Yes, I was just considering a possibility."

"What kind of possibility?"

"You don't suppose Maggie has done something, do you?" Ethan suggested.

"*Done something*?!" Tom jerked to his feet. "What do you mean by, *done something*?" He was definitely awake now.

"It doesn't sound like she intentionally walked away from her car. I guess I wondered if maybe Maggie had taken her away."

Tom paced, running his free hand through his hair, pushing it off his forehead. "Right. I'll bet Maggie pulled up, grabbed her by the hair and dragged her screaming from one car to the other, handcuffed her, strapped her in and sped away. And to beat it all, nobody witnessed it! Really, Ethan, what the hell is the matter with you?"

"I guess I was wondering if Maggie stopped and asked to talk to her or that they had run into each other accidentally on the lot and Abby could have gotten into her car to talk and Maggie drove away with her. I don't know. I'm just grabbing at straws."

"Well, you're grabbing at the wrong one, because you're not going to find her in Maggie's closet!"

When Tom ended the conversation, he sat back down on the side of the bed and remained there, hunched forward with his hands clasped together between his thighs. He was tired and he didn't want to move. Finally, rising to his feet, he shuffled downstairs in his sleeping shorts. Abby wasn't home, so he saw no reason to put on a tee shirt.

He started the coffee brewing and walked through the wide opening into the great room. After switching on the TV, he went back to the kitchen to prepare his cup with a few grains of sugar. Opening the refrigerator and checking the empty shelves, he decided he wouldn't have wanted to eat alone anyway.

The aroma of coffee was almost comforting to him. He leaned on a counter chair waiting for the dripping to cease. Looking through the doorway, the television caught his attention and drew him into the room. Without blinking, he stood, staring at Abby's smiling face on the large screen above the word, "MISSING."

Oh God, Abby! I'm so sorry. So very sorry. You know I loved you.

He fell to his knees and dropped his face into his hands.

Sharon Evans-Rose

CHAPTER

9

IT TOOK RAFE the entire day to get down the mountain. He had gathered his saw, axe, shovel and several other tools he felt he may need to clear the road of any debris. Abby packed him a lunch and filled a large bottle of water.

"I hope you don't encounter any unmanageable trees blocking the road," she said. "Are you certain you don't want me to ride along?"

"No, I'm sure I'm going to be very busy and you would be cooped up in the car alone, but thanks for offering."

Handing him the bagged lunch, she warned, "Please be careful."

"I'll be back before dark and you shouldn't expect me before then. Will you be okay?"

"Yes, of course. I'll be busy packing all my bags and choosing just the right outfit to wear," she said with a smile. "Don't worry about me, I'll find something to clean."

"Just stay inside. No one can get to you without me seeing them first. Nevertheless, you shouldn't open the door to anyone," he cautioned as he departed.

She tried to relax, but found the day excruciatingly long. Eventually, she lay down on the sofa and closed her eyes. The silence was broken only by a distant visiting bird. Its song lulled her to sleep where she found herself sitting in a swing watching a starling skittering about on the lawn. It was pecking at the ground in search of a worm.

She was pushing with her toes only slightly forward and back, keeping her attention on her feathered friend. Slowly she stood and putting one foot in front of the other, she tried to move without disturbing the hunt. She wanted to get a close look at the bird.

A six-year-old's small feet, walking heel-to-toe, would take a long time to cover the ground between herself and the bird, but she kept at it. When finally reaching the spot she felt was close enough, the animal's small head came up with a worm caught in its beak and took flight so suddenly that she jumped.

Her eyes opened as she instantly sat up, somewhat disoriented, and listened for the sound that roused her. She looked around to establish her whereabouts. As her predicament surfaced, she heard the uniform crunching of footsteps against gravel announcing that she was no longer alone.

She rose from the sofa with the intention of peeking out the window to see if it was Rafe, when the kicking against the entry began. Moving quickly to the door, she leaned against it. Waiting, it was silent now.

The kicking started again and she heard Rafe call, "Belle? It's me!"

She unlocked the door and threw it open. With great relief she grabbed his arm and said, "Thank goodness it's you. I was really frightened."

He was still standing outside the door as she suddenly released him and with a frown, said, "You scared me! Why didn't you let me know it was you before you kicked the first time? I didn't know what was going to happen. How could you do that to me?"

He stood with hands full of tools, stature sluggish, hair matted with sweat and eyes tired and regretful. She looked at him and was filled with shame.

"Oh, Rafe, I'm so sorry. I was sleeping when you got here so I didn't see you arrive. How selfish of me," she blurted as she tried to take some of his gear to lighten his load.

He held tightly onto everything as he stepped inside. "It's all right."

"You look exhausted. What can I do for you?"

"Just let me get cleaned up and then I want to get some sleep." He sounded dissipated.

"Aren't you hungry?"

"No. I only want to rest."

She ran the tub full of warm water while he put things away. Heating a can of soup and filling a glass with milk, she made him eat after his long soaking. He was too tired to argue when she insisted he take the bed.

"Would you like me to rub your back?" she asked.

"The water relaxed my muscles. I'll be fine," he replied, heading to the bedroom.

She followed him and picked up a pillow to take with her to the sofa. He plopped down onto his back and with eyes closed and ankles crossed, he locked his fingers together on his stomach.

Abby stood beside the bed looking at him as a soothing healthful cocoon of sleep enveloped him. She lifted a sprig of hair from his forehead and leaned down to kiss him lightly on the cheek.

The next morning was spent readying the cabin and their minds for departure. To Abby, it was leaving home as it was the only one she could remember. The only one, except that of her dreams, and she suspected there had to be some semblance of her youth in those dreams.

When all was ready, she pulled on a pair of old tennis shoes she had found in the closet, and looking like Clarabelle, she asked Rafe, "Could we walk to the place you found me?"

He took her hand and they wandered slowly through the trees. "It really is total seclusion up here, isn't it?" she stated.

"Until recently," he added with a wink.

She looked up at him and smiled.

As they neared their destination, she released his hand and turned to look back.

"We've come quite a distance. I don't think the cabin could have been seen from here that evening."

"That was my belief too. The lights weren't on inside and visibility was highly limited by the snowfall. Whoever brought you here thought you would not be found. You really were left for dead. Or to die."

She shivered. "Loss of memory may be a defense mechanism, don't you think?"

Without answering, Rafe watched her as she examined the small area.

"So, if it weren't for the keys and your fishing rod you would never know I had been here. It's sad and ironic," she said. "Someone intended for my life to end here, yet, for Belle, this is where it began."

She touched a few trees as her eyes followed the trunks up to where the limbs mingled so thickly that one was unable to tell which limb belonged to which tree. Briefly leaning against one trunk, she closed her eyes and listened for a sound she could take with her for remembrance. Nothing.

Shuffling about, she picked up a stick to examine before using it to brush debris about on the ground. She stooped down and fingered a few rocks before locating the one she wanted. Lifting it, she stood and dropped it into her pocket.

Rafe watched her performance with a mellow heart, knowing that she was creating a memory for herself. She finally tossed the stick away and with a final circular glance, returned to his side. He took her hand again and led her back to the cabin in silence.

She took a bath, put her own damaged clothes back on, heels and all, dampened her hair and blew it into a soft style, including a slight feathering of bangs, which she had never worn, bit on her lips and pinched her cheeks.

Looking at this slightly thinner face in the mirror, she asked it, "Just who are you? Where are you from and what did you do to get yourself in this fix?" Getting no answers, she shrugged her shoulders and left the room.

With hair dryer in hand she entered the bedroom where Rafe was putting his things together and asked, "Rafe, do you take this or leave it here?"

He picked up the luggage and turned to her. His eyebrows raised and he blew air through puckered lips. "Is this little Belle? You look like an executive. And a very pretty one."

She smiled. "Have I graduated from cute?" she asked, tilting her head.

"I'll say." He released the bags and walked toward her.

She held the dryer in front of herself. "Do you take this or leave it?"

He took it from her and tossed it onto the bed. "I leave it."

Taking her shoulders, he turned her around for an all over look. "You're taller."

"Almost three inches," she stated, smiling.

"A *take-charge* girl if I ever saw one."

"Well, thank you, kind sir."

"Okay, let's go," he said, indicating that she take the lead.

Abby stayed alert, watching for clues, as Rafe drove down the mountain and took Route 52 into Winston-Salem. Nothing was familiar. He drove her past the clinic and on to his home.

His house was located in a typically upper middle class residential area where lawns were cared for by the owners, everyone had a barbecue grill in the back yard, the children were bussed to school and neighbors knew each other's names. It appeared welcoming and friendly.

Abby sighed with relief. *Nobody here would want to kill anyone,* she thought. She smiled inwardly as he said, "We're home."

He pulled into his driveway, punched the remote and the garage door opened upward as he eased the vehicle inside and closed the door. Entering the house, she made mental notes as he escorted her through the laundry room, past a bathroom and into the kitchen/family room combination.

"This area, and of course my bedroom, is where I live. The living room is for, uh... I don't know... visitors?" he said.

She followed him to the bedroom that he indicated would be hers.

"Why don't you look your room over while I put my things away, then we can take you to do a little shopping, have dinner and finally get settled in here."

She did as he asked, then they made a quick run to a shopping center across from the clinic. Abby purchased clothing while Rafe picked up groceries. After loading the vehicle, Rafe ran over to the clinic while Abby stopped in Quick Cuts for a hair trim.

Rafe returned as she was walking out of the salon. "You obviously didn't settle for a simple quick cut!"

She smiled and touched her head with her hand. "No, I didn't. I've never worn my hair this short, and I decided to have the tips lightened. Now, Belle really *is* a new person."

"It's very becoming." He thought she looked pixie-cute, but he kept the thought to himself. "How about picking up hamburgers and taking them home for dinner?"

"I think that sounds fine. It's been a long day and my stamina is running low," she admitted. "Thank you for everything, Rafe. I'll reimburse you as soon as I get on my feet."

"Forget it! Let's consider all this a trade-off. While you're living in my house, you can practice your cooking skills."

"But—" she started.

"That's the end of it," he said sternly.

After a few days adjusting, Abby decided to get on with life and her initial stab at normalcy was to try the "cooking thing."

When Rafe arrived home that evening, the aroma that met him at the door brought back memories of his mother. He stood silently as sights of happy times washed over him.

"Rafe, are you coming in or not?"

He shook the scenes from his head and entered the kitchen where he lifted each lid before giving Abby a large appreciative hug.

She smiled happily as they dined on chicken and dumplings, green beans, pineapple salad, rolls and iced tea.

"Belle, you've really brought life into the dining room, and I'm not referring only to the food and company. It's really amazing."

"That's very kind, but I only made a few changes," she said.

"The house has really needed some serious female attention."

"I'd like to talk to you about that, Rafe. Look, I can't simply sit around here all day doing nothing. Would you mind if I spruced things up?"

"I have a lady who cleans once a week," he said.

"That's not exactly what I mean. I'd like to do some painting, rearranging and if you'd agree, have a few things recovered. Would you think about it?"

"Why don't you start on one room and see if you're up to it?" he suggested. Perhaps if she could think about something other than her situation, her mind might begin to recall things. "I've got a handyman that I'll get to help you."

"Thank you, Dr. Adams." She lowered her eyes, and repeated softly, "Thank you."

Sharon Evans-Rose

CHAPTER 10

S AM, ERIC AND Tom were clustered around a table at the police department. Eric had placed a cup of steaming coffee in front of each of them. Now, he set a carton of nonfat cream in the center and took his seat.

Sam lifted the cup to his lips for a gulp before they began. He returned the cup to the table so fast he splashed coffee over the rim and onto his hand. Opening his mouth to suck in air, he stared at Eric and said, "Yipes, boy, that just about cooked my tonsils. How did it get so hot?"

"I can't drink lukewarm coffee from that old pot, so I heated it in the microwave," Eric stammered.

"Well, I can. Don't do that to me again."

Tom watched the play between them. Sam was gruff with the young man but he didn't mean any of it. The scene struck him as a fatherly thing. Tom waited impatiently for them to turn their attention to his problem.

As Eric wiped the table clean, Sam picked up a small stack of papers and tapped the bottom edges on the table to bring them together in a neat form. Laying it in front of him, he scanned the first page quietly. Eric sipped his creamed coffee and smiled at Tom.

Without looking up, Sam said, "We seem to be standing in the dark without a flashlight. We've explored every avenue and can't find a solid lead."

Looking at Tom, he asked, "You got anything?"

"No, I've told you everything I know."

"We're going to have to dig a little deeper. It's been over a week now, and nobody has heard from Mrs. Cummings. Her car was abandoned. None of her personal things are missing. The dog picked up her scent in the car and followed it about two feet before stopping. It seems she just vanished, but I don't think it was by choice."

Tom said, "That same thought has been gnawing at me."

"With nothing pointing to what happened to her, the next thing we do is look for a motive for her disappearance. Who would you guess would have reason to want her out of the way?" Sam asked.

"I can't imagine."

"Does she have any disgruntled employees, ex-employees, relatives, friends or husbands?" Sam wanted to know.

"Are you suggesting that I'm a suspect?" Tom asked incredulously.

"Until we can unravel this puzzle, everyone is a suspect. Our present job is to eliminate each one until we're left with the guilty party."

Tom shifted uneasily in his chair. "Couldn't she have been abducted by somebody totally unconnected to any of us? It happens all the time. Haven't you heard about the Amber Alert?"

"Yes, that's true, but more often than not, the perpetrator is known to the victim. What about relatives? Are any of hers located here?"

"No. Neither Abby nor I have anyone close. Most of our relatives are older and we've never really kept in touch," Tom replied.

"If no one had a grudge against her, then we must consider who would profit the most from her being taken," Sam said.

"There isn't anyone but me. She has no siblings and we have no children. I don't know how anybody could benefit from her demise, if that's what has happened to her."

"Then you would be the sole heir to Mrs. Cummings' estate, is that correct?" Eric asked, setting his cup down.

Tom asked to use the phone. He made a quick call to his lawyer. "We're finished until my attorney gets here."

Sam and Eric left him alone while they waited. Jason Arbaugh was with a firm in Charlotte, so Tom had close to an hour to fret. He found it very difficult to sit still. He had quit smoking when he met Abby, but he sure would like to light up now.

Finally, his lawyer arrived and the four gathered around the table to continue. Sam explained at that time that this was a simple interrogation. Tom was only one of several people with whom they intended to talk. They were not focusing on Tom or anyone else. There was no proof of any crime having been committed, but Mrs. Cummings had been missing too long to simply assume that she was vacationing and they believed Tom was the last one to see her.

"Mr. Cummings, we want to find your wife and I'm sure you want us to do everything possible to accomplish that. You happen to have been the closest to her, which gives us the hope that something you might know, even subconsciously, could suggest a direction we should take. Now, if you don't mind, we'll get back to business." Sam looked at the lawyer for affirmation.

As Tom replied to the questions, his lawyer cautioned him to be careful. "Even the innocent can incriminate themselves," he warned.

"Just as the guilty can come off innocent," Sam replied, then turned to Tom. "That is not to suggest that you are responsible. We're only looking for answers. You may know something that would help, but in your mind you haven't linked it to what happened."

They continued for almost an hour. In the end, Sam thanked him for being cooperative and asked that he notify them if he remembered anything else. They all shook hands and Mr. Arbaugh departed while Tom made a stop at the rest room. He splashed water on his face and leaned onto his hands while trying to regain his composure. Anger and fear lay heavily upon him. He left the building and stood for a while trying to remember where he had parked the car.

Tom sat across the table from Ethan in a quiet corner of the bistro. He had asked Ethan to join him for dinner. The meeting with the detectives had been traumatic and he needed to talk to someone.

He picked up his Guinness, then set it back down. Leaning over the table, he looked at Ethan and said quietly, "I think they suspect that I have done something to Abby!"

"What? But why?"

"They didn't come right out and say it," he told him, "but the questions certainly were indicative of such suspicions."

"You must be overreacting, Tom." Ethan sipped his cosmopolitan looking down his nose and over the edge of his glass at his friend.

"You think? They hinted at checking out my car and house. They wanted to know where I spent the day after Abby left the office."

"And, where were you?"

"If you recall, I visited your office. Then I went home. I didn't go out again until Wednesday and that was only for a late lunch."

"Can you verify that? Was the housekeeper there? Or anybody else?" Ethan asked with lifted eyebrow. "Maybe you made calls that would show up through the phone company."

"No, Berta doesn't clean on Tuesday and no one else was there. Maggie has never been in our house, but I did talk to her that day," he said thoughtfully. "Wait, that wasn't until the evening."

"Tom, the husband is always the first suspect when something happens to the wife. Those were just routine questions. There is no reason for them to think you would want to be rid of Abby."

"Let's see! I have a mistress and Abby just found out. My livelihood, at this point, depends wholly on my wife, who had just asked me to move out. If I'm widowed, I have everything, whereas, if I'm divorced, I don't have a pot to piss in. Sounds like a motive to me!"

"We know you wouldn't hurt her. Well, you *did* hurt her, but you didn't do her any physical harm. Why would anyone harm her? A kidnapping I could understand, but you would have heard something by now." Ethan pushed his drink aside. "Unless she fought, and they, perhaps, killed her by accident. In that case they might be afraid to contact you."

"If that happened, the police would still be trying to pin it on me," Tom suggested, "because they have to find a guilty party."

"Abby's too smart to have done that anyway," Ethan said, concentrating. "She would have reacted calmly while trying to reason an escape."

"Oh, I don't know what to think and I can't believe this conversation." Tom turned the glass up and drained it. "I'm sorry Ethan, I simply can't eat." He stood, threw a hundred dollar bill onto the table and added, "Have yourself a good meal. I'll talk to you tomorrow."

Detective Robertson's call to Tom for permission to visit the mill and speak with the workers highly unnerved him. He wasn't sure what might have been overheard in his office, but Donald knew something awful had transpired and Donald disliked him so much he might accuse him of anything. Maybe he shouldn't have gone back to the mill so quickly. No, he had to get back. He couldn't chance having Donald digging around in his office. Perhaps he should have been a little nicer when he caught him there—after all, Donald was following Abby's orders.

Tom felt the detective had made up his mind to pin the crime, if he could prove there was one, on him. If Sam Robertson kept this up, he would charge the detective with harassment. What was the matter with him? If he made a fuss, it would simply invite more suspicions.

Damn Abby! She shouldn't have reacted so harshly. So he had been with Maggie, so what! Everybody messes around sometime. It would have passed.

"Very interesting!" Eric said.

They were leaving the Langford Mill's office, having gone there to talk with employees. The visit had not proven fruitful. However, they did get more of an insight into personalities involved. It seems that Abby was the favorite while Tom was considered to have an uneven temper. Of course, he held the position of control and would naturally be more objective and less friendly. Where it was difficult to get anyone to discuss Tom, everyone was more than ready to tell them, in glowing terms, about his wife.

Donald was the most open. Having been with the company and family so long, he appeared secure in his position. He was in total recall when passing on the events of his last conversation with Abby and his apprehension was obvious.

"Has Mr. Cummings remained on the job during his wife's absence?" Sam asked Donald.

"He was away for two days."

"What about the day she left? Did he leave immediately after his wife?"

"I don't know how long he remained here, but when I went out for lunch he was gone. I'm sure Alice can give you more information."

"And when he came back to work, how did you handle that?" Eric asked.

Donald described the scene that took place in Tom's office. He said he had tried to stay clear of Tom since then.

"Doesn't that make it difficult to run the business smoothly?" Sam asked.

"It had already become difficult for me. I seem to have been relegated to the basement, so to speak, and am only allowed to be involved in what *he* chooses."

"How did his wife feel about that?"

"The rapid growth of the magazine had so consumed her that when she was over here she was usually on a mission, but she always took time to say hello and visit a while. I didn't want to burden her with what was bothering me or be the cause of any friction between them."

"Did you witness any disagreements or ill tempers between the two of them?"

"When he first came to work here, shortly after their marriage, he was very attentive to her. They each seemed devoted to the other."

"And later?" Sam prompted.

"When the magazine began to take Ms. Abby out of the picture here, I seldom saw them together, so I can't answer that."

"In your own opinion, would you ever think he could hurt her?" Eric asked.

Don bowed his head and thought for a moment. "I don't know him well enough to reply with any honesty. I can say that I've never seen him be unkind to her."

"That's a positive sign."

"I hope you find her safe. I miss her," Don told them.

They stopped by Alice's desk and requested a few moments of her time.

Where Donald Freeman had welcomed their questions, Tom's secretary was somewhat more hesitant.

She asked them to have a seat. "I'm very concerned about Mrs. Cummings. What can I do?" she asked, glancing nervously in the direction of Tom's office.

"Last Tuesday morning, as she left, what was her demeanor?"

Speaking quietly she said, "She wasn't as distraught as she was angry, I think. Actually, she was very much in control. It's the first time in a long time I've seen the business side of her." She glanced once more at the door.

"Did you know or do you know what brought on this anger?"

"She arrived excited about something and was anxious to share it with Mr. Cummings, so she entered his office without waiting to be announced." Lowering her voice yet again, she added, "That put me in disfavor with him," she recalled, tilting her head in the direction of the door. "The next thing I knew, she came out and told me that as of that moment Donald was in charge," she whispered. "Then she left."

"And how long did he," Sam tilted his head toward Tom's office, "remain here after she left?"

"He walked to the front door and watched her depart then went back into his office, put his coat on and took off."

"Did he say anything before leaving?" Eric asked.

"No. That's all I know. I really have nothing more to add," she whispered, turning back to her computer.

"Just one more question, please," Sam said.

Over her shoulder she said, "Yes?"

"Do you know if Mrs. Cummings had any enemies or if there was anyone who really had issues with her?"

Alice did not turn away from the computer nor did she reply. She picked up a pad and pencil, made a quick note, folded the paper and handed it to Sam.

"If you'll excuse me, I must get back to work," she said.

"Of course."

Sam slid the note into his pocket and they left the building and walked to their car. As Sam closed his door, he retrieved the note and opened it.

Eric watched Sam as he looked at the note then passed it to him. Sam started the car as Eric read the words out loud: "M. Templeton!"

The two detectives were sitting in an unmarked car along the road outside the mill parking lot. This was the third day they had observed Tom and so far it had been very uneventful.

"This is getting to me," Eric said. "Something's gotta happen or I'm going to expire of boredom."

"You don't fish, do you, Eric?"

"No, why?"

"Because it takes patience," Sam said. "You have to learn to wait. You can't force events. Let the fish swim until he's ready. He's not going to take the bait right away. He's going to wait until he thinks he can safely make the move. Then you've got him."

Eric waited for Sam to make his point. Sam looked at Eric and raised one eyebrow.

The light went on and Eric blushed. "Oh, I know. It's like detective work, right?"

"Right! Now, relax."

"I'll try."

After a few minutes of silence, Eric asked, "What did the department in Charlotte find?"

"Nothing. Jefferies said the car was clean and the dog had trouble picking up anything more than a short lead. I guess she didn't go far, or the melting snow destroyed her scent. They made a pretty thorough localized search, but didn't find anything."

"Too bad. I had hoped they would provide us with something."

In that instant Tom's Lexus began to nose its way out of the lot.

96

"Here we go," Eric said.

They waited until he had gotten into the flow of traffic before pulling onto the road. Keeping two to three cars between them they had no problem following as Tom was careful not to exceed the speed limit.

"He's quitting early today. Maybe he has plans," Eric suggested.

Twenty minutes later, he turned up a driveway between two brick pillars and well sculpted yews. When they approached the entrance they neither stopped nor looked in that direction. Driving past and turning around at the next available place, they were now traveling in reverse.

The property was in view, so they slowed. Tom had driven up the curved driveway and was getting out of his vehicle in front of the house. He carried a briefcase.

"Sam, look! That's the house!" Eric almost shouted.

"What house?" he asked.

"In the pictures. Remember the ones Ethan showed us? You know, his shoot."

Sam leaned forward, coming almost to a stop, and squinted at the setting.

"You're right, but what would Mr. Cummings be doing there?" Sam paused thinking it over. "Maybe he knows this man and asked Ethan to pick him for the next issue."

"I've had an unsettling feeling about this place ever since Mr. Bland showed us those pictures."

About half an hour later, Tom returned to his car, put the briefcase in his trunk and drove to a restaurant in town where Margaret Templeton was seen entering shortly after his arrival.

"I'll tell you," Eric said, "that woman sure can smile."

"With his wife missing, you would think he would be a little less open with his affair!" Sam grumbled.

"Yeah, he should have enough respect for her to appear concerned." Eric had never met Abby, but he was beginning to have pity for her.

Eric left the car, ran a couple of blocks, and picked up dinner at a fast food eatery. Returning to the car, he passed out the sandwiches and drinks. They ate, keeping one eye on the restaurant door.

When Tom and Ms. Templeton reappeared, they went their separate ways. The detectives stayed with Tom until he was home and the house was dark.

Saturday morning, Sam, Eric, three or four people from forensics and half a dozen policemen arrived at the Cummings' home with a search warrant. Tom appeared shocked and became very upset at their arrival.

"We would like to put a couple of people on your vehicle or vehicles. How many do you own?" Sam asked.

"Other than the one Abby was driving," Tom said, "two. The car parked in the driveway and an SUV in the garage."

"Very well, Mr. Cummings. We'll get started now, and I'll speak with you before we leave."

Tom stood at the windows for a time. It was raining and he wondered how heavy the fog would be on the mountain. He turned briefly to watch everyone going through his things, then sat on the sofa and rested his elbows on his knees and his chin in his hands. He stared quietly into space.

Once a perfect specimen of the male jock, Tom had softened with time. He had become so busy that any effort at body building had become less important. He jogged many evenings, but that didn't build muscle.

Eventually, to avoid the intrusion, he moved to the kitchen and poured a cup of coffee, adding the usual cream and a few grains of sugar. After testing a sip he stirred in a little more sugar. Taking his cup, he sat at the table with the morning paper. He flipped the pages and twisted the cup while waiting nervously for the crew to finish. Sam walked in and joined him.

"Coffee?" Tom asked.

"No thanks. Today, it would just sour on my stomach."

I really wanted to know that, Tom thought, but asked, "Have you found the smoking gun?"

"We did locate a gun but it doesn't seem to have been fired lately."

"That gun was purchased for protection, and was used for practice only a short time. We've kept it in the bedside table at all times except when it's being cleaned."

98

"We'll be taking it with us for tests and will return it in a few days. This is all routine, Mr. Cummings. Unfortunately most spouses go through this kind of thing when something questionable happens to a mate. The reason is, that more often than not, they turn out to be the guilty party. Not in every case, by any means, but we have to start somewhere."

Sam set a small tape recorder on the table and turned it on. Tom looked up at Sam and asked, "Shouldn't I have my lawyer present?"

"Whatever you wish, but it'll prolong our stay. We could start and if you become uncomfortable at any time, we'll stop and let you get him before we continue," Sam suggested. "It's your call."

Tom thought about it a moment before replying. "Very well."

"The boys have found a spot on the floor of the passenger side of your SUV and several tissues in the right door panel with what appears to be blood stains. We'll be taking a floor sample and the tissues in for DNA tests. We also have gathered her hairbrush, toothbrush, makeup and a few other personal objects."

"The blood is Abby's. We were going out a few weeks ago when she noticed a hangnail. She always carries clippers and a file in her purse. When she attempted to cut the nail, I hit a pothole and she nicked her finger. She grabbed the tissues and we stopped at a drug store for band-aids. I didn't realize she bled on the carpet or I would have had it cleaned. Actually, I forgot about the entire incident by the time we got home from dinner."

"I see," Sam said.

"Besides, don't you think if I'd hurt her, I would have taken care of any evidence like blood?"

"You seem to be a sensible man," was all Sam offered. Picking up the recorder, he added, "Could we see you in the study, please."

Ignoring the activities of the search team, Tom followed him through the great room, up a few steps and into the study where Eric stood beside the desk. A female detective, bending over the desk top, was busy dusting and lifting prints off the briefcase that rested there. The adrenaline lifted Tom's heart into his throat and sent hot blood rushing into his arms. His legs weakened as he strained to show none of the symptoms he was experiencing.

Sam asked, "Does this briefcase belong to you?"

"Yes." Tom tried to keep his voice steady.

"It's locked. Where would we find the key?"

"The contents are only personal items," Tom offered.

"Nevertheless, we need to see what's inside," Sam insisted.

Tom pulled out his wallet and retrieved a key from a small inside pocket. He handed it to the detective.

"Are you finished, Kay?" Sam asked.

"Job completed!" she replied, straightening and stepping to the side. "After you open it, I'll get to the inside."

Tom eased backward and sat down in the wingback.

Sam turned the key and the latches flipped open. He slowly raised the lid, tilting his head to look inside as it opened and pressed the lid containing pen, pencil, note pad and calculator back until it held. There was a large manila envelope laying on top and Kay, in her latex gloves, picked it up. Sam's eyes widened as he realized she had uncovered stacks of bound hundred dollar bills.

He turned in the direction of Tom and asked, "What's all this?"

"Twenty-five thousand," was his answer.

"Is this a normal thing you do? Carry twenty-five thousand around in a briefcase?" Sam asked.

"No. Nothing is normal in my life right now."

"Would you explain this, please?" Sam said, nodding toward the money.

"I withdrew some savings and the rest is from various personal sources."

"For what purpose? Why would you carry this much around with you?"

"I've found it difficult to function rationally. You know, you think of everything. When the phone rings, I tell myself it could be someone wanting a ransom and I want to be prepared."

"You know exactly how much they'll want?" Eric asked.

"Of course not. As I said, I haven't been myself. I can't even think clearly but twenty-five thousand would be a start. If they wanted more, and I gave them that much in good faith, certainly they would keep her safe while I got the rest together."

"You carried the briefcase into the Ashburn home today. What were you doing there? I know the magazine is publishing a story on him. Isn't Mr. Bland handling that?" Sam inquired.

"Mr. Ashburn is a builder and is starting a new project. I turned in a bid on the job. And yes, I took the case in with me. Would you leave that kind of money in a car? I don't think you have any right to explore my business matters. I thought your concern was Abby's disappearance," he stated flatly.

"Actually our concern is to get her back and if that doesn't happen, it's our duty to find out who prevented it from happening," Sam informed him.

Turning his attention to Kay he instructed, "Take the briefcase in for further testing on the inside and go through the items found in her purse. If there is a pair of clippers and a file, check them for blood smears. Fill out the forms with the list of what we're taking and have Cummings sign it."

To Tom he added, "We appreciate your cooperation. I think that should do it. As soon as forensics goes over the case, we'll return the money." He thanked Tom and got everyone cleared out.

Tom watched their departure from the sunken great room. When the door closed behind them, he stood silently, letting the anger build until he brought his coffee cup back, sloshing the liquid over his hand, and threw it in the direction of the entry way. The ceramic cup hit the marble steps and shattered, leaving coffee dripping over the edge of the two bottom steps. He turned to the windows and folded his arms.

Sharon Evans-Rose

CHAPTER 11

RAFE PARKED AS close to the door of the hardware store as he could. Abby wanted to pick up some paint that would go with the fabric she had chosen. With only one person ahead of them at check out, the clerk looked toward Abby and smiled. Abby smiled back before she turned to see if maybe someone was behind her that the clerk recognized. No one seemed to be paying attention to the girl behind the counter.

When it was their turn, the clerk smiled once more at Abby and said, "Hi, how are you?"

"Fine, thank you. Do we know each other?" Abby asked with heart pounding.

"I'm not sure. You look so familiar. Do you recognize me?" the clerk asked as she went about her business.

Abby glanced at an apprehensive Rafe who stood stiffly beside her. His attention was focused fully on the two women.

"No, I'm sorry," Abby replied.

"It's nothing," she said with a flip of her hand. "I see so many people more than one time, everyone starts to look familiar. I've probably waited on you a few times." She began putting everything into the plastic bags.

"Thank you," she said as she handed him their purchases and continued to stare at Abby.

"I'm sorry," the girl said, "but there's something about your face. When I look at you, it almost comes to me. Oh well, please come again." She turned to the next customer.

"Maybe I'm from here," Abby said as they headed to the exit.

"Oh, wait!" They heard the girl call. She excused herself to her customer and ran over to them.

"I remember," she said. "You remind me of the missing lady."

"The missing lady?" Abby responded weakly.

Rafe's heart dropped. *It's beginning*, he thought.

"Yes. You know the... Of course you don't. She's from Charlotte. I was visiting a friend there a few weeks ago and every time the news was on, there would be a segment about the disappearance and her face would come up on the screen. I don't even know her name, but that's who you resemble."

She turned to Rafe and added, "I do apologize for disturbing you and your wife, but it was just driving me crazy."

"That's quite all right, but I'll bet she really wasn't as attractive as my wife," Rafe replied politely.

They drove home in silence, but Rafe could see Abby's mind working. Upon their arrival, he watched as she headed straight to her room. Without speaking, she dressed for bed and climbed in.

Rafe knocked on the door jamb as he walked through to ask if she was okay.

"Yes, thank you." She lay staring at the ceiling.

He moved to the side of the bed, took her hand, bent over and lightly kissed her forehead. "Don't worry the night away. We'll get right on this *missing lady* thing."

"I feel my life is about to change again. It scares me."

Rafe squeezed her hand and left the room.

Abby slept very little that night.

"Mr. Cummings, Mr. Bland is on his way in," the intercom announced. Alice would never again let someone walk in without notifying her employer.

Tom looked up as Ethan came through the door. "Don't you believe in knocking?" he asked.

"I assume you've settled yourself!" Ethan sat down and crossed his long legs.

Tom laid aside his pen and leaned back in the chair. "I'm uncomfortable being watched! They aren't going to be happy until they put me in the jail. If circumstantial evidence could convict a person, I'd already be there," Tom said, shaking his head as he closed his eyes and took a deep breath.

"Look, she's been missing two, two and a half weeks. People disappear for long periods all the time and then turn up. We must believe that's what will happen with Abby. I cannot entertain the idea that she's gone. I simply couldn't face that!"

"I hope you're right, Ethan. I sure as hell hope you're right," Tom said, then changing the subject he asked, "When will the new issue be on the shelf?"

"Friday. Everyone should be pleased. *The Climb* will do wonderful things for our man."

"Is the magazine on track? I hope everything is running smoothly," Tom stated.

"Like a well-oiled machine," Ethan answered. Putting both hands on the desk, he leaned forward and said, "Relax. If your nervousness doesn't subside, you'll have us all believing you're guilty of something. Besides, you look like you've been sleeping with the wolves. Why don't you take a day off? The rest might bring some healthy semblance back!"

"Too much work to do. Here, I've got a name for you," Tom said, opening his drawer and pulling out an envelope.

"Wonderful! I'm set for the next three issues and I need a subject for the fourth but we may even want to hold off another month for this one. We don't want to invite questions. Who is it?" Ethan asked, taking the envelope.

"Paul Harmon, from Greensboro. You ever heard of him?"

"No."

Tom pushed himself out of his chair and walked around his desk. "I've included a rundown on him. You can read it and tell me what you think."

"I'll get right on it." Ethan stopped at the door and over his shoulder he added, "Think about that day off," and he was gone.

Neither Rafe nor Abby had mentioned the incident at the hardware store but it had become a presence in the home. Almost a living thing, creating a wall that blocked out everything else.

Abby had been reserved and melancholy, wondering constantly about the "missing lady." She had to find out about her. There must be a way to research the story. Rafe knew it was weighing heavily on her mind, but his schedule had not presently allowed him to investigate. He tried to engage her in conversation about what could be done to the house, what kind of flowers should be planted outside, the upcoming election, the capture of Saddam Hussein or anything that might pique her interest, but got only indifferent responses. Knowing that he would be just as anxious if their places were reversed, he remained patiently attuned to her anxiety.

He knew, in time, they would have answers.

Due to a cancellation, he finished early the next day and, thankfully, his hospital rounds were short. He was anxious to get home, build a fire and enjoy the evening. He thought about picking up a movie on the way but decided to start one of the many unread books he had laying around the house. Until this recent interruption, he had begun to enjoy being at home.

He pulled into the driveway, looking forward to letting Belle know he was there. Every day, it seemed, he thought about her more. He regretted having gone to the paint store. He didn't care if she never regained her memory. That would prevent her from returning to whomever she left. How selfish was that? What if she had a family who was mourning her disappearance? What if there were children missing their mother or an ill parent who might die never knowing what happened to her? Then there was the possibility the person who tried to kill her would be waiting for her return.

"Where are you?" he shouted, finding the house too quiet. "Belle, where are you?"

He moved from room to room talking to her as he looked. With heart pounding, he retraced his steps. Frantically, he moved to the window in the family room and checked the backyard. He rushed back to her bedroom and walked around her bed to make sure she hadn't collapsed on the floor where he couldn't see her.

As he came back around the bed, he stopped at the dresser. There, on the right side of the top, lay a cheap comb and brush, a small bottle of cologne and a makeup mirror. These articles were bought at the store the night they returned. To the left, he found a square, two or three inch tall candle stand, and resting in the place of the candle was the rock she had picked up in the area he had found her on the mountain.

He felt a tightening in his throat. Were these things to be only memories of her? Could she have disappeared yet again? Had she gone to Charlotte? If so, would she come out of it alive? He was working himself into a panic.

The sound of a car turning into his driveway took him to the living room door. Opening it, he stepped out to find a contented Abby coming up the walk with a folder in her hand and a cab backing out into the road.

She looked up, saw him and waved. "You're home early," she said happily as she passed by.

He closed the door and asked, "Where were you, Belle? I've been so worried. I couldn't find you and I didn't know what to do, where to go, who to call. You scared me to death."

He hadn't given her time to speak while he continued the harangue. "You must be careful."

As she removed her coat, he was right behind her. He took her arm and pulled her around to face him. She looked at this man to whom she had grown so close. Her heart skipped a beat as she struggled to keep her feelings under control.

"Did you hear me? I thought he might have gotten you," he said right into her face, "or that you had run away." Holding both shoulders he shook her slightly and shouted, "Don't ever do that again!"

He jerked her to his chest and gathered her small form in his arms. He was trembling as he held her tightly to himself.

Listening to his heart pound, shame filled her for having caused such alarm. She should have told him of her plans, but she hadn't formed them until he had left for work.

"Rafe, I took a cab," she started quietly.

"Belle, anything could have happened. Don't go out alone." He pushed her back and leaned over to look into her eyes. "Did you hear me? Did you?"

"Yes." Tears were coming.

"Oh God, I thought something had happened to you." He leaned closer and she closed her eyes as one lone tear rolled down her cheek. He stopped speaking and stared at her sad, lovely face. He kissed that tear, then he kissed her eye and finally he moved to her mouth. Ever so lightly he kissed her soft lips, once. Closing his eyes, twice. Her arms came up around his neck and he encircled her in his. The next kiss deepened and she responded as each mouth hungrily searched the other.

The feelings they both had refused to allow to surface had finally overcome the battle with a vengeance. A warm heaviness surged into her vortex, a sensation she had not experienced for a long time. She could feel his need against her and it burned a yearning for complete submission.

They were losing control. Rafe was so hungry for her, he wanted to sweep her into his arms and take her to heights he knew she had never reached, but, it wasn't going to happen. Not yet! He didn't want there to be regrets later. Reluctantly, he lifted his face to rest his cheek on top of her head as she leaned against his chest, both their hearts racing.

"I'm sorry, Belle. I'm so sorry." He didn't know if he was apologizing for being so gruff with her or for giving in to his base sexuality or both.

They stood, holding each other and breathing in harmony, trying to gain control, until Rafe said quietly, "You scared the heebeejeebees outta me!"

"Would you spell that," she stated and began to laugh as he joined in. The spell had been broken.

Once more he looked down and turning her chin up with his hand, he kissed her delicately. *One day, my sweet.*

Nervously, they stepped apart, he, smiling intimately, and she, embarrassingly. He led her to the sofa and pulled her down beside him.

With a deep sigh, he shook his head clear and said, "Now, tell me where you've been."

Her trembling hands picked up the envelope and opened it. The feelings for this man that she had been pushing aside had erupted so suddenly and violently and now they left her shaken and weak.

108

"I went to the library." Turning to look at him, she added, "And if you had not come home early I would have been back when you got here. Anyway, I checked the past three weeks of *The Charlotte Observer* on microfilm."

Reaching into the envelope, she withdrew a handful of papers. "I made copies of what I found on the 'missing lady'."

She spread them out on the cocktail table as she said, "There were no pictures."

He read through them, making comments periodically.

"So, she's an heiress and there is a husband," he said, looking up at her.

Their eyes held. She was the first to look away.

"Yes, she's married," Abby said wistfully.

"We don't know if 'she's' you," he reminded her.

"They found her car, but this article doesn't tell its make. I wonder if it's a small car," she stated.

"Did you see this?" he asked her.

Turning to the clipping he was reading she said, "What?"

"It was parked in front of a Ground Beans!"

"I know!" Again, they looked at each other.

"Its not been determined if she left on her own or was taken," he said. "Other than superficial details, there's nothing here. Of course, the police don't let the public know everything. That helps them discard 'helpful' calls that give wrong information and if anyone confesses in details that don't fit the evidence, they know not to take it seriously."

"Maybe I should go to the police."

"Not now. If you *are* the 'missing lady' we know something they don't. Someone wants you dead—thinks you're dead, and until we can determine who that is, we don't want him or her to know where you can be found. Let's keep your predicament a secret for now. Meanwhile we'll find out if you *are* this person."

"How can we do that?"

"It's going to take some thought and planning. We have to formulate a way to find out, without giving you away," he said thoughtfully.

She looked at this man she hadn't even known three weeks ago. So much had happened. She was falling in love. *Can one fall in love in three weeks?* It wasn't because of what he had done for her. It was him. It was her attraction to him. It was his attraction to her. It was his kindness, his care, his heart, his beautiful dark eyes, his insistent mouth and body, the way he—

"Belle!" he nudged her. "You're not listening to me."

"Oh! I'm sorry. I was lost in thought," she replied guiltily.

"Did I give you those keys I found in the woods?"

"I think you kept them."

They both rose instantly and began a frantic search.

"I found them," Rafe said, holding up the prize.

"Good." Abby breathed a great sigh of relief, then asked, "Why do we need them?"

"Because they are the keys to the answer," Rafe stated.

Sam and Eric sat in the office reviewing all the evidence and notes.

Holloway had been on their backs. The Langford family was well known and the public wanted answers. The chief needed something to give the media.

"So the house was clean!" Eric said.

"Yep."

"And nothing to suggest a struggle outside?"

"Nope."

"The cars?" Eric asked.

"The crime lab is still working on them."

"How about enemies?"

"According to all accounts everybody loves her, including her husband who might possibly love his girlfriend more. No one, as far as we have learned, would have reason to want her out of the picture, unless, it's her husband, who would gain by inheriting everything and still have a girlfriend." Sam shifted in his chair, pulled his ankle up onto his knee and placed his hand on his ankle.

Taking a big breath, he continued, "It seems that Mrs. Cummings is gentle and easygoing, but a hard worker. All reports indicate that she gets along well with people." Lifting an eyebrow, he digressed. "Except for the big disagreement with her husband.

110

Finally, and most importantly, dropping out of sight is the kind of drastic action that is totally out of character for her."

"In other words, she would never walk off. She has no enemies and all her friends and relatives have no motive for harming her, unless of course, it's her husband," Eric suggested.

"Looks that way. But it's just too easy. He's smart. I wouldn't expect him to do something so obvious."

"Intelligent people do stupid things if they're hot tempered and/ or cornered," Eric said. "They often act on impulse, and remember, there was nothing in or around her car to indicate the presence of a stranger."

"Forensics found her blood on the clippers from her purse giving credibility to how Tom said the blood, if it is her blood, got into his car," Sam reminded him.

"Yes, but she could have cut her finger earlier and he grabbed on to that for an explanation," Eric suggested.

"You know, there was no blood in her car," Sam said.

"Perhaps she didn't drive her car there. He could have committed the crime in his car, disposed of her, then driven her car there himself and had Maggie pick him up. Or he might have stopped at the coffee shop, run into her in the parking lot and taken her away to do the ugly deed," Eric suggested.

"Ugly deed? That's the big question. What ugly deed? Has something happened to her? There's no body and no real evidence to support the suggestion that she has been harmed. The amount of blood found in the Cummings' vehicle could never be considered the result of a murder."

"There's her abandoned car and her disappearance," Eric reminded him.

"Here's another thought. Could she have arranged her own vanishing act to upset her husband?" Sam stated.

"And left her purse? I don't think so," Eric said. "Have you considered the idea of him having hired a hit man? Remember the briefcase full of money? That could have been a payoff for a job well done."

"I've thought about that too, but he didn't notify us until two days after she disappeared, so he had plenty of time to clear his account with the hired gun before we came on the scene. A killer wants payment right away so he can get out of town," Sam explained.

"You know there is another possibility, besides the one suggesting a stranger abduction. Maybe one of her distant relatives took care of her."

"For what reason? Tom inherits everything," Sam reminded him.

"Yes, but Tom just might be the next one to disappear!"

"In that case, it would be his relatives who would benefit."

"Right. Then, in other words, Tom Cummings could be guilty or not. On the other hand it could be someone else, who knew her or didn't know her. Or, maybe she could have skipped the scene herself," Eric itemized. "Well, we're just loaded with suppositions."

"And no real leads." Sam sighed heavily.

"I guess we keep digging?" Eric looked at his boss.

"Until we find the body," Sam said.

Sam picked up the receiver after the first ring. It was from the detective in Charlotte.

"Sam, Jack here. I did some checking on our man, Ashburn, and he came out as reputable as a newborn. There is nothing suspect in his past. He has a great family and is a hard worker."

"I figured. Eric's imagination has gotten a little too active," Sam said, looking at the young detective out of the corners of his eyes.

"Mrs. Cummings' car is as clean as a whistle. The vehicle had not been wiped clean of prints and there were very few other than her own. A few seemingly old prints were picked up inside on the passenger's side and in the back seat area. Some of these were her husband's and others' unknown. None but those we assume to be hers on the driver's side, inside and out, so my bet is that she was not taken from her car, but exited it herself."

"How about the position of the driver's seat?" Sam asked.

"The seat and rear view mirrors were right in line with her build. Looks like *she* drove the car there."

"I see. Shall I tell Mr. Cummings that he can pick up the car now?"

"We've done that. If there is something else we can do to help, just pick up the phone."

112

"Absolutely. Thanks, Jack. We'll call and catch you up when we get our man."

"Or woman," Jack reminded him.

"Or both," Sam suggested.

Abby and Rafe sat at the table with the checklist. They had gone over the plans for several days and he made arrangements to take the next two days off.

"Did you call the hotel?" she asked.

"Yes, I got a suite with one bedroom and two double beds. I didn't think you would want to be alone, but I could call back and get connecting rooms if you would be more comfortable."

"No, it'll be fine. Did you put fresh batteries in the flashlights?" Abby inquired.

"Yes, and I found the caps. As an extra precaution I picked up a pair of clear glasses for you. With your hair lightened and that short cut nobody will recognize you—from a distance anyway. Besides, we'll be in a car with darkened glass most of the time."

"The keys are packed? We don't want to get there without them," Abby said.

"Yes, and the camera. You nervous?" he asked.

"Are you crazy? Of course I'm nervous. What if I get shot again and this time it takes?"

Rafe's heart skipped as a surge of adrenaline spread through his chest and down his arms. He felt he was going to be sick.

"Come on, let's relax for a while before we try to sleep," he said, taking her hand and leading her around the counter and into the family room. He moved to the sectional and pulled her down beside him. Sliding his arm across the back cushion, he laid his hand on her shoulder. She tucked her feet beside her hips and leaned slightly against him.

He picked up the remote and clicked on Fox News. There was a story on the Laci Peterson case and Abby listened intently as though it were about herself.

"Do you think he did it?" she asked.

"I can't imagine anyone doing that," he answered, clicking the remote for something more settling.

She rested her head in the hollow of his shoulder and closed her eyes. He tightened his protective hold. His heart ached for her and he was afraid she belonged to someone else. She sat still for a very long time while he stared at the screen. Eventually she dozed off.

At some point in time, she felt herself being lifted off the cushions and she wrapped her arms around the strong neck as she was carried to her room. The television was silent and the lights were off. Her eyelids opened as he placed her on the bed. She did not release his neck as their eyes locked and neither spoke. Very smoothly, he eased himself down beside her and put his arm over her waist. He closed his eyes now, and the two remained so close each one shared the breath of the other. Her eyes closed and they both began to relax.

"I love you, Belle," he said quietly.

"And I love you back," she whispered.

They slept soundly.

Tom was in the bed with his forearm on the pillow above his head. He was awake and staring at nothing when the phone rang. He grabbed it on the second ring.

"Hello." He expected to hear Sam Robertson's voice.

"Are you sleeping in the nude, darling?"

"Maggie, I've told you not to call here. I want to speak to you only from a pay phone."

"I know, dear, but you haven't called all day and I didn't want to go to bed until you whispered something really nice to me."

He felt the stiffening of his manhood. That sexy voice making playful innuendos always started his engine. Ethan's warning echoed in his head but was put aside. He couldn't control himself. Was it because of her need to have him or the excitement of doing something wrong? Something *bad*. The thrill of taking chances!

"Look, I have a plan. I'll call you tomorrow. Arrange to stay home until you hear from me. Now say good night, Mags."

"Good night, Mags, and you too handsome," she growled.

CHAPTER 12

RAFE WAS DRIVING while Abby, enjoying the ride, studied the landscape. They were on I-40 West heading to I-77 South. They didn't leave until eleven o'clock because they wanted to have lunch before arriving in Charlotte. It really was silly to think she might be seen by someone who would know her in such a large city, but if it eased her apprehension, Rafe was more than willing.

"We should start watching the exit signs for a place to eat," Rafe suggested.

"It looked like there were quite a few at Statesville, but we passed it a few moments ago."

Soon, Abby read a sign on the side of the highway giving the mileages to the next few exits when she experienced a sudden visual flash. It was a bright, quick picture of a green sign overhead imprinted with the name of a town she had just seen listed.

"Rafe, let's get off at Prestonburg," she said hastily.

He glanced at her and knew something was up. Saying nothing, he traveled on but was more alert to her reactions. He took the exit at Prestonburg and pulled over at a neat diner.

"How's this?" he asked. "They probably have great 'unyuppy' food. Maybe chili. I'd love a bowl with a hot dog. Diners usually have great hot dogs."

"It'll be fine."

She put the glasses and the cap on, opened the door and jumped out.

After studying her, he couldn't resist saying, "Now, that's cute!"

"I thought you said these glasses were clear."

"I meant they weren't corrective. Besides, the tint is so light it won't be obvious to you indoors."

The waitress met them with two menus and said, "It's all no smoking, but do you have a preferred table?"

Rafe answered, "A quiet corner, please. And could I borrow your phone book for a few minutes?"

"Sure," she said, escorting them to a table and disappearing briefly before returning with two phone books. "I didn't know if you wanted the Prestonburg or the Charlotte book."

"I'll take them both, actually."

They looked over the menu while the waitress went for their drinks. After ordering, Rafe picked up the small phone book first. He flipped through it to find the page he wanted, then his eyes scanned down until he hit upon the name for which he was searching.

"Belle, the Cummings' home is here in Prestonburg, not in Charlotte. What made you suggest we stop here?"

She told him about her vision and added, "This is getting scary. What's the address?" she asked.

He pulled out a pen and grabbed a paper napkin. "I should have brought our notebook in." He repeated the address as he wrote it down. "Sound familiar?"

"No."

Lunch was set on the table and they put their plans aside until they had eaten. Finishing first, Rafe looked up the information on Langford Mill.

"When we leave here, we'll stop at a filling station and get directions and buy a map of Charlotte. All finished?" he asked as he laid the payment and tip on the table.

"Yes."

The young waitress thanked them as they passed and said, "You two certainly make a handsome couple."

Belle flushed. Walking to the car, Rafe bent over and picked up a rock with a napkin he had carried out and put it in the trunk.

Following the map, Abby directed Rafe and within ten minutes they found themselves in a very nice residential section. It took even less time to find the Cummings' home. They drove casually past it, giving little attention to the house itself, but scanning the surroundings instead.

"I'm going to circle around shortly and head back," Rafe said. "That will put you next to the house. Pay attention to the door and the area toward the side street. We're in luck with the house sitting on the corner. It's not close to the road but I want you to concentrate on the foliage in relation to the house from the side."

Abby studied the layout. Rafe turned onto the road beside the house for a quick study and continued past one intersection before he made a turn left and wound his way out of the area. He then drove to a fast food lot and parked. "Let's have coffee and talk," he said.

Upon entering, Abby looked around to find a table away from everyone else.

"Have a seat. I'll get the coffee," Rafe offered. "I have a feeling that acquaintances of Mrs. Cummings don't frequent this place, so don't worry about being recognized if, in fact, you turn out to be her."

She had been so involved in their purpose that she hadn't thought about the situation. Now, however, she wondered if she had just left her home. Rafe set the coffee on the table and took a seat opposite her.

He leaned forward and put his hand over hers and asked, "Still okay?"

"Yes, I'm doing just fine."

"I feel pretty good about the setup and don't expect any problems unless surveillance should be there when we go back."

"Surveillance?" she questioned.

"Look, when a wife disappears under suspicious circumstances, the husband, until he can be ruled out, is automatically among the suspects. We don't know if this man has been dismissed from the suspect pool yet, so the police could be keeping tabs on him, but we plan to arrive before he gets home. Now, if they're watching only him and not the house, that lowers the chances of our being seen."

They sipped their coffee slowly while searching the Charlotte city map. Abby marked the best route to the mill.

It took considerably longer to find their object of destination this time. Eventually, Rafe turned onto the lot beside the main office and drove past the entrance, then Abby's eyes widened as they approached the *Success* marquee over the door of the magazine office.

"I think I know this place. There's a familiar feeling about it," she said.

Rafe drove around the building only once before heading to the hotel. The suite was not large but it filled Abby's needs. It allowed her a little more privacy than a motel room provided. Unconsciously, she thanked him for that. The extra room gave them enough space to stay out from under each other's feet, but kept Rafe close enough to provide a feeling of being protected.

"I'm going to take a nice, leisurely shower," Abby said, removing the cap and shaking out her hair.

"Can I wash your back?" he asked teasingly.

"You want to leave here with two hands?" she answered.

Rafe went into the sitting room, turned on the TV and flopped down on the couch. He propped his feet on the coffee table and folded his hands behind his head.

"I'll try not to take too long," Abby called out, "then the bathroom is yours."

"Take your time. We don't have to eat early." Rafe turned his head in her direction as he answered. He could see across both beds and right into the bathroom. With her back to him, she was pulling her sweater up and off her head. He knew he should look away, but couldn't. Her arms came around behind her and she unhooked her bra. She hung it over a towel rack then turned and closed the door. The vision stayed with him. That classically perfect body. Even the redness of the gunshot scar was diminishing.

He closed his eyes, the ache for her mellowing into a need to simply hold her. What would he do if he loses her? His first marriage had been a young love and they had not really invested time in each other before his wife became ill. He had loved her and had gone through misery at her death. It had been a very sweet, but short marriage.

Until now, his single life had been satisfying. With the exception of his private time at the cabin, his focus was on the clinic and the future of the Inn had consumed him. Abby's presence was re-awakening feelings that had lain dormant and he was developing a deep attachment that he didn't want to let go. He sat there daydreaming about her until, he drifted off to sleep.

Abby blew her hair dry and put on the robe that she retrieved from the hook on the back of the bathroom door. She plugged in the curling iron and decided to move to the bedroom to do her makeup while it heated.

Her short hair was so easy and fast to manage, it would only take her several minutes to put a few wild hairs in place. She could dress quickly and they would be off—if Rafe were ready then. Maybe she had better check on him. He had been too quiet.

Rafe could hear his name being called faintly. He lifted one eyelid to find Abby standing in front of him with her hands on her hips. "The bathroom is free," she said.

He smiled, then jumped forward and grabbed her around the hips and lifted her up and onto the sofa with him.

Laughing, she asked, "What are you doing?"

"Having a little fun," he said, pulling her down and rolling on top of her.

"Rafe, you're crushing me," she giggled.

"Are you ticklish?" He had a mischievous glint in his eye.

"No, don't you dare. I cannot stand to be tickled! Besides, I can't breathe."

He quickly rolled off her onto his side at the back of the sofa, propping his head up with one hand and pulled her to face him, as he asked, "Better?"

"Very much so!"

He ran his hand behind her neck and pulled her face to him. Looking straight into each other's eyes, the smiles faded.

He loosened the terry belt on her robe and slid his hand underneath and around to her back. Her silky skin was warm and inviting. As he slowly and delicately rubbed her back, he could feel her relax. She lifted her head and kissed him on the mouth then pressed her cheek against his and whispered quietly into his ear, "You are so good for me."

They lay, embracing each other, entwined in a cocoon of total absorption. Nothing else mattered at this moment. He moved his hand down her back then up her side and around her, bringing it to rest on the front of her ribs under her breast. She kissed him again and this time he responded as his hand moved up to cup her breast. His thumb and forefinger took the soft pink nub and rubbed, bringing it to a hardened peak. Opening her mouth, she drew breath in quickly and pulled his head into her cheek.

He kissed her under her ear then at the base of her neck and pushing the robe aside, finally on the most sensitive part of her breast before bringing it fully into his mouth to caress with his tongue. She moaned and closed her eyes, riding the passion that threatened to disable her completely. She arched her back giving him full access as he took his time lifting her to heights of liquid euphoria.

His hand slid down to find her secret nugget of pleasure fully aroused. Teasing this most special place brought her to a breathless intensifying need. As the pleasure built, her breathing almost ceased. She had given herself completely to the ecstacy that was peaking. The release was sudden and all consuming as she gasped, opened her eyes wide in surprise while spasms of delirium shook her to the core.

Ignoring his own needs, Rafe released her breast and kissed it as he brought his hand up to rest on her stomach. *She may be married, but she's not been loved.* He looked into her glazed eyes and pulled her into his embrace, sensing and enjoying every little quake of her body.

When she was finally able to speak, she said, "I am so sorry, I don't know what happened to me. I had no control. Please, please forgive me."

"My sweet Belle, don't apologize. Pleasing you gives me more satisfaction than you'll ever understand." He put a hand on each side of her face and said, "I wanted you in the worst way, but I didn't want you to hate me for it later. I know you're worried about being married and doing something you shouldn't, so, if you *are* married, you have not disgraced your vows." He halted before adding, "If you aren't married, well, we'll talk about paybacks."

She laughed and hugged his head so tightly he had to pry her off.

"Let's not go out to dinner, let's stay here and hold hands," she said, smiling in deep satisfaction.

"I need instant gratification and food is the next best thing for that. Besides, I'm going to feed you well because tomorrow you'll probably be too skittish to eat."

They had a delightful dinner and Abby was happy and bubbly throughout the evening. Neither of them mentioned the next day's plans.

Abby went to bed with the hope that her dreams, which had become so strong and frequent lately, would not keep her from resting this night. The dreams seemed to be speaking to her and they remained in her mind for days. She did *not* want that distraction tomorrow so she tried to clear her head of everything that involved herself. She drifted off wondering if she would get to see the deer on the mountain again.

Rafe was relieved to discover that, unlike himself, she had no trouble sleeping through the night.

"I plan to pull around to the side of the house. Back near the pool area." Rafe was drawing an overview of the house and streets and pointing out the strategy to Abby.

"First, we want to find a gas station. I'll fill up and we can visit the rest rooms to put the dark coveralls on I picked up at the costume shop. They even have a company name on the pocket. And, of course our caps. We'll look like a repairman and his boy helper."

Abby was visualizing the scene.

"Next we'll go to the house. If we get there a little before six o'clock, it should be getting dark. We'll drive the block once to make certain no one is out walking, you know those hard-nosed joggers walk in all kinds of weather, then we'll park about here," he said, pointing to the spot.

"You carry the keys and mag light in your pocket and I'll carry the tool box, which is simply to enforce the suggestion that we're there for a job, if anyone happens to see us. I think we should walk around to the front and up to the door. It might be more conspicuous, but less suspicious."

"Now comes the tricky part. We have narrowed the keys down

to three and we feel pretty certain which one of those is the house key, so try that one first. Remember, I'll be standing behind the right side of your back and arm covering you while you work at the lock. I'll pretend to ring the bell and it'll look as if we're waiting for the door to be answered. If you think you need the pen light to see well enough, give it to me and I'll shine it on the keyhole."

"Try to insert it and if it slides in turn it first one way, and if it doesn't turn try the other. If that fails, move on to one of the other keys and repeat the process. If that one doesn't work, try the last one. When—if—one of them does unlock the door, don't withdraw the key immediately, quickly lock it back first.

All of this must be done with speed. I'm certain this house is equipped with a security system and in that case, after you unlock the door, we need to disappear before the alarm goes off, so we'll make a furious exit this way," Rafe said, indicating on his drawing that they would move from the front steps to the side and behind the privacy hedge that runs from the side of the house to the road and around the pool.

"There is a weak area in the hedge about here. That's where the car will be parked. We can squeeze through there and take the car and vanish. The alarm will sound before we get away but neighbors usually ignore this for a while because it happens quite often when residents forget to punch in the code or accidentally set the alarms off themselves. Even if it does draw attention, people automatically come out through their front doors to determine the source and we'll be leaving in back."

Abby indicated the rock laying on the napkin beside the sketch. "Is that for beating the enemy off if we're caught?" she inquired.

"I'm going to break a window on the side as we leave to give the impression that there was an attempted break-in. Even if the security system indicates the problem originated from the front door, the door will be locked, leading them to believe that an entry might have been attempted but was not successful. The broken window should make them think it wasn't done by anyone who might have had a key or they wouldn't have tried the window. It's an effort to confuse the trained."

"You make it sound so simple," she said.

"It is. Just remember, you hold the key and you want an answer, so be careful."

"If the key doesn't turn, I'm still lost, but if it does, what do I do next?"

"Don't get ahead of yourself. Let's take one thing at a time."

"But if the key turns, we don't have to worry about being caught because it would be my house. If that's the case, do I stay?"

"No! Absolutely not! You're leaving with me. We'll go home and talk it out and you can make decisions more clearly then. Remember, that's part of the plan. You leave with me, understand?"

"Yes."

Tom was looking forward to the evening. He knew Maggie would make it special *and* entertaining. He planned to drive to Martrands, pay the valet to park his car in the staff lot, tip the maitre d' well to simply escort him through the dining area to the back door. This would enable him to depart immediately without taking his shadows with him.

He laughed at the thought of those two sitting in their car watching the front door and waiting for him to leave. They were so inept, he figured they'd wait a couple of hours before becoming suspicious.

He was highly irritated with himself for having left a small gift he had ordered for Maggie at his house. He finished up as early as possible so he could get home, retrieve it and return without being late. Maggie didn't like her food to get cold.

"Damn!" Sam said. "These things give me indigestion before I even finish. If we don't get this case cleared up soon, you can just strike a match to my tongue and watch me go up in flames."

Eric, ignoring him, was on his second hamburger and enjoying every greasy bite. Sam looked at him and shook his head.

The silver Lexus pulled onto the road and Sam threw the remainder of his hamburger into the bag. "Here we go," he warned.

Staying a good distance behind Tom, they were still able to keep him in sight. He made one stop at a convenience store. They drove around the block and waited on a side street. When Tom came out, he was carrying a bag with what appeared to be a large bottle of wine.

Tom acted as if he hadn't seen the unmarked car. He got into his car and headed north.

"He must be going home," Sam said.

"Looks like he plans to drown his troubles tonight."

"Yep. We'll stay with him until he hits the highway and then call it a day." Sam was glad he was going to get home. Maybe his wife would have leftovers.

Tom noticed their departure. *Well, this will save time. Now I won't have to go through the Martrand's charade. Thank you, Detective!*

The afternoon seemed to have evaporated and Rafe and Abby soon found themselves driving to the Cummings home. Deep dusky skies erased all shadows and eased their apprehension. As they reached the neighborhood, they were again struck by, what was to them, an uncommon lifestyle. There were no children visible, the lawns and shrubbery were manicured to perfection and there didn't seem to be anyone outside.

"Must be dinner time," Rafe suggested.

After scouting the neighborhood, he turned the corner as he passed the home and pulled along the side of the wide road near the rear of the house and stopped. They gathered their props and pulled on the caps. Rafe leaned over the steering wheel and looked up at the sky.

"I see a faint moon. It'll soon be dark. We'd better get started."

Tom was approaching the Prestonburg exit. He was glad he had picked up the bottle of wine but wished he had included a box of Godiva in the event he did arrive a few minutes late. *Oh well, the wine will suffice.* Mags wouldn't mind. She was more interested in the after dinner events anyway.

Abby and Rafe got out of the car and moved down the sidewalk. Rounding the corner, they came almost face to face with a young woman walking her dog. Rafe turned his head to Abby and said quietly, "Look at me."

She turned her face up to his as he spoke.

"You'd better do a neater job on this one than you did on the last, son, or I'm going to have to find another helper," he said to Abby as they passed the dog walker.

They continued on their way as Rafe said under his breath, "Where the hell did she come from?"

Turning up the circular driveway, he glanced toward the woman who, by now, had crossed the street and was some distance from them.

The three steps took them onto the half moon shaped, brick portico where they stopped and pulled on the latex gloves. Abby had the keys in her shaking hand. Rafe stepped in front of the door as a buffer to any inquisitive eyes, flicked on the small light and shined it directly onto the door lock before he touched the finger on his other hand to the side of the doorbell button.

Abby lifted the key and carefully aimed the point of it into the lock. It slid in perfectly and she twisted her hand to the right but the key didn't move. She reversed the effort and it turned easily as she felt the bolt slide, then, instantly, she locked it and removed the key. Suddenly, and without warning, she experienced another, almost overwhelming, flash in her mind's eye.

She saw past the door she was still facing, past the marble floor in the entry, down the steps into the great room, through the large windows and onto the distant mountains. A complete feeling of deja-vu washed over her. She was on familiar ground.

Tom rounded the corner and spotted the new neighbor, Barbara Hancock, walking her dog. She was a real looker. He slowed and lowered his window. Waving, he called to her, "Hi, Barb."

She stopped. Squinting in the semidarkness, she recognized him. "Oh, hi, Tom. I'm so sorry about Abby. I think about you often. Let me know if I can be of help!"

"Thanks. I'm still hoping for the best. Have a good night." *And I wouldn't mind helping you do that.* He watched her in the rearview mirror as she strolled off before he moved on.

Rafe had returned the light to his pocket and he took Belle's arm and walked briskly down the steps at the side to guide her around the house and through the hedge. He then released her and moved to a window, found the pane in front of the inside lock, took the rock from his pocket and threw it. As the glass shattered, he grabbed her hand and ran to the outside hedge.

Abby was totally unaware of their movements. She was still lost in her recognition of a time past. As Rafe urged her forward, she looked back at the house, hoping for one more visual reminder of what had been, but darkness obscured the structure and robbed her of any link to yesterday. The beams from a set of headlights turning into the driveway swept across the tall hedge through which they had just stepped.

The alarm sounded as they climbed into the vehicle and started the engine. Driving to the corner without lights, the sound of the loud recorded male voice invaded their quiet escape. "Step away from the house, this is a warning..."

Tom heard the alarm before he turned off the engine. He grabbed his cell phone and dialed. *Where's the damn police when you need them?!* He jumped from his car, tried the front door and ran to each front corner of the house to check the sides. Nothing.

"This is nine one one," the female voice said into his ear.

"Well, this is Tom Cummings. Get your lazy asses over here."

"They're already on their way," the efficient voice replied.

Rafe switched the lights on as he turned left and traveled slowly to prevent any suspicions. The alarm could no longer be heard. Neither of them had spoken. They joined the traffic that fed onto a busy bypass.

Rafe reached across the gear shift and laid his hand on top of Abby's that were folded tightly together in an effort to reduce the trembling. He gave them a squeeze before taking the steering wheel again.

When they were safely on I-40 E, Rafe looked in her direction and asked, "Belle? Are you all right?"

"Abigail." She said staring ahead.

"What?"

"My name is Abigail Langford Cummings."

"Yes, it is."

Lost in their own thoughts, they traveled silently the rest of the way home. To his home.

Abby, now, had her own name. Maybe things would begin to fall into place. If that happened, what would she do? She certainly didn't feel at home in the cold scene she had just experienced and Tom was alien to her now. She was wondering what was going through Rafe's mind. Would he be glad to see her return to her familiar waters or was he concerned about the unseen sharks?

Rafe considered the emotions Abby would experience at either outcome, but he didn't realize how this new discovery was going to upset him. What impact was it going to have on their relationship? What would she do now? He wanted her to be very careful in making any decision. It must be the right one. The safest one.

Rafe and Abby carried their bags into the house where Abby headed directly to her room. Rafe put his things away and walked to her door.

"Would you like something to eat?" he asked.

She turned to him and shook her head no. "I'm very tired. I'm going to bed early. Thank you, Rafe, for everything."

He made himself a peanut butter sandwich and washed it down with a glass of milk. Turning the TV on, he sat down in front of it for a while. Realizing he hadn't heard a word that had been spoken, he turned it off and went to Abby's room.

She was lying on her back staring at the ceiling with one forearm resting on her forehead. That seemed to be her thinking position. She didn't acknowledge his arrival.

He pulled a comfortable chair close to her bed, left the room briefly and returned with a pillow and blanket under one arm and an ottoman under the other. He sat down, propped his feet on the ottoman, put the blanket over his legs and the pillow behind his head. He was set for the night. Almost. He slid his hand along the bed and picked up her small cool hand, closing his around it. She returned his grasp. He closed his eyes and soon they both slept.

Rafe's eyes opened as the warm promise of an early spring lightened the sky. He looked at Abby, who was still sleeping deeply. Considering the trials she had suffered these past weeks, it was surprising to see her looking so calm and unfettered. Of course, she was not conscious, when she wakes and her mind recalls everything, it could be different.

He pushed his stiff, sore body up and carried his pillow and blanket back to his bedroom, then turned the shower on to heat the water while he shaved. Checking the mirror for any spots he might have missed, he was made painfully aware that, unlike Abby, he did not look rested. Turning away, he stepped under the hot water, closed his eyes and stood there waiting for the heat to ease the muscular aches. Getting ready for work had really been a chore. It was going to be a long day.

Before leaving he looked in on Abby once more. She had rolled to her side, but still slept soundly. He pushed the hair off her face and stared for a long time, imprinting her image on his mind so he could pull it up at will. He bent down and lightly kissed her cheek.

Returning to the kitchen, he left her a note with his office number and said he would be home around six-thirty. He reminded her of his love and with an inner fear that she might return home, he asked her to wait for him.

Rafe trudged to his car, got inside and started it. He backed out of the garage and stopped, turned off the engine and got out. Walking toward the front door with head down, he moved briskly. At the porch, he stopped. After a short pause, he made an about face and took his leave.

CHAPTER
13

TOM ARRIVED AT the office late. It had been a dreadful night. The police had stayed hours searching for clues and found nothing but a rock. A dirty, ugly rock! The alarm showed there had also been a tampering at the front door.

The official report stated "attempted break-in supposedly for the purpose of robbery" but Tom didn't buy it. Someone was trying to scare him—to make him think Abby's ghost was after him, or, maybe she was alive and coming after him. *God, am I losing my mind!*

To beat it all, he called Maggie's house this morning to explain his absence the night before and she refused to take his call.

Walking through the front door of the mill office complex, Tom saw Donald talking to the receptionist. Donald turned at the sound of his footsteps, nodded his head at Tom and walked around the desk and along the wall to his office.

"Mr. Cummings, Detective Robertson has been phoning for you. He asked that you return his call as soon as you get here," Alice said.

"What was that all about?" he asked curtly.

"I'm sorry, sir, he didn't divulge his reason for calling."

"Not him," he said with exasperation. "Him!" he emphasized, looking in the direction of Don's office.

"Oh, I thought, I mean—"

"Alice!"

"Mister Freeman was asking if there had been any news on Mrs. Cummings. He's very fond of her, you know."

"Don't we all know *that*." Tom whirled on his heel, walked into his office and slammed the door.

He headed to his desk in a huff. Robertson didn't even show up at his house. So, he was off duty, they could have called him in. The police tried to explain that the situation was not related to the case the detectives had been working on, but Tom knew better. Robertson should have been there.

Well, what could this nuisance of a detective want now? After the fact! He flipped on the intercom and asked Alice to get Sam Robertson on the phone.

Soon, Alice notified him that the detective was on line one.

"Tell him I'll be with him shortly," Tom said.

"Yes, sir."

Tom sat down, put his ankle up on his knee and leaned back to rock slightly while he let Sam wait. This was one of his favorite tactics to put anyone he considered beneath him in his or her place and he *really* wanted to do this now. After what he thought was the right amount of time, he lifted the receiver and said, "Detective, I'm sorry I—"

"Excuse me, Mr. Cummings, Detective Robertson will be right with you," a female voice interrupted before putting Tom on hold.

Tom seethed, but held the receiver in his tight-knuckled fist while he waited.

"Hello, Cummings," Sam finally said.

"Did you want something?" Tom asked flatly.

"I understand you had a problem at your home last night."

"I did." A statement.

"I'm sorry I wasn't notified at the time, but I've gone over all the reports and it seems everything that I would have done has been taken care of."

"Whatever you think!" Tom was highly irritated with the department and didn't care that Sam knew it.

"I just wanted to let you know that I was made aware of the incident."

130

"And now I know! I'm buried in work, so if you'll excuse me." Tom hung the phone up without waiting for a response.

This was not a fuckin' glitched robbery attempt! If you can't see past your own stupid noses, then I sure as hell don't have anything to worry about. I'll simply take care of this myself.

"Alice, I've got to get out for a while. If I get calls, just say I'm in meetings." Tom had not even removed his coat.

"Yes, sir," she replied as he walked out the door. She kept right on with her typing as she shook her head in exasperation. She truly hoped everything would hold together here. At her age, she didn't want to start looking for a new job.

Rafe resisted calling home to see if Abby was still there. His appointment schedule was brutal and the hospital rounds were heavy. There had been an influx of his patients while he was off and he had some catching up to do. When he was finally free to start home, he climbed into the Land Rover, exhausted.

It was after nine and the house looked dark and quiet. Rafe's heart sank. He pulled into the garage, put the door down and entered the unlit kitchen through the laundry room. He could see a faint, flickering light coming through the doorway.

Taking his coat off as he went through the great room, the glow in the dining room attracted his attention. He glanced in that direction and came to a stop. The candles, still burning, were now very short. There were two large salad bowls filled to the rim on the table between the good silver and cloth napkins. Red wine filled the goblets. Rafe's heart and spirits lifted.

Turning his head to focus on the sofa, he spotted the small figure. She was lying on her side with her hands clasped beneath her cheek. Her breathing was regular and deep. Walking into the dining room, he extinguished the candles and took the salads to the kitchen.

Abby continued to sleep as Rafe lifted her into his arms and carried her to the bedroom. He laid her on her bed, removed her dress, located a blanket and covered her. He stood smiling down at her briefly before walking to his bed.

The aroma of bacon and coffee roused Abby from sleep. She opened her eyes and looked around the room. Her happy, safe and comfortable room. Sliding out of bed and finding herself in her underwear, she slipped on a pair of Rafe's sweat pants and a long sleeved shirt, then toddled into the kitchen sporting her familiar smile.

The table was set with fresh burning candles, the cloth napkins and two wine glasses filled with orange juice and champagne. Rafe, with his back to her, stood at the stove frying bacon.

"Hi!" she said brightly.

He turned quickly, smiled at her in response and said, "Good morning, sleepy head. I'm sorry about last night's dinner."

She walked briskly to him, wrapped her arms around his waist and rested her cheek on his chest.

"I missed you, Rafe. Do you have to work today?"

"Today is Saturday. I have a few patients at the hospital I must check on later, but that's all. Why, Belle?"

"Abigail!"

"Excuse me. Abigail."

"Call me Abby. That seems more familiar to me."

He turned immediately to the bacon. It was getting too brown. He wanted it crisp but not black. "So, you're getting to know yourself?"

He set the skillet aside and turned his attention back to Abby, who stood by, watching his agility with the kitchen ware.

"Only slightly. I thought it would be nice to spend the day adjusting to the other me." She stepped back away from him and her face turned serious.

"I visited a part of my past yesterday, and I did *not* feel welcome. I sensed that I have been happier here. Someone that I didn't meet there, wants me dead. Thinks I'm dead. I don't know who or why, but one day I shall."

Rafe stepped forward and opened his mouth.

Abby raised her hand to stop him. "Wait, I'm not finished. I'm ready to take on whatever is after me. I can't let fear take over my life." She touched his elbow and ran her fingers down his arm to take his hand before continuing, "I don't expect you to put yourself in jeopardy and I don't want you to feel you have to stay involved. I'm strong enough now to move out and I could hire a private detective to help me."

"Is that what you want?" He looked sadly at this new person.

Her eyes were beginning to shine with tears as the lump grew in her throat. She didn't want this to happen. How could she be convincing if she stood in front of him and cried?

She looked down and swallowed deeply before replying. "No," she said honestly, "but I don't want to become your albatross." Now she returned her gaze to his face.

He hesitated as he looked down and raised upturned palms. "I have helped free you and now my hands are empty. If you leave, you'll leave my heart the same," he said as his eyes found hers. "I'm not complete without you. I want you to understand that I love you with my heart, my mind, my soul and I don't want to spend another day without you beside me."

He moved close and looked pleadingly into her sad face. "I know I'm risking an enormous heartache if you go back to your home when you gain your full memory, but I also know it's not the home you hoped you had. Don't go, Abby."

Her throat tightened again. She couldn't speak.

Rafe put his hands on her shoulders. "I love you. You, Abigail."

"Oh, Rafe, that's what I wanted to hear, but I don't want you to be burdened with my problems as I work them out."

"You could never burden me." He wrapped her in his arms.

She knew he was speaking from the heart. A dread fell from her and she felt a happiness she hadn't experienced since before the death of her parents.

Abby spent the next couple of weeks studying the news clippings she had obtained earlier as well as the current papers that Rafe had made arrangements to have delivered. The attempted break-in at the Cummings home was reported, but only as a side line to the story on the continued absence of its mistress. It seems, the paper stated, that her husband is being questioned intensely about her disappearance. There also has been speculation about the relationship between Tom Cummings and Mrs. Margaret

Templeton. Pictures were included of Tom and herself. She read the news stories over and over. How could she be involved in such a sordid situation?

According to the articles, she was the publisher of the magazine, *Success*. This so intrigued her, she had Rafe pick up a copy. It was a beautiful book, but other than her own, the only staff name that seemed to bring up a feeling of recognition was Ethan Bland.

She flipped to what apparently was a regular article written by him. After reading it, she thought she was fortunate to have him on board. He must be running the magazine now. She had suspected that he was more to her than simply a co-worker. Tom's name was nowhere to be found. This must be totally her project.

Her efforts to bring lost memories to the forefront were exasperating. She was beginning to have a sense of knowing these people but it could be that she was building an association with them out of studying all the information she had collected. Giving up, she packed it all away.

With no evidence substantiating foul play, it seemed that Abby had simply vanished. Her presence erased. Eric told Sam he knew it wasn't the Rapture because he was still here. Sam shook his head. There were days that other crimes took precedence and they were relieved to get away from it for a while. As soon as the interfering problem was solved, Sam would be on it again.

"What the hell are we missing?" he said, hitting the desk with his fist before standing.

Eric jumped and looked up at the frowning face as Sam paced.

With hands clasped behind his back and shoulders slumped, Sam stopped and said almost to himself, "Has he committed the perfect crime? Is he going to get away with it?" He turned to Eric and asked, "Did we check on other disappearances in the area?"

"Yes."

"All the way from Fancy Gap to Myrtle Beach?"

"Yes."

"What'd we find?" Sam asked.

"With the exception of a few runaways and a lost- in- the woods, everyone seems to be where they're supposed to be," Eric answered.

"So there's no serial thing going on here! What do we do next?" Sam asked, popping a Rolaid.

"Ya know, Boss, one day we're gonna be sittin' here and it's gonna come to us clear as a bell," Eric promised.

Ethan sat in Tom's office waiting for him to pour the coffee. "Cream?"

"Tom, I've been here four years and you still can't remember I drink it black?"

"I know that, I wasn't thinking. How's it going next door?" Tom asked, adding the usual few grains of sugar and cream to his own coffee.

"We're adjusting." Ethan accepted his cup and sipped at the coffee. "I don't understand your aversion to tea."

"It tastes like brewed tobacco."

"What about your shadows, are they still around?"

"Not like at first. I think Holloway has told them if they can't solve it to move on, but the case is still open and I know I'm their 'person of interest', but they have nothing to connect me to her disappearance," Tom said.

"You should count your blessings. I'm surprised they haven't picked you up on circumstantial evidence. Your personal and active association with Maggie would certainly point to motive. You need to get your desires under control," Ethan warned.

"We've been through this before," Tom admonished. "I haven't seen or talked with her for a while. I know I need to be in my home at night, for now, and I don't think she should visit there," Tom told him.

"By the way, did they find out who tried to break into your house that night?"

"No, and I think that attempt is suspect. Every home in the area has security. Why would anyone undertake that problem? The police said the front door had been tried as well as the window."

"I guess those who do that kind of thing know that areas with security have it for a reason, so if they can get into a house there, the profits will be better. You have no idea who it could have been or what they were looking for?" Ethan asked.

"If it weren't for the broken window, I would say that Abby, or her ghost, came home, then changed her mind," Tom suggested.

"You have to be joking, Tom."

"If she could, don't you think she would want to punish me? Maybe haunt me for the rest of my life?"

"Ooooh, now it's payback time? You can bet it's not Abby causing your discomfort. It's you. Guilt is a powerful debilitater. It can eat at you until you go completely off. In your case, however, I don't think you understand guilt. Your problem is fear and right now, until the police give up on you, you're scared."

Tom quietly studied this man of whom Abby was so fond. He couldn't remember how his involvement with Ethan had gotten started. They were so different, yet, from the same mold.

Guiding the conversation back to the subject, Tom said, "I don't know what to think. Maybe it was a couple of the detectives coming back for the money they had just returned."

"Speaking of which."

"You know I can do nothing about that until everything is back to normal. I know they aren't watching me constantly, but I'm not sure when they're there and when they're not," Tom told him.

"Just wanted you to know I hadn't forgotten. Actually, I came over to see when you plan to introduce me to Mr. Harmon?"

"I much prefer that you make the contact. It's better if I'm brought into it as an afterthought," Tom told him.

"Of course that's preferable, but since you've met him already, why don't we simply attack this one in reverse?" Ethan suggested.

"I'll set it up. Maybe a dinner meeting."

Ethan stood. "I think that's good. The relaxed atmosphere is much more conducive to establishing a favorable rapport, which in turn, is more profitable."

CHAPTER
14

ABBY PUT HER basic black on for the evening. Rafe brought the dress and a few other items home as an "appreciation gift" for cooking and caring for the house. Her hair, having been trimmed once again, was very short with the highlighted tips accenting the natural auburn growth. Small wisps of hair touched the circumference of her face.

This cut, in conjunction with her high cheekbones and small chin, had taken a couple of years from her appearance. The loss of weight accented her facial bone structure and seemed to have diminished her entire frame. A little light makeup and she was ready.

She carried the glasses in her purse so they could be put on when she arrived at the restaurant. She entered the living room where Rafe was sitting on the sofa, remote in hand, watching the news.

He looked up and whistled. "You look fantastic."

Surprised, she responded, "I'll bet you say that to all your lady friends."

"As a matter of fact, I have found that to be the gentlemanly thing to do." He stood, and pulled a long black box from his coat pocket, added, "I thought that dress called for these."

Abby looked into his hand and back up to his smiling face. He flipped the top open to reveal a strand of pearls and matching earrings.

With a quick intake of breath, she brought her hand up to her chest and said, "Oh, Rafe they're beautiful."

"You make me so happy. I had to do something for you."

"*You* had to do something for *me*? You, just had to do something *more*, for me! I don't know what to say. Thank you, Rafe."

He took the pearls out of the box and fastened the simple strand around her neck as she put the earrings on. She turned to face him.

"Beautiful," he said. "Absolutely beautiful!"

She was beaming. Her anticipation of a night out was proving to be more satisfying than she dreamed.

He turned the TV off, threw the wrap over her shoulders and offered her his arm. *This should be a horse driven pumpkin*, she thought as he helped her into the vehicle.

"I need to make a short detour by the clinic. I picked up an x-ray at the hospital for Dr. Cantrell and he may need it in the morning before I get there."

"That's no problem. It's still early," Abby answered.

Rafe parked in back of the clinic and insisted that Abby join him inside. He didn't want to leave her alone in an empty parking lot.

She stood, looking out the window in his office, while Rafe delivered the x-ray to Dr. Cantrell's desk. Upon returning, he joined her at the window.

"Mission accomplished!" he said, standing behind her.

She pointed across the side street to an empty lot and said, "That's an awfully nice space beside you. It takes up the whole block. I'm surprised something hasn't been built there. This is such a prime area."

"It belongs to the clinic doctors," he told her. "We have plans for it. We just don't have the funds yet."

"What kind of plans?"

He turned her around, put the small purse in her hands as he answered. "A small hotel with an Inn atmosphere."

Picking up her wrap and taking her arm, he continued as they left the building, "The dream is to have a place where parents or spouses can stay with their loved ones while they're undergoing treatments. It will include dining facilities, a small open kitchen for drinks and snacks, a play room and game room as well as an area for families to gather for comfort talk. A very homelike place. The idea is to get financial support through philanthropic organizations so the cost for staying there can be kept to a minimum."

They were heading east as Abby asked, "That will be wonderful. When do you expect it to be built?"

"Not sure, but we're working on it," he answered. "Okay, what are you in the mood for? Japanese? American? We've done Italian. Mexican?"

They finally chose a restaurant by its appearance, taking a chance on the cuisine. It was a classy intimate spot located away from the hustle and bustle areas. Resting smugly on a quiet street heading into town, it was surrounded by flowering trees and shrubbery. Had it not been for the small white lights that adorned the greenery behind the darkened glass of the dining areas they might have missed it. The parking was located in back, and homes that had resisted commercial growth stood on either side.

The dining experience was perfect. Lights were low, the waiters wore black dress pants, white shirts and their own choice of colorful ties. Low ceilings carried the soft musically appealing sounds from the piano in the back corner. It was a dreamy and luscious evening.

Rafe insisted on appetizers before the entree and they shared a dessert afterward.

Rafe laid his hand atop hers. "This is your coming out party," he said, smiling.

"And a wonderful one, it is!" She was radiant.

She had herbal tea while he sipped Amaretto and coffee. They were quiet now, basking in the glow of the other. Completely at ease, neither of them wanted to break the spell.

Rubbing his fingers lightly over the back of her hand, he looked into the depth of her being and said, "I can't live without you, Abigail."

She did not smile. "And you won't," she told him seriously.

"Let's go home," Rafe stated.

He held her chair then followed as she maneuvered among the tables. She was almost out of the dining area when she glanced to her left to find a familiar male face staring directly at her. Without exhibiting one iota of recognition, she transferred her focus to the exit and moved smoothly past.

Rafe laid her shawl across her shoulders, then held the door as he escorted her out. He sent the valet for the car then turned to Abby. He took her hand, and said, "You really are beautiful tonight and my heart is so full." Lifting her hand to his lips for a kiss, he felt the trembling.

At that instant, the valet pulled up in the vehicle and jumped out. Rafe opened the door, held her elbow until she was seated, tipped the young man, then moved around to the other side and got in.

"What happened?" he asked her anxiously.

"I just saw my husband."

"What? Where?" he asked, astonished. The adrenaline surged through him.

"In the restaurant. He was seated at a table we passed as we were leaving."

"Did he see you?" Rafe looked into the rearview mirror to find a man rushing out the front door.

"Oh yes! He was staring almost open-mouthed," she emphasized.

"Did he recognize you?"

"He evidently thought he did and I recognized him." She looked at Rafe. "Did you hear me, Rafe? I recognized him. I was very careful not to show it. I didn't even acknowledge his look. But I knew who he was!"

Rafe adjusted his rearview mirror and checked behind them once again. The man seemed to be writing something down.

"I can't think he would positively have known it was you," Rafe suggested.

"Oh, he thought it was me. His shock was evident. What if he finds out who you are?" she asked, frightened at the thought.

"I paid cash, so I didn't sign anything. The waiter wouldn't know me," he assured her. He didn't want to add to her dilemma by reporting what he had just witnessed.

140

"Okay."

Rafe laid his hand on her knee and gave it a little squeeze. She looked at him and forced a wan smile.

"Excuse me," Tom had said. "I left my wallet in my overcoat."

He walked past the maitre d' and out the front door. Looking at the back of the Discovery, he squinted at the departing license plate and jotted down the numbers. Hurrying back, he stopped just inside. Facing the table he had vacated, he stood there until Ethan glanced up and Tom caught his attention and motioned him to follow.

Ethan looked at Mr. Harmon, who was studying the menu, and said, "I'm sorry, Paul, but I see someone I must speak to before he gets out. I'll be right back."

Mr. Harmon acknowledged Ethan's statement, but kept his attention fully on the menu.

Ethan caught up with Tom as he was entering the rest room. Tom checked below the bottom of the wooden stall doors. They were alone.

"Tom, what's the matter with you! This isn't girls' night out. Can't you go to the rest room alone?"

"Shut up, Ethan. I saw someone that I'm not sure wasn't Abby."

"What?" Ethan asked, confused. "Could you rephrase that so I can understand what you said?"

Tom took him by the lapels and got into his face. "I said, I think I may have seen Abby," he hissed through his teeth.

Pulling Tom's hands off his coat, Ethan straightened with a bewildered look on his face. "How many drinks have you had?"

"One!" He walked in a small circle. "It was her face, it wasn't her hair, and her eyes were not clearly visible behind those glasses. Thinner, but it was her face." He was speaking in thoughts.

"Abby doesn't wear glasses."

"I know that!" He stopped briefly and spoke into Ethan's face, "She could have changed her hair and picked up the glasses to disguise herself."

"From whom? And for what reason? This is Greensboro, not Charlotte or Prestonburg," Ethan reminded him.

"I know, I know," Tom repeated, reversing his circle.

"Did she see you?"

"Yes, she looked right at me. God, I was just sitting there staring like an idiot."

"And did she recognize you or speak to you?" Ethan questioned.

"If she knew me, she hid it well, and no, she didn't speak to me."

"Most attractive women tend to ignore gaping oafs," Ethan scolded.

"Am I losing my mind? It couldn't have been her, could it?" Tom asked.

"Pull yourself together. We've got an important client out there and any breakdown you feel coming on is going to have to wait," Ethan stated firmly. "Do you hear me, Tom?"

Tom stared at the floor for a moment, thinking. Then he lifted his head and shoulders. "Of course," he answered. That must be what was happening. He was having delusions. He could probably put Abby's face on just about anybody. It was his fault she was gone. He should expect to suffer.

Rafe was sitting on the sofa looking out the front window and Abby was lying with her head in his lap. The room, lit only by dim street lights filtering in by way of the windows, provided concealment while allowing Rafe to watch for any suspicious activities.

"I felt nothing for him. Actually, I haven't loved him for a long time. There was another woman. I can't remember her name but she's been his mistress for several years," Abby offered.

Rafe didn't respond. He sat quietly, watching each passing car and running his fingers through her hair. She needed to let her mind work it out.

"I wonder how many people knew what a fool I was? He promised me it was over. I knew it wasn't. I don't know how I knew." She hesitated in thought. "Maybe I didn't know, maybe I just hoped it wasn't over because I wanted the marriage to end. How could I stay with someone who had been carrying on an affair for some time. He must care about her, she wasn't just a one night stand."

She was pressing her mind to focus back and it was exhausting her. "I tried to forget, but I never felt the same. It was over. I told him it was over." She closed her eyes and was quiet for a moment, then speaking more softly said, "I had my magazine, that's what kept me happy. It wasn't him. He didn't care about me. I don't think he ever did. He was lonely, as was I, and we thought we needed each other."

Rafe looked down at his hands in her hair oblivious to the silken feel of it. He was quiet while she continued her murmuring.

Almost whispering to herself now, she said, "Maybe I caused it. Maybe I made him want someone else." She was silent, but only briefly. "I don't know who failed whom?" She paused a little longer. "I don't know." "I..."

Rafe closed his eyes and rested his hand on her head.

Abby had searched the Charlotte papers thoroughly for days following the sighting of her husband. If he had recognized her, she was sure he would have gone to the authorities. Of course, that doesn't mean they would've believed him. If they were beginning to point a finger in his direction, his report of having seen her would certainly be suspect. If that had happened she felt sure he would then have gone to the media, but there was no mention of it.

On the other hand, if he were the one who had harmed her, he wouldn't want her found. He would, instead, be searching for her to do what he failed to accomplish on his first attempt. The thought made her ill.

It was difficult, however, for her to believe that he had lost total control, as he was not one to express emotion of any kind. The morning she left, he told her he loved her and that was probably one out of a dozen times he had said it throughout their six years of marriage. Even during their most intimate times, he was involved only in the act. No caressing, kissing or talking. Simply satisfying his needs and if hers happened to reach that point, then, she was most lucky.

It's funny how an incident can bring memories rushing back. Her activities that followed her departure from Tom's office on that fateful morning, however, were still elusive. *I wonder what event will have to present itself to help me there?*

Rafe had warned her once more not to answer the door nor to speak when picking up the telephone receiver. He had started calling several times a day to check on her. She began to watch the cars that passed and noticed one that drove around her block several times on a particular day. Trying to calm her fears, she told herself this person was simply looking for a certain address, then fright reared its ugly head again and said, "Yeah, *yours!*" Her predicament was currently occupying her every thought.

In an effort to redirect her actions, she began to concentrate on the house. Rafe told her it needed attention. He was right. It was just a house, not a home, but that was all he had needed. It was a place to sleep, a place to wait for the next day. It had no charm, no personality or life.

After walking through all the rooms and considering every aspect, she decided to make the living room her first project. It was the room not presently being used, therefore, she could work without stressing out about the disorganized state that would result before the change was complete.

She found a sewing machine in the attic, pieces of cast off furniture and a trunk full of what she assumed were, as yet, unused and probably forgotten wedding gifts.

As she returned from the attic, the phone rang. She rushed to answer it without actually answering per se. Putting the receiver to her ear, she could hear herself breathing heavily into the mouthpiece due to being out of breath.

It was not Rafe and whoever was on the other end said nothing. She held her breath now to listen carefully for peripheral sounds. Nothing. She hung up and looked at the phone as if it had life. Rafe didn't even have caller I.D.

She sighed and told herself it was probably one of those automatically dialed telemarketing calls and the someone was simply late connecting with her. Maybe they don't speak until they hear a "hello." She was determined not to let this spoil her day.

She and Rafe had just finished dinner one evening when Abby spoke to him of her ideas.

After telling him of her plans, she said, "I need a man. Your handyman!"

"Good, I'll make a call tomorrow. What day do you want him?"

"As soon as he's free. Can you tell him I'm your designer? I wouldn't want him to think you were living with someone."

"No, we certainly wouldn't want to give him that impression. A beautiful, self-sufficient, adorable young woman, why, that just might destroy my reputation. His name is David. I'd guess he's in his mid-fifties, balding, but wears a ball cap—backwards—and white coveralls. Don't open the door to anyone but him."

"I won't."

Rafe was relieved. She seemed to be excited and anxious to get involved. Damn Tom Cummings!

David arrived three days later and Abby presented her ideas to him and asked, "Can we do it?"

He was a short but husky man. His pinched face studied her sketches a moment before nodding slowly in thought. The clear blue eyes blinked before looking into her questioning features, then a smile broke through to affirm that he was the man for the job.

Before the day was out, they had become good friends, and in the days to come, she worked right along with him and he accepted her help without hesitation. They had nothing in common but a creative instinct, but this thread connected them quickly. She was enjoying herself without a thought of her past intruding.

Rafe had told David a few details of Abby's situation without giving away her identity. He informed him that she had been attacked and could be in danger. She was staying in his home only temporarily. He felt it only fair to let him know the circumstances before taking the job. Abby had agreed.

David accepted and promised to keep an ear attuned to anything unusual. This made Rafe feel better about leaving her alone.

It was late morning on Friday when Abby headed to the laundry room to get a few more rags. The movement of a car in the driveway drew her attention. She stepped closer to the window to find the car she had previously seen driving around the block. The drivers door opened and Tom stepped out. The next thing she knew she was in the living room grabbing David by the front of his coveralls. She was having trouble breathing.

"What is it, Miss Abby?" he asked. "You look like you've seen the Ghost of Christmas Past!"

"I have and he's coming to the door. He could be trying to find me." She was trembling and her fear was evident. "I very much don't want this man to know I'm here."

Suddenly he was all business. "Okay, missy, get yourself into the bathroom and lock the door. Don't worry, I'll take care of everything."

She stood in front of him looking over her shoulder and then back at him, still clinging to his straps.

"Did you hear me?" he said sternly. "Listen, you have nothing to fear. I'll take care of it. Now, disappear."

She shifted into gear, obeying him as the doorbell rang.

David waited until she was out of sight, then picked up a screw driver and strolled to the front door. He opened it, stepped between the jambs and peered at the man on the threshold.

"Yes?" he said.

"Isn't this where Raphael Adams lives?" Tom asked.

"That's correct!"

When David offered nothing else, Tom continued, "Is he in?"

"He's in his office."

Tom waited. David said nothing.

"Look, I'm an old college friend of Raphael's. I just happened to be passing through and thought I would stop by to say, 'Hello.' I don't suppose you could mean he is in his office at home?"

"He doesn't have an office at home." David stood, impatiently holding the screwdriver as if a job were waiting for him.

"I see. Well, what about Mrs. Adams, is she here?"

"She works in his office."

"I'm very disappointed. I've never met her. Have they been married long?" Tom shifted from one foot to the other with his hands clasped behind his back. His smile was forced.

"Long as I've known 'em." David did not relax. He lifted his arm to look at his watch.

"And how long has that been?" Tom pressed.

"Since the first time he called me on a job!"

"And that was—?"

David rolled his eyes upward as if in thought. "I don't know. A busy man doesn't count time. What's your name? I'll tell him you stopped by, see if he remembers you."

"That's not necessary. I'll just come by the next time I'm in the area," Tom said.

"I'm sure he'll be glad to see you," David said as he closed the door and locked it. He stood by the side of the window and watched him leave.

"All right, you can come out now. He's gone," David called out. He heard her leave the bathroom as he moved in her direction.

"Come on," he said, "let's pack up for the day. We'll have lunch in the kitchen where we can watch the road and I'll visit until your 'husband' gets home."

She hugged him.

The next week, Rafe arrived home one day to find Abby waiting in the kitchen with eyebrows raised and smiling from ear to ear.

"Oh no! Did you swallow the mouse?" he asked.

"Rafe, you stand right here until I call you."

"What's going on?" he asked as she turned and disappeared through the kitchen doorway.

"Okay," she called out.

He took his jacket off and threw it over a chair before moving through the house to the living room. During the makeover, he had been banished from this room. Now, Abby was standing with her back to the far wall with that silly grin spread across her face. He stepped into the room and stopped.

The butter-colored walls were the background that pulled the entire scene together. The sheers over the windows were topped off with padded valance boards covered in a large stripe of muted reds, yellows, creams and sage. The dreary beige wing backs were now in a cheery floral print of the same colors that adorned the valance boards. Before Abby started, the furniture had simply been placed boringly around the walls, but it had now been rearranged with a few pieces from the attic storage added. One could almost detect a conversation between them.

There were containers of greenery scattered about and a fresh flower arrangement on the cocktail table in front of the red sofa. Under this table rested a large deep cream, plush rug. A mirror hung over the fireplace, establishing the focal point, with a medley of various heights of candles burning on the mantle. The existing pictures had been brought together to form an arrangement on the wall with no windows. The original light sage carpeting took on a fresh new look with the overhead light off and the three lamps lit.

His astonished gaze took in the entire room before looking back at that wonderful stupid grin on that anxiously awaiting designer of his.

"This is absolutely unbelievable! There is no resemblance to the room you've kept hidden from me. I'm speechless." He walked to her and took her hands. "You really have a talent. It's beautiful, simply beautiful!" Leaning forward, he kissed her on the cheek. "Thank you."

She said, "No, I thank you!"

CHAPTER 15

ABBY READ THROUGH the current *Success* several times and after thoroughly scrutinizing Ethan's article, she handed the magazine to Rafe who was watching the same news stories he had seen twice before on the half hours.

"Read this and tell me what you think," she suggested.

He took the magazine which was opened to *The Climb* and sat back, placing his ankle on his knee. As Abby rose and headed to the kitchen, the phone rang. Rafe reached for it with his attention still on the article.

"Doctor Adams here," he said.

"I would like to speak with Mrs. Adams, please," a man's voice replied.

Rafe looked toward the kitchen and said quietly, "I'm sorry. She's in the shower. If you'll give me your name, I'll have her return your call."

"I'm just about to go out. I'll try her another time," the man told him.

"May I tell her who called?" Rafe asked as the phone line went dead.

Abby had cut Rafe a piece of homemade pecan pie and added ice cream. She put the delicacy and a cup of coffee on a tray and took it back with her, placed it on the table and sat down.

He lowered the magazine to discover what was on the tray.

Turning to her he asked, "Are you sure your name isn't Martha?'

"Martha?" she asked.

"Stewart. You don't remember who she is, right?"

"Right!"

He scooted forward and picked up the plate and fork, laid the magazine on the table and read while he ate.

Finishing both, he sat back and said, "He's very good. His articles must be financially beneficial to the subject."

"That's what I thought. Give you any ideas?"

"Excuse me?"

"This magazine is sold all over the east coast and is being picked up in the Midwest. That's what I went to Tom's office to tell him that dreadful morning. Anyway, my point is, that the piece on this man," she continued, pointing to the picture in the magazine, "is worth a million in advertising. Don't you expect that his company must pick up a lot—and I mean a *lot*—of business because of it?"

"Absolutely! And?"

"And doesn't it give you any ideas?"

He looked at her questioningly for a moment before it dawned on him.

"No! Never," he said, standing. Gathering the tray, he headed to the kitchen, then came right back and sat down. "How could you entertain such a thought? What if he were in the restaurant that night with Tom and saw me? Besides, your husband knows my name and he may have told this Ethan Bland."

"No one saw you that night. It was me that Tom spotted and he didn't see anything else. He has gotten your name and address through your license number and doesn't even know you're a doctor. He's been told you are Raphael Adams, not Raphael Andrew Musgrave Adams. So, identify yourself as Doctor Andrew Musgrave. It could be very good for your clinic. Perhaps by the time they would get to you, all this bad business will be cleaned up and there would be no problem using your name."

"And if it isn't?"

Abby hesitated before answering. "I guess it wouldn't help you but maybe it could benefit me. I want to know what's going on and you could be my eyes and ears."

"Abby, I think only trouble could come of it."

"More trouble than I'm in now? Look, Tom has already been here looking for me and I don't know if he fell for David's story or not, but I don't want to wait around for another unexpected visit. I would rather we make our own. See what we can learn."

He looked into her pleading eyes, and sighed. "I don't know, Abby."

"Sleep on it, please," she said, taking his hand and squeezing it.

"All right." He wanted to think about it on his own. He had trouble keeping his thoughts objective around her.

"Rafe, do you think I'll get in trouble with the police? You know, for not contacting them after I learned they were looking for me?"

"The police would still have been investigating, as they are now, even if they knew you were okay, because there was a crime committed. The attempt on your life was made by the very person they're trying to pin your disappearance on, so let them do their job. If they make an arrest, then it would be your duty to go forward, but until that happens or you remember what occurred that day, you have to protect yourself."

"Could a mind totally and forever block out a tragedy? Could it be possible that I'll never remember who tried to kill me?"

"I don't know, but if it's necessary, I'll see that you get in to see someone who can professionally help you."

She leaned forward, wrapped her arms around his neck and kissed him on the ear. He twisted his chair about and pulled her onto his lap.

"Ummm, you smell so tantalizing," he said.

"No, I don't. It's only a little cheap cologne I dabbed below my ears."

"What's it called?" he asked.

"*Daisy Water*! No, it's not. I really don't know. I picked it up at the drugstore and it was simply the least offensive of their offerings, so I bought it."

"Must be your natural scent I'm enjoying," he said, nuzzling her neck.

"I found a perfume I loved, called *Minuit Etoile*, when I was living in Paris. It's French. It means 'Midnight Star'."

"Paris!" he said with surprise.

"That's where I was when my parents had their accident. Anyway, I haven't been able to locate it here, so I've had to order it from Paris."

"That's a shame, but I don't think it would matter to me," he said.

"But, it matters to me."

Abby had just returned from a walk to the convenience store to purchase flowers for the patio when she heard the phone ringing. She rushed from the garage into the house to answer it. Since Tom's little visit, she was nervous about any unsolicited contact. She lifted the receiver and held it to her ear without speaking.

"It's me," Rafe said.

"Hi!"

"How about pizza tonight?" he asked.

"My favorite," she replied. "Are you bringing it home or are we going out?"

"I'll pick you up."

Now, she was going to have to hurry to get the flowers planted and still have time to clean up before Rafe got home.

The impatiens would be the most trouble. The patio, edged with mulch, begged for color. These flowers would multiply and fill the edge with bountiful blooms. She worked diligently placing them at properly spaced intervals to cover the allotted area.

Next, she made haste to get the ferns in the pots placed at each side of the patio. Finally, it was finished with time to spare. Dusting herself off and gathering her gardening tools she headed to the garage where she put everything away and entered the kitchen. She stopped there, as an uneasiness caused a chill to come over her. She had an uncomfortable feeling that someone had been in this room. Frowning, she looked around. Things were where they were supposed to be, but maybe, just a little out of kilter. The catchall drawer was not quite totally closed and the blinds were tilted at a different angle.

This is ridiculous! I'm so jumpy I could probably imagine words written on the walls in blood. Straighten yourself up girl, or you're going to lose it.

She reached for the paper towels, then stopped instantly, arm still outstretched. The sound of a drawer being pushed closed reverberated in her ears. Her heart began pounding. Someone *was* in the house.

Fear surged through her. She had carelessly left the garage door up in her effort to get to the phone and the door into the house was unlocked. As another drawer was pulled open, she wondered what this person was looking for. Jewelry?

You idiot, why are you just standing here? She heard footfalls moving out into the hall. The fear of facing another gun turned her legs rubbery.

Frantically, she looked around. The nearby pantry had folding doors and one of them was pushed open. She stepped through it and slid behind the closed one. She braced herself for what might happen. Lifting a can of vegetables off the shelf, she raised it over her head and waited.

Footsteps came through the great room and into the kitchen before they stopped. Abby tried to contain the shaking. She was afraid she was going to knock something off the shelf and draw attention to herself. Her heart sounded like a drum. Could the intruder hear it?

The sounds moved about the room. Cabinet doors were opened and closed, then it was quiet again. Now she was conscious of the fact that she was not totally hidden. From a small area in the kitchen, a portion of her could be visible to whomever was there. She tightened her grip on the can.

Abby heard the soles squeak as feet turned. Her raised arm was beginning to ache as the intruder moved closer. She could feel the presence just on the other side of the door. Holding her breath, her heart flip-flopped in her chest.

Suddenly a strong male hand reached in and grabbed her free arm as his other hand pushed the folded door aside. Her hand began its protective descent when the door was released and her arm was halted in midair. A swift whack of her arm against a shelf dislodged her makeshift weapon. With quick movements she was pulled out and flipped backward with her arms crossed in front of her. Strong hands trapped her backside tightly against his body.

She lifted a foot and came down hard on his toes. Gasping, he jumped and tightened his grip. She threw her head back hitting his chin hard. He yelped and she recognized the voice.

"You, you *are* her, aren't you?" he asked. "Stop fighting, I—"

She had been preparing for another strike when a sound from the garage stopped the struggle. Clamping a hand over her mouth and dragging her with him, he backed toward the living room.

"Hey!" Rafe called out. "Are you inside or out?"

Her captor was pulling her along as he moved quickly to the front door. He was now focused on getting away before Rafe discovered him.

Gripping her tightly while unlocking the door, he turned the knob and eased them both to the side of the door frame. For an instant, she feared he was going to take her with him, but suddenly, she was released and forcefully pushed forward. She went sprawling onto the floor hitting one arm on the coffee table as she went down. Rolling to her back, she grabbed her aching elbow as her fingers tingled. The front door stood ajar, but her husband was gone.

"Abby, where are you?" Rafe had walked through the kitchen and great room before calling down the hallway to the bedrooms. He then peered into the living room to find Abby lifting her head off the floor and turning to look at him.

"I'm right here," she said belatedly.

He ran to her and knelt down. She told him what had happened and how stupid she had been to leave the garage door up.

He pulled her close. "I promised I wouldn't let anyone hurt you. I haven't been careful enough."

"You? You weren't even here!"

"Thank God I got here when I did."

"Yes." She turned a questioning look toward him. "Why are you here so early?"

"I'm hungry!"

Tom drove back to Prestonburg with his head reeling. *It was Abby. I think. Maybe not. I don't know. I can't let anyone know what I did today. Ethan thinks I'm losing my mind already and if it got out, it might cause me even more scrutiny. Ethan, you bastard. You think I'm not suffering from guilt? It's making me crazy!*

On their way to Luigi's Pizzaria, Rafe pulled into a shopping area.

"I want to stop in here before we eat. It won't take but a few minutes." He opened his door and when she didn't move he said, "Aren't you coming?"

She pulled the handle and slid off the seat, saying to herself, "I didn't know you wanted me to."

Taking her hand, he led her through the doors. "I want to get a couple of cell phones."

"Why?"

"I never felt like I needed one until now, and I want you to pick one out for yourself," he told her.

"Why do I need one? I have no one to call but you and I always seem to be with you!"

"You never know when the need will arise. Look what happened today."

"Rafe, there was a phone in the house," she reminded him.

"But you couldn't get to it. If you keep one in your pocket you can get me in seconds and I can always call and you won't ever have to answer the home phone. Now, don't give me a hard time or we'll never get dinner."

The transaction was quickly completed and while they were enjoying the pizza, Rafe asked, "How would you feel about going to the cabin this weekend? You can give that elbow a rest and I'll do the cooking," he suggested. "It's been weeks and I like to check on it every so often."

"I'd love to," she agreed.

Putting the frightening episode out of her mind, she was making a determined effort to enjoy the weekend. She laid her head back and, with closed eyes, enjoyed the music as Rafe drove out of town. She was so comfortable with him.

As he left the interstate, she sat up to enjoy the scenery. After driving through a small inhabited area, Rafe turned onto the narrow dirt road that began winding up the mountain. The drive to the cabin took longer than it should, considering the distance they traveled. However, due to the small rugged unkempt roadway, they moved more slowly. Abby suspected her attacker must have simply stumbled onto this deserted path. Had it not been for the cabin, it was the perfect place for his crime.

"I hope I get to see this place during other seasons. I'll bet it's beautiful in the fall!" she exclaimed. "Rafe, look, there goes a deer." She turned in his direction. "Did you see it?"

He smiled. "Yes. There are many here, but you don't see them until early evening. That's when they come out to feed. And they can be quite a nuisance. As they begin to accept sharing their home with two legged inhabitants, they become more bold and it's hard to have outside flowers or nice plants because they eat everything."

"Have you tried hanging baskets?"

"Leave it to Martha!"

He pulled in close to the cabin and they carried everything inside. Abby felt like she had returned home.

After Rafe regulated the heat, checked the power and looked for any possible signs of unwanted inhabitants, he suggested they take a walk.

"It's a little nippy. Better get your sweater," he told her.

He picked up an old comforter, folded it and tucked it under his arm, after which, he opened a drawer and withdrew his hunting knife.

"You never know what you might meet out here," he said, putting it into his waist band.

He took her by the hand, leading the way. Traveling behind the cabin and away from the road, he pointed out two trees into which he had installed large hooks. "Those are for the hammock. On hot summer days it's great to bring along a book and iced tea, climb into the hammock and fall asleep before you reach the second chapter."

A pathway, cushioned by nature's mulch, had been defined by human hand and foot. Rafe moved over it by instinct. Each time Abby stopped to view something of interest, such as the birth of a

156

new tree or to pick up a huge pine cone to compare to a tiny one she had pulled off a fir tree, Rafe waited patiently. He had done the same things when he first visited here.

"Do you see that pile of river rocks?" he asked, pointing to the left.

Peering into the direction he indicated she said, "There's a river up here?"

He laughed. "No, silly, we're at the top of the mountain." He turned left and they walked over a knoll where the land dropped down slightly. They descended the incline about fifty yards and stopped. To their side and very close beside a large tree, running freely over rocks, appeared a crisp, clear spring which fed a small brook that rippled downward.

"This leads to the river below. After a good rain, this brook triples in size and joins others and if you lie quietly in the hammock you can hear the water rushing downhill, splashing over rocks, snaking its route to lower ground. It's almost hypnotic. Very relaxing and sleep inducing."

"You come up here to rest, don't you?" she asked.

"It's a place to escape, and rest and sleep is the ultimate way of divesting oneself of life's pressures." He pulled her back up in the direction of the rock pile. "Anyway, I brought the rocks from the river with the idea of building a barbecue pit, but after they laid there for a while, I wasn't sure just how I wanted to use them."

He indicated the vast area and said, "Who would I cook for? There's nobody here but me. So, I've considered a walkway, a patio and a fish pond, among other things. When I think I've decided how to use them, I tell myself I need to consider all the angles, so, I get in the hammock."

"And relax!" she said.

"And relax," he laughed.

They walked on in silence, returning to his original path and continued until they came to a wall of low pine trees and brush. Rafe used his knife to cut away a few sprigs of briars, then pushed aside an opening for her to step through. When she had cleared it, she stood in awe. He moved through and stopped beside her as she grabbed his arm.

"Magnificent, isn't it?" he said.

"My goodness, you can almost feel the gravity pulling you over the edge."

The drop-off must be a mile or two almost straight down. Ledges and angles, of course, widen outward on the decent, but they couldn't be seen unless you moved to a dangerous point to look down.

They were standing on a wide outcropping of rock. There were areas of dirt and mulch which provided a perfect resting place to simply sit and enjoy a grand overlook of miles and miles of country. The beauty was staggering. He spread the comforter on the ground and folded it over for more cushion. They both seated themselves.

"You really can't see the end of this view. It fades out almost into a fog." Abby stated. "Stepping from the dense woods onto this is such a shock. It's really breathtaking!"

Rafe put his arm over her shoulder and asked, "Are you warm enough?"

She nodded. He picked up a stick and drew into the dirt indicating where they were in relation to Charlotte, Winston-Salem, Prestonburg and the view in front of them. She asked a few questions before they sat quietly enjoying the scenery.

"I'm always astounded at the natural beauty of our country," Rafe said.

He looked at Abby when she made no reply. "Maybe I'll get the chance to show you more," he said.

"I hope so."

They fell into a comfortable silence, with each other and their setting. She had grown up in this area, but had not enjoyed, nor even seen, what was beyond her back yard.

As the sun began to give way to the evening, Rafe suggested it was time to head to the cabin.

"You're right, it's getting a little chilly, let's go back and start dinner—" she began.

"I'm cooking, remember."

"Oh, I haven't forgotten."

About halfway to the cabin Rafe took her arm and stopping her, held his forefinger to his lips. Leaning close to her, he brought his finger away from his face and pointed in the direction off to the left. Abby turned her head to see a small deer and its mother munching on new foliage about a hundred feet away. The adult animal kept her eye on the two intruders and stayed close to her charge as they dined.

Abby let out a quiet sigh of pleasure before smiling at Rafe. They watched in fascination as the animals moved unafraid from bush to bush. Finally, Rafe urged Abby on toward the cabin.

"It's beginning to get dark and I don't want you to lose your footing," he said quietly, as he held her good elbow.

"I can't believe we didn't scare them away," Abby stated.

"They're used to seeing me out here. We're friends. They can become quite tame, you know. That's not always a good thing for them, because trust can lead to getting themselves shot."

"Yeah, tell me about it!" Abby said.

Soon they were all washed up and settled in the kitchen. Rafe busied himself over the stove as Abby sat down at the table to help chop vegetables. He had covered a large sheet pan with foil and was adjusting the oven shelf for broiling. A pot of hot salted water had been placed over the heat and the angel hair pasta stood by. Olive oil, pesto sauce and freshly grated parmesan cheese were awaiting the chopped mixed fresh vegetables.

"I thought you could call Ethan Bland's office and ask for an appointment when we get back," Abby suggested, picking up the knife and reaching for the cutting board.

Rafe turned to her. "Abby, stop that. I'm doing the cooking, so I should do the preparation also." He took the knife and joined her at the table.

"And when they ask for the purpose of the meeting, I tell them what? That I think I'm a perfect subject for his magazine?" Rafe asked.

"Not exactly. You could simply say that you wanted to talk with him about his article. Identify yourself and tell them you specialize in oncology, so they won't think you're some strange person trying to talk to him about an off-the-wall idea. I'm sure they get calls like that all the time."

Rafe added the chopped yellow bell pepper to the other vegetables and poured a little olive oil over them. He turned and popped a cherry tomato into her mouth, placed his hands on the table, leaned over it, kissed her nose and asked, "Exactly what do you think we'll learn from my visiting the office?"

"I don't really know," she answered honestly. "I guess I'm thinking you can bring something back to help me. Since I can't safely surface, I need assistance."

"Do you remember anyone else from work?"

"Not from the magazine. I know the name Donald, but I think he's associated with the mill," she said thoughtfully.

He turned back to the stove as he said, "I'll call Monday and see what happens."

She put her head down onto her arms that were folded atop the table and told him with gratitude, "I don't know what to say. You're so good to do this for me. I hope I learn that I've been a good person. I'll not be able to face you, if, in the end, I find that I didn't deserve anything that you've done."

He laid the knife down and came around the table. Bending his knees to lower himself to her level, he lifted her head to look into her face and said, "I know you're a good and kind person. You could not have been any different, it would show somehow."

She wrapped her arms around his neck and said quietly, "Then why did someone shoot me?"

It had already been a long day. Sam and Eric were working a case involving a stolen car from a dealership and had been out since early morning. Holloway had insisted they spend less time on the Cummings case, as the local interest had diminished, and he didn't foresee anything developing from the evidence collected.

Sam couldn't put it out of his mind and Eric was obsessed with trying to put his finger on whatever it was that was eluding him. It was late afternoon and they were sitting in the office, having completed the day's paperwork. Eric was, once again, flipping through the issue of *Success*.

"Would you put that magazine away! You think some of that culture is gonna rub off on you?" Sam asked.

"I can't get rid of this until I figure out what it is that bothers me about these pictures."

Sam sighed.

"By the way, Boss, I got you something," Eric said, closing the magazine and reaching for a bag behind his seat. Opening it, he pulled out a box of Prilosec.

"Happy St. Patrick's Day or Easter or whatever it is that's coming up," he said, setting it upon the desk.

"Why do you have to be so nice?" That was the only way Sam knew how to say thank you.

"Just trying to keep the boss well and happy. Makes my life easier," Eric replied.

Sam didn't have any children. He and Wilda had wanted them but it simply wasn't in the cards. If they had been blessed with a son, he would have wanted him to be like Eric. He was good through and through. Patient, liked everybody, always tried his best at whatever he was doing, didn't complain. A real good boy.

"Eric," Sam said, pushing his chair back to prop his legs on his desk. "You got a girl?"

Eric turned a sly look Sam's way and smiled. "Sure I got a girl, Sam. Did you think, maybe, I didn't like em?"

"No, I didn't think that." Sam smiled and clasped his hands behind his head. "You don't ever talk about her. What's the matter, is she ugly?" Sam teased.

Eric scooted up to the desk where he rested his elbows on the front edge. Cupping the heels of his hands together, he put his chin in them. Sam waited for him to speak, because he knew it was coming.

"You know, boss, she's really special." Eric was looking somewhere over Sam's head as he spoke. "She's a nurse. Real pretty, too. Clear blue eyes, dark brown hair and eyelashes. Those lashes! Wow, they really make her eyes spectacular. She can be a little fussy though, but that's because she worries about me. You know, with my job and all."

"You two got big plans?" Sam asked.

Eric closed his eyes as he continued. "We hope we'll have enough money saved to get married in a couple o' years." Opening his eyes now, he scooted back into his chair and looked seriously at Sam. "Boss, you know my daddy died last year."

"Yes, I'm real sorry about that, Eric. How's your mom doing?" Sam had removed his feet and sat erect at his desk now.

"She's still having a hard time. Anyway, I was going to do this later, but since you brought it up, I may as well ask you now."

"Yes?" Sam prompted.

"Well sir, I really respect you and I would be honored if you would stand up for me at the wedding. You know, like best man," Eric asked with an anxious face.

"You bet. I'll be proud to do it, son," Sam replied.

"Thanks, thanks a lot, sir."

Finally, Eric stopped talking, lost in thought. He was smiling broadly and Sam thought, *Yep, a perfect son.*

"Did you get cold last night?" Rafe asked Abby.

"Are you kidding! It could be twenty degrees in there and I'd be warm under that down comforter. How about you? You should have joined me, we could have cuddled."

"When I join you, it's not going to be to cuddle. I turned the heat up but it didn't seem to make a difference. I think I'll call the repairman when we get home and see when he can get up here."

Abby smiled. "Good. Can we come back then?"

"I'll try to arrange to have him come when I'm off, if you like," he answered.

"I like!" she said. "Let's build a fire tonight. It will keep your sleeping quarters comfy. Do we have any marshmallows?"

"No marshmallows, no chocolate and no graham crackers. No s'mores tonight. Sorry!"

"Oh, well. Next time!"

They were sitting on the porch being entertained by a bunch of busy squirrels who were digging for the acorns they had buried in the fall.

"How do they know where to find them?" she wanted to know.

"They don't. They're simply taking a chance of finding one wherever they dig, I suppose!" he replied.

"How would a human know what animals think, or *if* they think?"

"I don't do animals. My specialty is humans," he said, rising, "and you are the one I want to work on."

He pulled her out of her chair and threw her over his shoulder.

She cried out and he quickly put her down.

"Oh, Abby, I'm so sorry I forgot about your side. Are you all right? I didn't mean to hurt you." He was immensely concerned about her and upset with himself for doing such a foolish thing.

She took his face between her hands. "It's okay. It's okay. Really, It's still just a little tender. You didn't injure me." She gave him a reassuring smile.

He looked at her steadily for a moment before speaking. "You have changed my life and you have changed me." He laid his knuckles on her left cheek and caressingly moved his thumb under an adoring eye. "I love you Abby." He pulled her close then bent to kiss her gently before holding her to him again.

She longed for this feeling to be permanent. Her past was becoming a stumbling block. She wanted it out of this new life.

"Shall we go inside?" he asked.

She opened the door and stepped aside. "You first," she offered.

He walked past her and she grimaced, held her side and followed him in.

CHAPTER
16

D R. MUSGRAVE," Patsy said, "Mr. Bland will see you now. Right through that door," she added, indicating the one bearing the plaque engraved with 'Ethan Bland.'

Rafe walked in as Ethan rounded his desk with his hand extended. They shook and Ethan said, "Please, Dr. Musgrave, have a seat."

Ethan returned to his tufted leather chair behind the desk. With elbows resting on the chair arms, Ethan took his usual position placing his fingertips together just below his chin and tipped his head slightly to the right. "What can I do for you?" he asked.

"I have enjoyed your articles in *Success*. It's very inspiring to see how hard those who weren't born with a silver spoon in their mouths have worked to get to the top. The literary works of the upper echelon usually spotlight the lives of the born-wealthy, but this format is much more interesting. It was a very good idea for the magazine," Rafe started.

"Thank you very much, Doctor. I don't like to blow my own horn, but it's nice to hear someone else do it," Ethan said with a smile.

"Well, it deserves praise, but I didn't come here simply to pat you on the back. I do have an ulterior motive."

"And that would be?" Ethan lowered his arms to clasp his hands in his lap and resumed his business face.

"It's to discuss a possible subject for *The Climb*." Rafe was almost embarrassed. He didn't want to come off making the suggestion that he was on the level of Ethan's past selections.

"Yes?" Ethan held his position.

"It would be a little twist on your usual fare, but I think it could benefit us both."

"I have always felt my articles have benefitted both the magazine *and* my subjects," Ethan pointed out kindly.

"That's very true. I wasn't suggesting otherwise, I simply meant that even if you proceeded with a somewhat different tilt to your success story, it could also be good for your magazine," Rafe explained.

"Doctor, why don't you tell me what you have in mind and let me make that decision!"

Rafe began by assuring him he wasn't seeking attention for himself or his practice but for an endeavor to benefit the afflicted and their families. He gave him a brief background on himself and his partnership at the clinic. Ethan leaned forward, picked up a pen and made a few notes on his legal pad.

"We own a large piece of property beside the clinic where I'm hoping to construct an Inn..."

Ethan interrupted him as he looked up, "You're going to do some building?"

"Yes," Rafe answered, then continued to explain the intent of the building.

"I see," Ethan said. "So you are in hopes that if we did this, it could help you get funding to support this endeavor?"

"To put it bluntly, yes."

"My immediate reaction to this, is, if we did use your story for *The Climb*, I suspect many requests would follow with the same theme, which would change the intent of the article. By doing regular benefits in place of our usual story line, I'm afraid we would turn readers away from one of the big draws for *Success*. And if we refused them, would we be attacked for favoring one need over another? There could be a domino effect that would cause irreparable damage to the magazine."

"Or it could go the other way. You could be praised for daring to divert your usual story line in the interest of others," Rafe offered.

Ethan added a few more notes then hesitated before speaking, "I'll need to think about this," he said.

"Of course," Rafe replied. "I would be happy to send you the proposal on our plans so you can have a clear understanding of what we hope to accomplish," Rafe offered, knowing he wouldn't but wanting to appear believable.

"That would be helpful. I really will give it consideration."

Rafe stood. "I appreciate you taking the time to see me, Mr. Bland. Shall I check back with you in a couple of weeks?" he asked as he began to move away.

"Before you go, I'd like to take you over to the Langford Mill office. Mr. Cummings may be able to help with your building expenses. He's a kind man and very civic minded. Whether we do the article or not, I'm sure every penny you save would help."

Rafe was stunned. He had no idea that he would be meeting Abby's husband. He was trying very hard not to show his anxiety. What if Tom Cummings had seen him with Abby at the restaurant or at his home? The jig, as they say, would be up. This was definitely not a part of their plans.

"Uh, well," he looked at his watch. If he ran out now, Ethan might not believe his story. Abby had asked him to look around. "Yes. That would be kind of you."

With his stomach in knots, Rafe followed Ethan.

As they entered the mill office, Ethan approached Tom's secretary.

"Is he alone?" he asked her.

"Yes, shall I see if he's busy?" Alice replied.

"Please."

Alice glanced toward Rafe as they stood silently awaiting their admittance. She gave Ethan an agreeable nod. He then led Rafe through the door, addressing Tom with, "I'm glad you have a minute for me, Tom. I'd like to introduce you to a most interesting man, Dr. Andrew Musgrave."

Tom smiled and moved closer offering a handshake. Rafe was immediately relieved to find no recognition in Tom's eyes. The usual cordialities were exchanged before Ethan explained that Rafe would soon be building a structure for a humanitarian purpose and he thought Tom should hear about it.

Ethan turned to Rafe and said, "I'll leave you with Mr. Cummings now and we'll talk after I've given your project some serious thought."

"Thank you," Rafe replied.

Rafe turned back to Tom. His eye saw an attractive, well dressed business man smiling affably; he was the portrait of a perfect gentleman. His mind saw an adulterer hiding behind this fake pseudonym and he couldn't help but wonder if he had tried to kill his wife. *Poor, sweet Abby.*

In order to get through this without giving himself away, Rafe assumed the mindset of being in another office speaking with a complete stranger. After a lengthy explanation and discussion on Rafe's dream facility, Tom made a suggestion.

"Dr. Musgrave, I admire what you want to do and I hope you're able to see it through. I would like to make you an offer that could be of some help. I don't know exactly what the blueprints will specify, but I think I can safely estimate a deal on the lumber for the project. Since this is for such a beneficial cause, I might be able to sell you what you need at a forty percent discount."

Rafe was gratified at such an offer. Too bad he wouldn't be able to take it. "Mr. Cummings, that's a very generous gesture on your part. I'm simply astounded that you would be willing to do this." He couldn't believe that he would even have considered doing business with this man, but what a deal. Maybe he wasn't all bad.

"Before you agree to accept it, I have to tell you there are two conditions upon which this would hinge."

Rafe drew in a deep breath as he waited for the catch. "And those are?" he questioned.

"First, I would have to ask you to agree not to let it be known, or everyone would be coming by to seek the same deal."

"I understand."

Tom pushed himself out of his chair, walked around to the front of his desk and leaned back on the edge, crossing his feet at the ankles and folding his arms. This, he felt, put him in a superior position.

Rafe tensed. *Okay, now I'm going to see what he's made of. His true colors.*

He looked down at Rafe and added, "Second. Most of this would have to be a cash transaction. Ten percent to be paid by check to Langford Mill, for which you would receive a receipt, and the first half of the balance to be cash in advance, the second half, cash on delivery. One more thing. The company would need a receipt from your group stating we made a donation of lumber in the amount of your forty percent savings."

Rafe stared at him.

"You must see that if I ran it all through the books, it would falsely raise my income, which could hurt me on April fifteenth. Also, by the time I took the sales tax out of the small profit, I would probably be losing money on the deal. So, you see, this would be the only way I could help to this degree."

Tom straightened and returned to his chair before adding, "It really wouldn't matter to the Internal Revenue Service anyway, because it would simply be credit that would cancel out a debt." He smiled, knowingly, at Rafe.

Rafe tilted his head to the right as he considered what he had just heard. "Mr. Cummings, I certainly do thank you for your generous offer," he replied, tapping his fingers on the right chair arm. "I'm not in the immediate planning stages at this point. I guess I didn't make that clear to Mr. Bland."

He continued as he stood up. "There are still so many financial arrangements to be ironed out, but as soon as everything is set to go, I would like to come and talk to you again."

Tom joined him, placing his hand on Rafe's upper back as a gesture of friendship and accompanied him to the office door. "Of course, just give me a call," he said, stopping as Rafe stepped through the door.

"Thank you," Rafe answered, turning to shake his hand once more before taking his leave.

Rafe climbed into his Range Rover, closed the door and said, "How did Abby get hooked up with this scumbag?"

Rafe arrived home to find Abby on the bedroom floor on her stomach with her torso under the bed. She had been sweeping and had knocked the lamp plug from the outlet. This was the only way she could reach the power to reconnect it.

Rafe smiled at the sight before speaking. "Abby, what's going on?"

She jumped, bumping her head on a bed frame slat. A muffled "ouch" drifted from beneath the bed. Rafe took each of her ankles in his hands and pulled her into view.

Abby rolled onto her back and with a disgusted gleam in her eye, she spoke to him. "Thank goodness you're back. I've cleaned this whole house. I thought I was going to have to start on the outside."

"Nervous energy?" he asked, taking her hands and pulling her to her feet.

"Absolutely!" She brushed herself off. "Why didn't you call me on your cell phone after the meeting?"

"I was lost in thought, I guess. It really didn't occur to me. It's been used so infrequently that I forget I have it."

"How did it go?" she asked.

"No problems." He removed his coat and tie and tossed them onto the sofa as he passed.

She followed him into the kitchen where she seated herself while he retrieved a bottle of water from the refrigerator. He opened it, took a drink, then sat down opposite her.

"I met Mr. Cummings," he said.

"No!" Her eyebrows raised as she stiffened.

"Yes. It came as a shock to me, too," he offered, as he rolled the bottle between his hands.

"But, your appointment was with Ethan Bland!" she stated.

"Yes, and we had a very nice meeting. I don't think, however, that he is interested in the idea of helping a group of doctors and/ or the ill."

"Did he put you off? Was he unkind?"

Rafe smiled. "Not at all. He felt that if he published a 'benefit' article, all the needy causes would be demanding equal time. He did say he would think it over, but I know a brush-off when I hear one."

"I was hoping that when everything got cleared up he would do it. I really thought he might be interested, but I guess he's right."

Abby was leaning on the table, watching his every nuance. With a need to know about her connections, she wanted to hear everything.

"How did Tom get into the picture?"

"I was taken to the Langford Lumber Mill's office to meet him. It was Bland's suggestion. He seemed to think your husband could help us save money on the building."

"Oh?"

"Tell me, how much do you know about the mill's business?" he asked Abby.

She thought about it briefly before answering.

"I was very involved for a few years after my parents were, well, after their deaths. Then, Tom and I were married and he took over. I think I spent a lot of time there while he was learning the ropes, but as the magazine began to demand my attention, I left it all in his hands."

She walked away from the table to look out the window. Rafe waited. After a moment, she turned to him and continued.

"Donald! Yes, I remember it was Donald. He was there and he knew the business inside out, so I felt good about leaving."

"Did you ever consult him about how things were going?" Rafe asked.

"No, I don't think so. I guess I always thought Tom would have told me if there were any problems."

"Then you trust your husband?" Rafe wasn't certain if he meant that as a statement or a question.

She laughed out loud. "Are you serious? Really, are you serious? He has been sleeping with another woman for almost two years. Do I trust him? No!"

"Do you think he would steal from the company?"

She frowned as if not understanding.

"Are you aware, or were you a part, of any unethical practices?" he asked.

"Unethical! Me? I count my change to make sure the cashier doesn't give me too much! Why are you asking such questions?"

"Tom's offer to help us save on building materials had strings attached."

"What kind of strings?"

"He offered to sell me the lumber we need at a forty percent discount."

"Wow, that's quite a cut! The strings?" she prompted.

"Ten percent would go into company funds for which we would receive a receipt. The balance, because of financial reasons, would be cash only—a no receipts transaction."

Abby didn't respond. She was trying to mentally digest this proposition.

"But, why?" she finally asked.

"He offered a lame explanation, but technically, he cooks the books and comes out with tax-free income."

"How could he do that?"

"I just told you," he stated.

"I guess I should have said, how *dare* he do that!" She walked away from the kitchen into the family room and sat in a chair with her elbows on her knees.

Rafe pulled out a bottle of Zinfindel and filled two glasses. Abby was a light drinker but this was a favorite of hers. He carried them into the family room and set one in front of her. As he sipped on the other, he paced about the room giving her time to adjust to what she had been told. An affair, and now, this!

He walked back and seated himself on the sofa. Setting the wine on the coffee table, he leaned back, propped his ankle on his knee and stretched his arms along the back of the cushions.

Abby looked up at him. "Do you think, maybe, this is the only time he's made this offer? Because it was for a beneficial cause?"

"Do you?" Rafe responded.

She didn't answer immediately. Without looking away, she told him, "I think it's time I talked to the police."

"I gave that some thought myself. If your husband is doing something illegal and it's uncovered, you, too, could be implicated," he said. "I think, however, at first, you should talk to them through me."

"His name is Tom. I don't like to hear him referred to as my husband. Now, how could I talk to the detectives through you?"

"By breaking your silence through supposition only. No facts. Just feel them out. You know, let them know you could be in trouble if your circumstance should be made available to the public."

"Go on," she said with interest.

"I would strongly suggest that you could be hiding in fear for your life and if what you had to say would go any further than to whomever you will be speaking, our discussion would abruptly end."

"Do you think that's necessary?" Abby asked.

"There are always leaks. The story would thread its way from one to another until every policeman in the department would be discussing it over coffee and donuts. Then someone would secretly pass it on to his wife who would tell her best friend and so on."

"I see," she said thoughtfully.

"If it goes past the detective working the case it would eventually get to the media and then everyone would be privy to what you had divulged and we don't want the fact that you are alive and well and willing to talk to be made known to the wrong person."

"Tom?" she questioned.

"Tom. The paperboy. I don't know, but it was Tom who came here looking for you!"

"If you hadn't come in, do you think he would have harmed me?"

"I don't know enough to have an opinion, but I do know that someone tried to more than harm you. Are you sure you didn't have suspicions or that you hadn't uncovered something and he may have found out?"

"Which would give him reason to want me gone? No, unless, like the shooting, it's still hiding in the deep recess of my mind. The last thing I remember was the discovery that his involvement with Margaret Templeton was ongoing."

"That, too, could be motive," he offered. "And he *has* made two trips here to discover the identity of the female living here!"

"Yes, he has." She thought for a moment before continuing. "But he would want to know if it were me; whether he was guilty or not, wouldn't he?"

"I suppose so."

"I have come to realize that Tom is not an honorable man, but I can't believe he is a vicious person. Of course, if you're cornered!" She seemed to be thinking out loud.

"We could be wrong. Maybe his offer to me was simply an unselfish act of generosity that he didn't quite know how to accomplish without losing money," Rafe suggested.

Abby picked up her glass of wine and sat back with a sigh. "Okay, talk to the authorities." Abby sipped from her glass while absorbing everything she had just learned. She had to find out what had been going on right under her nose. After careful consideration, she made a decision.

"Rafe, I'm going to have to go to the mill office with a camera and see if I can locate anything suspicious."

He stood and faced her with his hands on his hips. "How the hell do you think you could do that? I'm sure there are alarms and I wouldn't know how to get you out of there. Besides, you never know when he could walk in on you and finish the job! No, I can't let you put yourself in jeopardy."

Abby sat forward. "I don't mean to upset you, but I'm tired of living from day to day, trying to sort out yesterday. I want to think about tomorrow." She looked up at him. "Considering the alarms, they're turned off by the front door key and I have one. It's an old system," she said.

He moved to sit on the cocktail table in front of her. Taking her wine glass and setting it beside him he held both her hands and said, "Let me talk to the detectives and we'll go from there. I'll feel better knowing that someone in authority is aware of the situation. At least we'll have them to advise us. They must know things that we don't."

She looked into those caring eyes, then pulled his hands over to her cheek. When this was all over, if she were still living, she was going to thank the gunman for putting her into the path of this wonderful man.

"Okay," she said.

"Oh, I almost forgot." Rafe walked back to his coat where he pulled a small gift wrapped box from his pocket.

She had followed him. "What's that?" she asked.

"It's for you. Open it," he said, smiling broadly.

She carefully removed the bow and paper, then flipped open the lid. Inside lay a small bottle of perfume.

"*Minuit etoile*," she said excitedly. "But where did you find it?"

"I can't take the credit. I put my secretary on the problem and she let her fingers do the walking. She located it in a small boutique in the middle of nowhere. I, however, had the hard job of locating the shop."

"Do you know how wonderful you are?" she asked sincerely.

"It wasn't totally selfless on my part," he suggested. "I'm quite anxious to give my approval."

Sam was seated alone in the "Rabbit Hole" having an early lunch. The television, attached to a base mounted high in the corner, was tuned to Fox News. He was finishing the last of a fried apple pie and watching an update on the latest bombing.

Eric stuck his head through the door. "You're wanted on line two," he said.

"I'm not in yet," Sam replied, "but, who is it?" His eyes had not left the news.

"I don't know. He asked to speak to the detective working the Cummings disappearance."

Sam swept up his empty coffee container and sandwich bag and dropped them into the trash, and, as he moved past Eric, said, "Why didn't you tell me that?"

"I just did," Eric replied, following him down the stairs and into their office.

"Detective Robertson here," Sam said into the receiver.

"Hello detective. I'm calling about Mrs. Cummings. I was told that you're in charge of that investigation?"

"That's right. What can I do for you?"

"I'd like to meet with you to discuss the matter," Rafe said.

Sam sat forward in his chair and picked up a pencil and pad. "Would you like to come to the station?" he asked.

"No, I'd rather not risk being seen entering your station house. I think it might be better if you come to me."

"May I ask why?"

"We'll talk about that when we get together. I'm free tomorrow after two. Would you be able meet me in Winston-Salem?" Rafe asked.

"What time and where?" Sam asked.

"Are you familiar with the location of a bookstore near Hanes Mall? It's just below Michaels."

"Yes," Sam replied, scribbling a note.

"I'll be there at three o'clock. I'll be wearing jeans, a white button down shirt and a navy sport coat. You'll find me sitting in the coffee area. Will anyone be with you?"

"Yes." Sam continued writing, "Detective Eric Burke. We've both been on this case since day one."

"I understand. However, I am going to ask you to keep this between the three of us. You can do this without telling your chief, can't you?"

"I can, but..." Sam started.

"If you must talk to him or anyone else about me, I'll not be there." Rafe told him sternly.

"We'll keep it private," Sam assured him as he tore the note off and stuck it in his wallet.

"Thank you, Detective. I'm looking forward to meeting with you."

Eric had closed the door and taken a seat.

Sam was studying the caller ID on his receiver. "Rats, a pay phone!"

"What was that all about?" Eric questioned.

"Just between you and me?" Sam asked.

"Sure, boss."

"Eric, I mean it. This has to be just between us," Sam said seriously.

"Geez. Yes, you and me. I promise," Eric replied.

"We're back in business. It could be a break in the Cummings case. Or at least a lead," Sam offered.

"What did he tell you?" Eric asked with interest.

"Nothing yet. He wants to meet us in Winston tomorrow afternoon."

"Exactly what did he say?" Eric pushed.

"He said he wanted to discuss the case with us."

"Oh." Eric looked almost stricken.

Sam watched the younger detective as the air seemed to go out of him.

"There is a reason he wants to talk to us, Eric. No one picks up the phone and calls simply to discuss a case they may have read about. He knows something."

"Aren't you taking a chance? What if it's the killer?" Eric asked.

"Eric, think! I don't believe the killer would make an appointment to harm me and set it up in a public place."

"Unless he plans to get us in the parking lot then disappear!"

Sam looked at him curiously. "Well, you have a point. And, if it's done there he would hope it wouldn't be connected to the Cummings' case. What would be the point? We don't have enough evidence to arrest anyone. Actually, there isn't even enough evidence to prove that she has been harmed. We're leaning toward one person as a suspect in the disappearance and everything we have on him is circumstantial."

"So you believe he's for real?" Eric stated.

"I believe that, yes."

"What do you think he has to talk about? Maybe it's someone who saw something and has decided to reveal it. Did you recognize his voice?" Eric's excitement returned and had him so agitated he couldn't sit still.

Sam watched him, remembering his own youthful thrill of finally putting the last piece in the puzzle. Eric is much more demonstrative than he had ever been. Perhaps that's why Eric wasn't the one taking antacids.

"No, his voice was not familiar. He spoke well. You know, educated, experienced, pleasant. I guess we'll soon know what he has to say," Sam stated.

"I hope he doesn't turn out to be an educated, pleasant nut!" Eric said.

Rafe arrived at the bookstore early. He purchased a cup of coffee and called Abby to check on her, something he had done every day since Tom's visit. Once more, he cautioned her to lock the doors and keep her cell phone at hand. He told her he would be late coming home but didn't reveal why. Rather than have her distressed all day, he would give her the details when he knew them.

At three o'clock, Sam and Eric walked into the book store and headed to the coffee bar, their eyes searching for the man in jeans. Sam spied him and continued to the counter for coffee. Eric followed. After ordering for both Eric and himself, he laid the money on the counter and said to his partner, "Bring the coffee over when it's ready." Turning, he walked to the table where the jeans were seated.

"Samuel Robertson," Rafe said. "Won't you join me?"

"Thank you," Sam replied. In a second, he had sized this man up.

Rafe had hung his jacket on the chair and his shirt sleeves were rolled up to reveal strong muscular arms. His hands were large and only slightly calloused. Short dark hair, not neatly combed, but shiny clean. A pleasant smile in an honest and strongly handsome face. His speech, very articulate.

Sam thought he had the build of a construction worker but the mind and presence of a professional. Probably a lawyer or banker who jogged and worked out when possible.

They shook hands and Sam added confident to his assessment.

Eric arrived with the coffee and Sam thanked him. To Rafe, he said, "This is my partner Eric Burke."

"Mr. Burke," Rafe said, shaking his hand. He looked at both of them and added, "I hope you don't mind if we skip the use of titles in public."

"Not at all," Sam replied. "Other than a title, is there a name we can use when addressing you?"

Rafe smiled. "I'm Raphael Adams."

"Thank you, Mr. Adams. What can we do for you, or what can you do for us?" Sam asked as Eric pulled out a pencil and note pad.

"Before we get into anything, I want you to know that someone's life may depend on our working together without involving others. Can I be assured that this will be confidential?"

"Mr. Adams, without knowing what you are going to reveal, I cannot promise that. I can tell you that nothing will be divulged as long as the law is followed and I'm not going against the rules of the department," Sam said.

"Fair enough," Rafe replied.

"You just used the term *working together*. That implies that there could be more than a discussion that you want to have," Sam stated.

"This will be just the beginning. Do you have any idea who may be responsible for the lady's disappearance?" Rafe asked.

"We have suspicions, but that's all they are. Strong suspicions."

"Are you at liberty to tell me whom you may suspect? No, don't insult me with your answer. I know you can't tell me anything."

"What is your interest in this case?"

"Let me just say at this point that I have one," Rafe replied.

Eric's fingers were beginning to squeeze the pencil. He was still waiting for something significant to jot down.

Sam offered nothing.

"Okay," Rafe started. "I'm going to speak hypothetically."

Eric wrote the words, "hypothetically speaking—Mr. Adams."

Rafe had picked a table in the middle of other tables, all of which were currently unoccupied. This prevented anyone who might be standing behind a book case from overhearing the conversation, nevertheless, he still lowered his voice when he asked, "What if the missing person actually is not missing?"

Eric straightened, wide-eyed, and looked around to make certain they were alone, then scooted his chair closer to the speaker.

Sam carefully observed Rafe, trying to read behind his dark eyes. He could tell the man wasn't sure he should be talking with them. He sensed a frightened hesitation, but Sam didn't think he feared for himself.

"All right, let's suppose that's true. If the missing isn't really missing," Sam shrugged his shoulders, raised his hands and glanced around, "then why can't anyone see this person?"

Eric wrote, "missing not missing, invisible? Sam."

Sam leaned toward Rafe and asked, "Are you suggesting this is a David Copperfield hoax?"

Eric wrote the words, "David Copperfield hoax, Sam."

"Suppose this person had narrowly escaped being killed and the intended murderer thought he had succeeded in his attempt to take the life? Wouldn't it be wise to remain on the missing list?"

So caught up in the intrigue, Eric had lost all interest in taking notes.

Sam's brows knitted as he turned these suggestions over in his mind.

"But why would this person remain silent? Wouldn't it be safer to put the perpetrator behind bars?" Sam asked.

"If the intended victim's memory wasn't also missing, yes."

Eric frantically resumed writing.

"Hypothetically, the missing person doesn't know who, let us say, tried to end her life, so it has become necessary to remain out of sight and presumed dead, in order to protect herself," Sam reiterated. "Is that what you are suggesting?"

"Yes! Furthermore, much of the memory of her past has returned but the attempt on her life, evidently, is too hard to face, so the mind is protecting her from going through it."

Sam leaned close and said, "Your title is Doctor, right?"

Rafe smiled.

"We," Sam started as he looked sternly at Eric, "can assure you that this will not go beyond us until the time is right, Mr. Adams," Sam promised. "Now can we get out of this suppositional mode so we can be more helpful to each other?"

Rafe breathed a sigh of relief. "Gladly."

"Where is she?"

"Hiding."

"How do you know about her?" Sam asked.

"Are you familiar with the Wilton Mountains?"

"Somewhat," Sam answered.

Eric was now absorbed with his notes.

"I have a cabin and property at the top of Pine Knob."

"I've been hunting on that mountain. It's beautiful up there."

Rafe told them of the events that took place with Abby's arrival and recovery. Sam interjected several questions and Eric jotted short quick notes that he planned to complete later. When Rafe finished, both detectives remained quiet as if waiting for more.

"That's it!" Rafe told them.

They both exhaled and relaxed.

Rafe stated, "Now, I'd like to ask you a few questions, if I may."

"Fire away," Sam said.

"It's going on two months since she vanished. How are her husband, partner and business associates handling their loss?"

"It's pretty morose at the magazine office, except for Bland. He has high hopes that she'll return. Mr. Cummings is hard to read. He has been more defensive than heartbroken around us. Of course, he knows that the husband is always a suspect. He seems to have a lot on his mind."

"Right," Eric said snidely.

"Like Margaret Templeton?" Rafe inquired.

He had gotten the attention of both detectives.

"She remembered that?" Sam asked.

"Yes, on that morning, after discovering he was still involved with her, Abby left the office. Her mind has blotted out the rest of the day."

"I see," Sam said.

"Is Templeton on your list of suspects?" Rafe asked.

"Not at the top. Why do you ask?"

"I think a female would leave quickly after a shooting. I don't think she would want to get too close to the ugly part of her actions. You know, shoot and run, don't check to make certain your actions were completed satisfactorily."

"That's possible," Sam responded.

"Does Mr. Cummings drive an SUV?" Rafe asked.

"He has one that I'm sure he drives in bad weather, but he also has a Lexus."

"The weather was bad the day she disappeared," Rafe reflected.

"And that means?"

"The attempt on her life was made by someone driving an SUV. I saw it leave the area after the shot was fired."

"What was the color and make?"

"Visibility robbed me of that knowledge," Rafe explained. "I know it wasn't black."

"That's not enough to pin the attack on her husband. I'll bet eight out of ten families have an SUV or a van of some type," Sam said.

"I know. I guess I thought if he wasn't one of them, it would rule him out."

"Is Mrs. Cummings at your cabin?" Eric asked.

"No, I wouldn't leave her there alone."

"Where is she?" Sam asked.

"If you don't know, you wouldn't be able to divulge her whereabouts, even if you were threatened, would you?"

"I guess I wouldn't. Guess I could be killed for not telling."

"You would be killed for telling too, so what's the difference? I'll tell you. The difference is that she would be safe!"

"What do you want us to do?" Sam asked.

"I don't know. She wanted to let someone in authority know she's alive and afraid. We decided to have me break the news so she wouldn't be forced to do something she wasn't yet ready to do."

"Do you think that she might meet with us to answer some questions?"

"If you met with her and saw with your own eyes that this really isn't hypothetical, would you feel it your duty to make a report to your department?" Rafe asked.

Sam said nothing while he considered the question. "I'll tell you what," he said, "let us think about all this for a day or two and you talk it over with her, then give me a call and we can get together again."

"That would be fine. There are a couple of things you need to know before we part." Rafe told them about the restaurant encounter and Tom's two visits to his home.

"He didn't harm her the second time?" Sam asked.

"Her face was not directly visible to him nor did she speak, so I'm not sure he knew for certain it was her."

"Very puzzling. Was there something else?" Sam asked.

"I have reason to believe that Mr. Cummings may be involved in some dubious business dealings. His wife has had nothing to do with running the mill, so if corruption is discovered, she had no knowledge of it. That's another reason she wanted the police informed of her current situation."

"What kind of dealings?" Sam asked.

Rafe looked at his watch, then said, "I really need to get back now. How about if we take that up next time? I'll call you day after tomorrow."

"I would appreciate that," Sam said. "It was a pleasure to meet you, sir."

They stood, shook hands and Rafe reminded him once more how important it was that this not reach the media.

"I'll see that it doesn't. Meanwhile, if anything changes, you know, with her memory, call us immediately."

"Absolutely," Rafe assured him and left.

Sam looked down at Eric who was still writing, then, once again he took his seat—to wait for him.

"Some break! Huh, Boss," Eric stated without looking up.

"Yeah," Sam answered, then added to himself, "The doc's in love with her."

Rafe walked into the kitchen and lifted the lid off a big pot of vegetable soup, releasing the wonderful aroma of home cooking. He opened the drawer, pulled out a large spoon, stirred the soup and tasted it. "Very good," he said aloud, but to himself.

He was tired. He called to Abby but got no answer. Assuming she was going through things in the attic again, he moved into his room, undressed, grabbed a sweatsuit and headed to the bathroom. He felt a nice hot shower would release the tension.

The door was half closed. Whistling, he pushed it and stepped inside. Coming to a sudden halt at the sound of water, he saw Abby's form through the glass as she reached for the knobs. She turned the water off and faced the door, placing her hand on the handle in preparation to exit. A gasp escaped as her vision settled on Rafe through the mottled glass door.

"I'm so sorry!" he said. "I didn't realize you were in here."

"Did you see me in the kitchen?"

"No," he replied.

"In the family room? Or any other part of the house?

"No."

"Then, where did you think I was?"

"In the attic. I'm so tired and tense, I thought I would get a hot shower while you were out. I was whistling and didn't hear the water. I'm so very sorry," he said again.

Looking at that tall muscular form through the glass raised her heart rate and sent a warm surge through her groin.

"So, I think you're in the position to make the first move," she suggested.

"You're right," he said, opening the shower door and stepping inside.

"Oh," she said, edging backward.

He smiled and moved a little closer.

"Oh," again. She took a big step away and her backside touched the cold tiles.

"Yikes!" she squealed and lunged forward right into his arms.

"You've been to the beauty salon, right?"

"Yes, I really needed a trim and when the stylist finished, all the blonde was gone," she said, turning her face up to him. "Is it okay?" she asked hesitantly.

"I told you, I don't care if it's blue!" he answered.

"How was your day?" she muttered nervously. She couldn't believe this whole scenario.

"It's getting better by the minute."

"I see. Well." She started to move them around so she would be next to the door.

"Going somewhere?"

"I'm giving it a good try," she replied. She *needed* to get away from him yet she didn't *want* to.

He leaned over and kissed the side of her neck. The touch of his lips sent chills, down her arm to the tips of her fingers.

Lifting his head, he looked into her beautiful, longing, yet frightened eyes. Little streams of water wiggled over her forehead, down and around her full pink lips and dripped from her chin.

Even without makeup, she glows, he thought.

Her heart began to pound as he tasted her mouth, her ear lobe and the side of her neck. He put his hand behind her head, pushing his fingers into her hair and leaned back to look again into her eyes. This time it was sadness looking back at him. Holding her head he rubbed his cheek against hers and whispered into her ear.

"I love you Abby. I won't do anything you don't want me to do." He touched his lips to her soft, warm, wet mouth. His gentle kisses encouraged a careful response. His hand slipped around her shoulders and his kisses became more urgent and as his tongue began to probe, she tensed slightly. He withdrew.

Breathing deeply and with eyes closed, she tried to relax. He backed off by simply holding her lovingly and lightly rubbing her back. He felt small quivers run up her spine.

"Your skin is so smooth. It feels like silk," he whispered. He lifted her hand and kissed her palm then the inside of her elbow. He moved his hands to her waist and along her hips, memorizing the delicate figure that caused such a burning within him. His eyes followed the clear rivulets running freely down her full breasts and flat stomach, touching every enticing curve and secret area that he longed to claim. Cupping a breast, he kissed her once more before bending to taste the rosy bud that had peaked at his touch.

"Oh, oh my goodness, Rafe."

His hands slid down her back and pulled her close against him. His need for her had grown and Abby was made aware of his desire as their bodies melded.

He kissed her now with a sensuous fire that ran from his own mounting drive down to the center of her being, melting her defenses with the growing heaviness of sexual anticipation that took over. She had passed through her nebulous wanting into a clear craving to be entered.

Aware that she was losing control, she turned to Rafe. With desire and shame, she looked pleadingly at him and he loosened his hold.

He brought his arms up to encircle her shoulders and holding her tightly, he bent his head forward to rest his cheek at the side of her temple. He could feel her tremble.

"I want you so badly, so badly," he said with eyes closed. Dropping his hands, he then looked into her face and added, "but I don't want you until you're ready."

"I want to, but I can't. I'm not free to do this," she said softly. "I'm hurting, I want you so much. I just can't. Not yet."

He put his hand on her head and ran his fingers through her hair. "I understand, and I don't want it to be like this, I want it to be the most wonderful thing to ever happen to you."

"You *are* the most wonderful thing to ever happen to me." She stepped back and looked gratefully into his yearning eyes. "It won't be long."

Taking her hands, he inhaled deeply. "Oh God, I hope not!" came almost as a whisper on the exhale.

That evening they were sitting together, Abby reading and Rafe watching the news channel, when Rafe told her he had talked with the detectives.

"Already?" she said, laying her book aside.

Rafe switched the TV off and turned his attention to her. "Yes. Detective Robertson asked if you would talk with them. They agreed to keep it quiet for now."

"They?"

"Robertson and his partner, Eric."

"Only the two of them?" she pressed.

"That's right. They gave me their word it would not go past them for the present," Rafe emphasized.

"Are you sure I'm not in trouble for not speaking up before now?"

"No, they understand. What do you say?"

She frowned slightly while thinking.

"I'll make you a proposition," she said.

"I tried that earlier and got nowhere. What makes you think it'll work for you?" he asked.

She smiled and continued, "If I talk to them, would you take me to the mill office? I want to look things over. We can do it late at night."

The thought was disturbing but perhaps it was time to bring all this to a head. "Okay," he agreed.

She looked at him startled. "You will?"

"We did the house thing right, so, as long as we can make clean plans and not put you in danger, I'll agree."

"Great! Call them and set it up," she said.

Tom was in need of company. Ethan had been of no help to him. They more or less had business that brought them together, but with the long time friendship he and Abby had shared, Ethan always wound up lecturing him about his infidelity and he was tired of it. His strained relationship with Ethan was rapidly eroding.

Actually, never having thought about this before, he now realized he had no friends. Abby had been the closest to a friend he possessed. Thinking back, he recognized that he had always been a loner. After his parents passed away, he was so involved in putting himself through college that he never had the time to cultivate a friendship.

That left Maggie, who had remained miffed over his failing to keep their date the night of the break-in and he, in turn, had been short with her but he was upset that she had expected him to be so available when he shouldn't even be talking to her during this investigation. She certainly should have understood that! He had begun to miss her and now, he needed her. Be damned what people may think.

He picked up the phone and carried it to the sofa where he slouched into a comfortable position with his feet on the table and his head resting on the back cushion. This would be a pleasant surprise for her. He smiled at imagining how her face would light up. Dialing her number, he listened to the ringing while he considered where she might like to go for dinner.

"Hello," she answered smoothly.

"Maggie, I'm missing you terribly. It's been too long."

"And who's fault has that been, Tom?"

"I know. I've been neglectful, and I deserve a good scolding, but right now I need to see you. Let me take you somewhere nice for dinner and," softening his voice he added, "we can talk about dessert."

"Doesn't that sound tempting," she replied, "but I can't. I'm busy this evening, Tom."

"Busy? Doing what, your nails? You're angry and going to punish me, right?" he asked.

A devilish laugh rose from deep within her. "Darling, you know punishing is not what I do best. I've missed you, too, but I've already made plans for the evening. I'm sure you understand."

"No, I don't understand," he said angrily.

"Well, then let me explain it to you." Her voice becoming less syrupy. "I've met a quite attractive and available attorney. He's been very kind to me, so I've decided to let him handle all my 'affairs.' Now do you understand?"

He sat up abruptly, tightening his grip on the receiver. "You fucking bitch. Do you know what I've done for you?" he asked.

"What? Gotten rid of a wife you didn't love? I'm sure that wasn't done for me. That, my dear, was to gain total control over what you were about to lose because of us. Whatever you did, Tom, took care of both the women in your life."

"The only thing I did was you! That's my crime, you stupid broad. Do you know what you're giving up? I'm going to be rich!" he shouted. "Rich! An attorney will never support you the way you want."

"Do you think I'm broke?" she asked. "I didn't say I was marrying this man, I said I was having dinner with him, but if it comes to marriage, we won't have to get rid of a wife first."

He pulled the phone from his ear and threw it across the room where it struck a portrait of Abby's parents, the glass shattering before it slid down the wall coming to rest upright with Mr. Langford's eyes staring at Tom.

Abby, with a tam on her auburn head and the glasses resting on her nose, found herself the center of attention in a sitting area of the bookstore. She had answered questions from Sam and Eric as best she could. They were extremely attentive and seemed genuinely concerned for her safety. Rafe listened quietly to the vocal play between them.

"I've been very candid. Now, would you mind if I made a few inquiries?" she asked.

"Not at all," Sam offered.

"Do you have any solid evidence as to who may have taken me?"

"No."

"But you have a suspect in mind, don't you?"

"The spouse is always a suspect."

"Anyone else?"

"There could have been more than one person involved, and there is always the possibility that you were abducted by a stranger." Sam tried to soften any shock she might experience with the realization that her husband could be involved.

"That's true. But why would a stranger take me? Wouldn't he have had a purpose other than to kill me? I mean, why not seek a ransom or keep me with him on some kind of insane attention-driven scheme?" she asked, with a dozen other questions running rampant in her head.

"Then, you suspect your husband, too!" Sam stated.

"He certainly had motive," Abby offered, leaning back with a sigh. "And he's made two trips to Rafe's home in search of me."

Rafe put his hand on the back of her neck and gave a soft squeeze.

"If a man's wife has gone missing and he thought he may know where to find her, he would make that effort, don't you think?" Sam hesitated while she thought about it. "Your friend told us that you suspect Mr. Cummings is involved in some kind of wrongdoing at Langford Mill," Sam said, changing directions.

"That's right."

"What makes you think so?"

"Are you familiar with the magazine *Success?*" she asked.

"Yes," Eric answered quickly before looking at Sam as if to say, *I told you!*

Abby informed them about sending Rafe to talk to Ethan Bland, then turned to him for the details of the meeting. He described Tom's offer.

"Do you think he has done this before?" Sam asked Abby.

"Why would I think otherwise? I've never known him to be generous to any good cause. But then, he has always kept business matters to himself," Abby said.

"You never suspected anything?"

"Nothing!" she responded. "I should never have turned the reins of the mill totally over to Tom. I regret that. My father started that business and put his life's blood into it and I should have taken better care of anything that meant so much to him."

"I'm sure you did what you trusted was a good thing," Sam assured her.

"It was selfish of me to turn my back on what he left me and put myself so totally into what I wanted."

"Your dad would not have wanted you to spend your life taking care of his business to the point of ignoring your needs," Rafe added, taking her hand.

"Perhaps, but if Tom is taking advantage of his position for his own personal gain at the expense of the company and me, I want to know," she told Sam.

Sam understood her dilemma. "Are you going to open this case up so we can investigate?"

"Not quite yet. First, I plan to do a little investigating myself."

"What do you mean?" Sam asked.

"I'm..." she hesitated and looked toward Rafe. "We're going to make a visit to the mill office this evening," she said.

"Can you do that safely?"

"I guess we'll find out, but I think so."

"What if your husband is there?" Sam asked.

"And how do you plan to get in?" Eric added.

To Sam she said, "He won't be there. He only worked late when he needed to give me an excuse for his absence," then to Eric, "I have a key. For some reason, I turned up on Knob Mountain with nothing but my set of keys."

"And you left your purse," Sam said.

"It seems I did. The departure from my vehicle must have been abrupt. Anyway, the key will get me in and turn off the security system. I'll have a flashlight, but I already know my way around pretty well, I think. Rafe will stay outside to watch for any arrivals and we have cell phones in case either of us needs the other." She smiled at Rafe and added, "He even put his number on quick dial so all I have to do is push two to get him."

"You have this well planned," Sam said.

"This isn't new to us," Abby told him.

Sam and Eric looked at each other, back at her, then stated simultaneously, "Your house!"

Abby smiled.

"What if your husband or another employee shows up unexpectedly?" Eric asked.

"You won't be armed, will you?" Sam added.

"I feel that I don't have to carry a weapon. After all, it's my building. Rafe would join me if someone should arrive, which would deter anyone from harming me, don't you think?" Abby inquired.

"At this point, I don't know what to think," Sam said, shaking his head.

"What's to stop someone from killing you both?" Eric inquired then looked at Rafe and asked, "Do you have a weapon?"

"Yes, I have a weapon. Will I have it with me? No! But I won't let any harm come to her," Rafe stated.

"I think you're taking a big risk. Why don't you come in and let's go through the proper channels?" Sam suggested.

"And take a chance of allowing the perpetrator to silence me permanently before I can identify him?" Abby responded.

Rafe spoke up: "If she returned and Tom knew she would be renewing her demand that he leave, he would get rid of the incriminating evidence that we may locate tonight. When Abby first suggested this, I didn't like the idea, but the more I thought about it, I began to realize that it made perfect sense."

"So, tonight is the night?" Sam asked.

"Tonight's the night," Rafe repeated.

"I'd like to say we could be there to back you up, but if we had to step in, I would have to do some explaining to the chief and it wouldn't go well for us if he found out we were working this without his knowledge."

Abby turned to Sam. "We would never ask you. We'll not take any chances."

"But you are taking a chance since you don't remember who shot you!" Sam told her.

"We'll take every precaution possible, short of a gun, and be very quick in the execution," Rafe assured him.

Abby nodded. "Any incriminating evidence we may find will be turned over to you immediately. I want this resolved. I'm tired of living in fear."

"Okay, anything you can give us to help would be great because I really don't know how long we can keep your reappearance a secret," Sam warned. "This needs to be wrapped up before anything else happens."

"We know," Rafe said. "After we leave the office, if Abby has gotten anything on film that could be important, we're going to take the camera for one hour developing. However, in the morning we're heading to Knob Hill. I seem to have a heating problem at the cabin, and we won't be back in town until Saturday night or Sunday."

Rafe continued, "We'll take special care to see that nothing is left out of place so Tom won't be able to tell someone has been there. Any danger to Abby should be eliminated since we'll be away. I'll give you a call Monday."

Sam took Abby's hand as they prepared to leave. He covered it with the other and said, "You are a very brave young woman. I'm terribly sorry about all you've suffered these past few years. Nobody deserves that. Until Monday," he squeezed her hand. "Enjoy your weekend and be careful tonight."

Turning to Rafe he added, "Wish I were going up that mountain with you. It's a beautiful place." He handed Rafe his card. "If you need me, I'm on duty through the weekend."

"Thank you, Detective Robertson," Rafe said before turning to Eric. "You too, Detective Burke."

Eric offered them a crooked smile.

After the detectives left, Rafe and Abby picked out a couple of books for the trip to the cabin, then talked over a cup of coffee before leaving.

"Are you sure you want to go through with this?" he asked.

"Yes. I'm almost looking forward to it. You'll be there, so I'm not afraid. Well, that's a lie. I *am* afraid, but your being there will help calm me. I hope."

"I can't work miracles, Abby. You have to be ready to react if something happens. Just remember, all you have to do if you need me, is push number two."

"I know. After I turn off the alarm, I'll hand you the keys and you can lock me in. That way, if I need you, you can get in."

"Yes, I remember the plan."

Their initial idea was to enter the building very late or during the night, but they decided that could be suspicious to any police or security patrols who might happen by at that time. A decent hour seemed to make more sense.

"It's six-fifteen. Will he be gone by the time we get there?"

"The mill and magazine offices both close at five, so it should be clear now even if someone left late."

"Okay, let's go."

CHAPTER
17

RAFE PULLED OFF the road onto a wide shoulder partly obscured by trees, but giving himself an unobstructed view of the mill's front door. There was a small grassy area between them and the business grounds.

With the time approaching seven, it was not yet dark. Abby was thankful daylight savings time had gone into effect. Although the weather didn't require it, Abby had put one of Rafe's jackets on and wrapped a large scarf over her head and around her neck. She felt this would camouflage her normal appearance in the event she should be seen by anyone who might otherwise recognize her.

"Do you have the light and camera?" he asked.

She nodded.

"Where's your cell phone?"

"It's all in here," she said, patting the shoulder bag in her lap.

"Keys?"

"Yes." She held her hand up and jingled them. "Let's wait just a minute. Check carefully for movement," she suggested.

"Getting apprehensive, right?"

"Right!"

Abby looked the building over carefully. It was all so familiar now. She could visualize the layout in both businesses. A flood of faces and sounds washed over her and they were all happy. No, not all of them. The sound of her own words resounded in her head. The words she last spoke there.

"Abby, are you listening?" Rafe was leaning toward her.

"I'm sorry, what?" she asked.

"I'm going to take the door key off your key ring. I don't want to have to fumble for the right one if I need to make a fast move. Besides, you should take the keys with you in case you need the one to Tom's office."

"I should have thought of that," she said almost absently.

He removed that key and handed her the others. Pocketing them, she then took the door key.

All right, she was no longer apprehensive. She looked at the man beside her with resolve. Placing the bag over her shoulder and with a deep breath and a sigh, she said, "I'm ready."

"Wait a minute," Rafe said, taking her upper arm.

She turned to him as he smiled, brushed a kiss over her lips and said, "Be careful."

They walked right up to the door where she unlocked it, slipped in and disabled the alarm. Handing the key to Rafe, she waited for him to lock the door before she turned. She stood for a couple of moments allowing her eyes to adjust. She didn't want to use the flashlight until she got inside Tom's office. When she could see well enough, she carefully made her way in that direction.

Her cell phone rang and every muscle attached to her bones jumped in a different direction. Her trembling fingers unzipped the bag. Grabbing for the phone, she put it to her ear.

"Hello, hello." He didn't respond. Another ring and she turned her head to look at the flashlight she held in her hand. Throwing it back into the bag, she located the phone.

"Yes?"

"Abby, someone is pulling up in front of the door. Find a place to hide quickly and don't disconnect me," Rafe advised her.

Scanning her surroundings, she moved to the closest object: Alice's desk. Moving behind it, she crawled under the desk and turned. After seating herself, she pulled the chair under the edge of the desk top. The lights were still off, so she felt sufficiently hidden.

The lock clicked and the door swung open. Abby recognized Tom's familiar footfalls as they moved to the alarm, then headed to the office door. Stopping just past Alice's desk to unlock the door, he was aware of nothing out of the ordinary. Abby held her breath. He entered his office and Abby waited.

He picked up his briefcase and started to leave. Abby's nervous trembling caused her to bump her elbow slightly. Having exited his office, Tom stopped and looked about in the darkness.

"Arthur, are you there?" he called out.

It's too dark. Arthur wouldn't be cleaning without lights. He moved beside Alice's desk and listened for a moment before making his exit. Abby let her breath out slowly as he locked the front door.

"That was close!" she said to Rafe.

"Just sit tight until he's in his car and down the road," he cautioned her.

Soon she inched herself stiffly from underneath the desk. She sighed and then shook the fear from her limbs. *Get yourself together girl, you've got a job to do.*

She tried the door and found it locked, as she knew it would be. After withdrawing the keys and pulling up the correct one, she felt for the lock above the knob. Locating it, she placed her fingers in the center to help guide the key in. The lock turned easily and she entered the office. Pulling the door almost closed behind her, she moved to the desk where she removed the scarf and jacket, sat down and opened the middle drawer.

Flipping on the flashlight, she leaned forward and very carefully searched the contents, finding nothing but what one would expect in a desk drawer. She closed it silently and moved to the drawer on the right. It was locked. "Damn," she whispered, then, "Oh, I shouldn't have said that." On reflex, she looked about to make sure she was alone.

She checked the middle drawer for a desk key but found none. Reaching for the drawer on the left and expecting to find it locked, she almost jerked it out of the desk as it opened. "Damn," she repeated. She covered her mouth briefly before stating, "Oh hell, who heard me anyway!"

Nothing of interest there either. And no key. Standing, she moved to the smaller desk that Alice sometimes used. Every drawer was locked. What was she to do now? Sitting silent while trying to come up with a solution, she almost jumped from the chair when her cell phone rang once again. Immediately turning off the flashlight, she shakily fumbled for the phone. Why hadn't she thought to put it into her pocket? Because she didn't expect it to ring, that's why!

Finally, she had it in her quivering hand. She pushed several buttons before hitting the right one. "Yes?" she whispered.

"Abby," Rafe said, "he's back and is approaching the front door. It appears he has his key ready."

Abby could feel her heart beating in her ears. "Yes, he's unlocking the door."

He heard me hit my elbow and must have gone for a gun!

"He came around the side of the building. Must have parked in back. Sit tight but leave your phone on so I can hear what's going on. I'm out of the car and ready to run."

Abby stood, and in the darkness, eased herself toward the door. She wanted to get her back against the wall. As she approached the door, she heard a movement on the other side. She looked at the bottom of the door but could see no light filtering underneath. Continuing toward the wall beside the door, she froze as the footsteps came closer. The door was flung open and he stepped through, bringing them instantly face to face. The screaming began.

Rafe was running to the building. His shaking hand unlocked the door and he was in.

Following the hysterical screams of both male and female, he headed in the direction of Tom's office. Before he reached the door, he slowed. Was he hearing correctly? The screaming had begun to sound less urgent.

Confusion accompanied him into the office. Closing the door and flipping on the light he was stunned. Abby and the stranger were hanging on to each other and laughing uncontrollably.

Abby spun in his direction and gasped out, "Did you turn the alarm off?" knowing that he had not, because he didn't even know where it was. She grabbed the key from him and raced out. The laughter died away and Rafe, although slightly relieved, looked menacingly at the man. He didn't recognize him, but the fact that he was neither Tom nor Ethan began to settle his nerves.

"Hello, I'm Donald Freeman," the stranger said.

196

Rafe broke into a smile as he moved in to hug this man. "I can't tell you how nice this is, Abby has spoken fondly of you."

"This is Rafe," Abby said upon returning.

Donald was smiling widely. "I can't believe I'm looking at you," he said to Abby. "I was beginning to lose hope."

She stepped to him and held his hands. "I'm not back yet, so you have to promise you won't tell anyone you've seen me," she pleaded.

"I'll do anything you ask, Ms. Abby. It's been miserable around here without you," Donald said.

"Don, I need your help. I want to get into that desk," she said, pointing to the smaller one. "It's locked and I think the keys to it could be in the private drawer in Tom's desk. When I left and turned my office over to you, I left a set of keys to his desk in one of my drawers."

Before she could ask him to check, he was on his way. It took only a moment and he was back with a pair of eyeglasses and the prize.

Abby located the right one and opened the drawer, where, as expected, she found the item for which she was searching.

Moving to the small desk, she unlocked all the drawers and each of the three began to look through one.

"Keep everything in order. I don't want it to be obvious that someone has gone through this stuff. That's very important, Donald," Abby cautioned. "If you see anything suspicious or obviously illegal, point it out to me. I want to photograph it."

"I've felt for a long time that something was not right," Donald said. "Mr. Cummings had become so secretive with some of the clients."

"Here," Rafe said. "Take some shots of these." He spread several sheets out on top of the desk.

Abby snapped away.

Donald leaned over the papers, picked up one and said, "I know this name." He moved to the filing cabinet and shuffled through the C's. Pulling out an invoice, he exclaimed, "Here it is! Cumberland!" Carrying it over to compare to what they had found, the three of them studied what was before them.

"Look," Donald pointed out. "According to the confidential

report, Mr. Cumberland received eighty-five thousand dollars worth of lumber for which he paid fifty-one thousand. There has been a ten percent and a fifteen percent deduction from that."

"What for?" Abby asked.

Don consulted the business file and picked up a pad and pencil before replying, "According to Langford's documentation, Cumberland made a payment of five thousand one hundred, which is the ten percent taken from the fifty-one thousand, and he received a goodwill donation of twenty-five thousand dollars worth of lumber from the company. The mill papers show he obtained thirty thousand one hundred dollars worth of lumber."

"How would he explain what happened to the missing forty-nine thousand nine hundred dollars worth of materials?" Rafe asked.

"There's always throw away lumber that goes unaccounted for," Abby said.

"Throw away?" Rafe said.

"Bad wood. Most is totally destroyed or donated for bonfires and such," Donald explained. "Of course this inflated amount of bad wood could call up questions, but someone would have to be searching hard to notice. I'm certain he is being very careful not to make too many deals to avoid unbalances."

"What about the fifteen percent?" Rafe asked.

"There's no explanation, but I assume it went to Ethan. That left Tom with forty three thousand three hundred and fifty dollars."

"Miss Abby, I swear to you I had no idea," Don said.

She hugged him. "Of course you didn't. If you had known, you would have told me."

"Yes, Ma'am, I would."

They spent close to an hour, working quickly. She was glad to have six hands. When finished, they carefully straightened every drawer, closed and locked them, returned the key to Tom's desk and locked it.

"What were you doing here tonight, Don?" Abby asked, returning the keys to him.

"I left my reading glasses."

Abby looked at Rafe and said, "How lucky was that?"

She turned to Donald, swore him to secrecy and promised to return soon. They parted and Rafe and Abby drove back to Winston.

Relief and the assurance of the desolation of the past filled them with an almost childlike giddiness.

"That went smoothly, didn't it?" Abby stated upon arriving home.

"After you scared the life out of me!" he answered.

"You mean the heebeejeebies?" she said.

"Yeah, that, too! Did anything jump out at you tonight?"

"Besides Donald?" She started to giggle in complete relief and abandonment.

He smiled. "Okay, enough of that."

"No, it isn't," she said, pushing him onto the sofa and straddling his lap.

She put her hands on the cushions behind his shoulders. Leaning forward, she placed her mouth on his neck and kissed it before giving it a good nibble.

Rafe pushed her away, bringing his shoulder up to his ear. "Now, I've got chills all over," he said.

She laughed. "Oh, really?" She pulled his shirt up. "Let me see," she teased.

Placing her hands on both sides of his rib cage, she said, "You're right. I can feel them."

She slid her arms around him, laid her head on his chest, closed her eyes and said, "I feel reborn." Holding her close, he pulled her down with him, onto their sides. She slipped her arm from underneath him and bent it under her head as he slid his leg over her ankles with a sigh.

"It's good to hear you laugh," he said, raising his head and laying his cheek on hers.

She closed her eyes and, lifting her arm, wrapped it around his neck.

"You make me so happy, Rafe Andrew Musgrave Adams. I love you dearly."

He smiled as he studied her sweet lovely face before closing his eyes. Now, he held her vision in his mind.

They clung to each other in a quiet surrendering of troublesome matters. It wasn't exhaustion but a complete relaxation that soon brought sleep to both. It was sometime during the night that Rafe carried her to bed, lay down with her and pulled her close. They slept peacefully through the rest of the night.

"Aren't you two going home this evening?" one of the men on night shift asked Sam and Eric as he passed Sam's office.

"Just about to leave," Sam replied.

"Do you think it's over?" Eric asked his boss.

Sam looked at his watch. It was eleven thirty and there had been no reports of a disturbance of any kind at the mill. He hoped Abby Cummings was now safely on her way back to Winston.

"Yeah, I think so."

Sam stood up, straightened the articles on top of his desk, stretched and walked to the window. Eric watched in admiration of this man who took his job and the people involved so seriously.

Peering through the window panes, Sam said, "We sure could use some rain. The spring flowers won't be as colorful if it stays so dry."

"Everything's all right, Boss. Let's go home," Eric said.

CHAPTER 18

O N THE WAY to the cabin, Abby reviewed the pictures. She looked through each one carefully, then started again.

"You know, several of these clients are men that have been featured in *Success* as the subject of *The Climb*." She looked at Rafe. "Ethan definitely is involved in this," she stated.

"Yes, he suggested I could be helped with the lumber costs before turning me over to Tom. I don't think Ethan even entertained the thought of using me as a basis for one of his articles, but, knowing that I needed a good break on building materials, he probably thought I would jump at Tom's offer. I wonder if he gets a finders fee?"

"No doubt! There are others who weren't featured in the magazine. I wonder who located them?"

"Probably Tom, but I'd be willing to bet that Ethan has been in on the execution somehow. They had to have been very careful about making these deals. If the wrong person had been approached, he might have reported them to someone who would have instigated an investigation into what was going on."

"But Tom made the offer to you without much scrutiny," Abby said.

"Maybe he thought Ethan had checked me out or that I would be so desperate to save money that I would jump at the offer."

"As I'm sure others have done!" she said, studying some of the pictures more intently. There were folders for each transaction and a record book including names, dates, payments and other pertinent information, but no receipts. "The last name entered, a Paul Harmon, must be Tom's next target because there hasn't been an order or payment for him. There were deals made with approximately six businessmen in the last two and a half years with two payments from each one. Wasn't that the arrangement that Tom suggested to you? Half of it upon ordering the lumber and the other half at delivery?"

"Yes."

"The total of payment from each person ranged from somewhere just under fifty thousand to close to a hundred thousand," she said, looking toward Rafe. "Do you know how much he has stashed away? And the loss from the lumber sold was absorbed by the company and me!"

"That ten percent he put in the company was to help cover his a... butt. I guess he didn't want the mill to go bankrupt because his free ride would be over."

She continued to research the papers.

"Rafe, he took out ten to twenty percent each time for B."

"Bland!" they said simultaneously.

She then stated, "So, as Donald explained, out of every hundred thousand, the mill gets ten, Ethan ten to twenty and Tom walks away with sixty to eighty thousand, tax free."

At first she felt betrayed. Now, she was becoming very angry. "He's going up the river," she said.

Rafe smiled as he glanced at her. "Up the river?" he asked.

"That's what my parents used to say. Up the river, to the big house, be put away, do time, whatever," she said. "I'm going to turn the evidence over to the police and let them do their job. Donald will help."

"Way to go!" he replied.

"Give me Detective Robertson's phone number. I'm calling him."

"Don't you want to wait until we get back? I told him we'd call Monday."

"No! I'm going to let him know. What's the number?" she asked again.

202

Rafe pulled the detective's card out of his pocket and handed it to her. She made the call. After reporting that the contents of the desk showed Tom had been making deals on the side and collecting for them under the table, she described briefly how he handled it. Assuring him they would turn everything over upon their return, she asked if it would take long to bring Tom up on charges. Sam explained that the Federal Agents would most likely be involved due to nonpayment of taxes on the money taken. He asked that she send the evidence in by Rafe on Monday so he could evaluate it.

"You know you have uncovered, yet another, very strong motive for Tom to do whatever he thinks he must in order to keep his position, don't you?"

"Oh my goodness, you're right," she answered astonished. "I'm not going to feel safe again until he's locked up. You won't divulge my presence until he's arrested, will you?"

"Mrs. Cummings—" Sam started.

"Don't call me that, Detective Robertson. If you would, please use my given name, Abby. I would greatly appreciate it. *Mrs. Cummings* somehow makes me feel unclean."

"Of course. Anyway, I don't want you to be frightened. If it has to come out that you're back before he's taken in, we'll keep you safe. I, personally, don't think that will happen. Your presence is going to be a huge awakening that we'll want to keep as a surprise for Mr. Cummings. Meanwhile, we'll hold off on all this until you return."

"Thank you." Abby was relieved.

"You are most welcome. I must tell you, I feel compelled to go to the chief with this. It really is something for which he needs to be fully informed. I hope you understand. I can assure you it will go no further. The media will hear nothing until legal charges are filed, then it will become public record," Sam explained.

"I understand."

"Good," Sam replied.

"By the way, Ethan Bland is involved in some way. He may be the one who's locating the men for whom Tom offers the 'big deals'," Abby said.

"Is that right? Well, Eric and I will pull the files and review everything. There may be incriminating clues that we missed because we were investigating another matter."

"Thanks. You have been very kind and reassuring. I guess that's it until we see you next week," she said, signing off.

"Okay, I feel better now," she told Rafe, putting the pictures away.

"Good," Rafe replied. "Now, we're going to forget all this until Monday and enjoy the cabin."

"Right!" she said with her mind working over every possible angle of the deception that had been perpetrated at her expense. Until this very moment, she really did not believe in her heart that Tom would have actually tried to kill her. Now, she wasn't sure. The realization that, after all these years, she hadn't truly known him, had made a deep impact on her.

Abby was busy tidying things while Rafe followed the repairmen, who were trying to locate the problem. The cabin was a little cool, so Abby found one of Rafe's old comfortable cardigans and put it on. She rolled up the sleeves and buttoned it halfway from the bottom up. She swept the kitchen and cleaned the counter tops before dicing the meat and vegetables for a stew. After searing them, she added water and a can of chopped tomatoes, seasonings, and turned it on.

"Rafe!" she called, searching for the men.

"We're out back," Rafe replied loudly.

She moved to the back door and pushed it open. "Are you guys hungry? Would you like a sandwich?"

"We brought lunch, but thank you, ma'am," the taller man replied.

"How about you, Rafe?"

"Call me when it's ready," he said, watching the men intently.

She looked at one of them, winked and said, "I'll try to hurry."

Rafe joined her for grilled ham and cheese sandwiches and soup.

"How's it going?" she asked.

"They've located the problem but don't have all the parts they need for the repairs. I guess they'll be quitting for the day and will come back tomorrow to finish the job."

Erased

"It'll be nice to have a fire tonight," she said.

"Yes, it will."

"By the way, would you cut a couple of branches and sharpen the ends for me this afternoon?" she asked.

"What for?"

"S'mores!"

Ethan called Tom to invite him to share lunch. He was anxious to know what had transpired with Mr. Harmon. Tom informed him he was too upset to eat. Abby was his source of agitation. Ethan insisted on joining him if only to air out his fears. He was worried that if Tom didn't get himself under control he would ruin everything.

Tom agreed to order lunch in and Ethan could come to his office. He simply didn't want to go anywhere. Lunch and Ethan arrived at the same time.

"Don't open the food containers yet," Tom requested. "Stand in the middle of the room for a minute."

Ethan did as he was told, thinking Tom must have gone over the edge.

"Breathe deeply through your nose," Tom said.

Ethan complied.

"Can't you tell?"

"Tell what?" Ethan asked.

"That Abby has been here," Tom stated nervously.

"Tom, I don't get it. What are you saying?"

"When I walked into my office this morning, her scent permeated the air. Its been two months since she left this office, so why would my senses be picking up her perfume now? It wasn't apparent yesterday or last week, why today?"

Ethan inhaled, but tuna was all he could smell.

"Tom, you may be headed for a nervous breakdown. You must stop dwelling on Abby's disappearance," Ethan suggested.

He spun on Ethan. "I'm not dwelling on it. She keeps bringing it up. And I mean Abby, or Abby's spirit. Which is it Ethan? Can you tell me?"

"Calm down, Tom. Let's have lunch and talk about what she has been doing."

Ethan turned the club chairs to face the table between them and opened the lunch boxes. He took one seat as Tom placed himself in the other. Ethan passed a tuna salad, aluminum wrapped hard rolls, plastic silverware and bottled water to Tom.

"Now, tell me exactly what's happened."

Tom picked up his fork and stabbed a piece of lettuce as he said, "You didn't see her in the restaurant in Greensboro. I did!" Holding the fork in front of his face, he stared at Ethan and continued, "If you had, you would have known that those glasses and blond hair were on Abby's face."

Ethan swallowed then said, "Tom, I'm sure you thought—"

Tom slammed the side of his empty fist on the table, causing the lettuce to fall from the fork into his plastic salad container.

"I didn't *think* anything. I *know* what I saw. I looked right into her eyes and they were Abby's eyes looking back at me. No matter what state of mind you think I was in, and regardless of the fact that you thought that it was making me hallucinate, I have no doubt now! You were wrong—it was Abby!"

Ethan lifted his napkin, dabbed his mouth and said, "Settle down, Tom, or you're going to have Alice listening at the door. Look," he raised his hand to indicate Tom's salad, "you haven't even started on your lunch." Lifting the bottle of water and pouring a glassful, he watched Tom, who sat with brows knitted.

Tom pushed his salad forward and, folding his arms, leaned on the table.

"I got the license number that night, discovered the owner, and made a visit to his home."

In stunned disbelief, Ethan jerked his head up and asked, "Tom, are you crazy?"

"Maybe so, but she was my wife and I have to know if she is alive or dead."

"I hate to dash your hopes, but it has been too long, Tom." Ethan turned back to his lunch. "I think if she were alive she would be here, not living with some man. And disguised? For what reason? It simply doesn't make sense."

"I had to check."

"Obviously, you didn't find her." Ethan dabbed at his mouth before laying the napkin back onto his lap.

"Unfortunately, I was unable to confirm my suspicions as my visit was cut short," Tom said, recalling the events.

"You're lucky you weren't jailed as a *Peeping Tom*." Ethan smiled at his pun and picked up his water.

Totally oblivious to the fact that Ethan continued with his lunch, Tom continued, "Remember the attempted break-in at my house? I think the window was broken to draw attention away from the front door. There were no visible signs of tampering to the door. However, the security system indicated a breach there. I think she used her house key. If you remember, her keys weren't in her purse when they located the car."

"Why didn't she simply open the door and turn off the security alarm?" Ethan asked while fiddling with the cap on the bottle.

"I don't know."

"If it was her, don't you think that would have been the logical thing to do?" Ethan stressed.

Tom stood and began to pace. He was obviously mentally reviewing and connecting these incidents.

"The moment I entered the building this morning, I got a whiff of her perfume."

"Were you the first to arrive?" Ethan asked, knowing he would, as usual, have been the last.

"No, Alice and Donald were here," he said, watching Ethan push the eggs to the side of his plate. "How can you sit there and eat?" he asked.

"I'm hungry!" Ethan said, working the fork into the salad. He suggested, "perhaps Alice was a little too generous with her cologne today."

"It was *Minuit Etoile*. Abby is the only one I know who wears that, and she always ordered it from Paris." Tom was standing across the table with hands on hips, and leaning toward Ethan.

"Are you sure? Maybe it was a cheap copy," Ethan suggested.

"After six years of the expensive scent, believe me, I'd know the difference."

Ethan laid his fork aside and leaned back in his chair. He looked into Tom's unblinking eyes.

Tom emphasized, "I would know!"

Ethan put his napkin on the table and placed his fingertips together while he considered this.

"Did Donald or Alice notice it?" Ethan asked.

"Alice thought so, but she couldn't be sure. Donald, naturally, disagreed with me. He's always in opposition to everything I do or say, so you can't rely on him. But I know, without a doubt, she has been in this office."

Ethan stood now. "Was anything missing?"

"No," Tom replied.

"Were your desks locked?" Ethan walked behind Tom's large desk to check his drawers for keyholes.

"Yes, the drawers that needed to be, were secured."

"Did she have a key to them?"

"Not that one," Tom said, indicating the small desk. "I don't know about this one. She did at one time."

"And I'll bet that you, with your muddled mind, put a key to that one," pointing to the small desk, "in this one." Ethan now indicated Tom's personal desk.

Without speaking, Tom simply looked at him.

Ethan ran his hand over his head and through his hair as he paused to let it all sink in.

"It doesn't make sense, Tom. If she is alive, why hasn't she let someone know?"

"Yes, why?" Tom dropped into his desk chair and with hands folded in his lap, he stared at nothing. Now, lost in thought, he no longer acknowledged Ethan's presence.

"I've been away from the office long enough," Ethan said. "I've got to get back and make sure they haven't planned a takeover."

He walked briskly through the door, exited the building and headed to his car. He drove to *The Ground Beans* and went in for coffee, then returned to the car, where he sat in deep thought sipping the dark liquid. Could it be possible? Did she live? He was going to have to return to the mountain. As much as the thought repulsed him, he had to see if her remains were there. He lifted the cup to his mouth and when the aroma of the coffee penetrated his senses, he made a face, opened the door and emptied the cup.

Picking up his phone, he notified his secretary that he would not be back due to a debilitating headache that required he go home.

208

He informed her that he was going to take pain medication and go to bed. He would not be accepting any calls.

Ethan knew he had replaced the gun but due to his need for checking details, he opened the glove compartment anyway.

Tom picked up both salads and threw them into a garbage bag. He twisted the top and put a rubber band around it. The odor of tuna was making him sick. Or was it the perfume? He didn't know. He couldn't concentrate anymore. When did things start to spiral out of control?

Had it started with Maggie? Maybe it was when Abby began work on the magazine and abandoned him. Perhaps it was Ethan's arrival. If Abby hadn't brought him in to the magazine staff, Tom may still have had his clean character and an honest business. It was all of them! They turned his head and now he was in such a state that he felt his existence crumbling beneath him. The thought that he might have had anything to do with the current circumstances didn't even remotely enter his mind.

He threw the bag down beside his wastebasket, put his suit coat on and walked out of his office.

"I'm leaving for the day," he told Alice without a glance and strode through the door. *Damn, I need a martini!*

Eric sat in Sam's office paging through the same issue of *Success* that, to him, had been so bothersome. Sam was scrutinizing the notes he made while talking to Abby.

"Looks like Tom Cummings is going to jail one way or the other," Sam said.

"I wonder if Mrs. Cummings had discovered what he was doing before she disappeared?"

"To what are you referring? His indiscretions or his pilfering?" Sam asked.

"We knew she found out about Ms. Templeton the day she left. I mean did she have any inclination that he was involved in company wrongdoing?"

"She said she knew nothing about it until now. Actually, not until her husband made an unethical and illegal business proposition to Adams."

"Didn't she say that Mr. Bland had taken the doctor to see her husband?" Eric asked.

"Yes, it looks as though the two of them are working this together. Maybe photo man finds the ego-builder who wants the publicity so much that he's afraid if he doesn't take the good deal on the lumber, he won't be featured in the magazine. He still comes out ahead because, he not only gets the lumber he needs at an excellent price, but the publicity increases his exposure, therefore, increasing his business and financial gains. Everybody wins," Sam stated.

"What does Mr. Bland get out of it?"

"Mrs. Cummings said he receives a percentage of the deal and it's probably more if he's the one who locates Mr. or Ms. Money-pockets. I'm sure he's made no less than ten to fifteen thousand off every hundred thousand Tom takes."

Eric whistled. "Nice little tax-free income, I'd say."

"Yep, pretty good deal all around," Sam said.

"Except for Mrs. Cummings and Langford Mill!" Eric added.

"I really think if she had gotten wind of these transactions before, she would remember that now. She seems to have recalled everything up to catching her husband whispering sweet nothings to his mistress. In her present state of mind, that's where the day ended."

Eric was studying the pictures in *The Climb* article so intently that he was only half listening.

"What'd you say about your mistress, Boss?"

Sam turned his head in Eric's direction and frowned. "My mistress?"

"Yeah, what were you saying about her?" Eric repeated as he kept his eyes on the article in front of him.

"Eric, if you don't get rid of that magazine, I'm going to put you both through the shredder."

Eric took the magazine to Sam and laid it in front of him.

"Remember this house?"

"Yes, that's where we caught Tom leaving with the briefcase full of money."

210

"It's also the one that Mr. Bland told us he photographed, or in his words, *shot*, the afternoon that Mrs. Cummings disappeared," Eric prompted.

"I remember."

"Look at those pictures."

"I am looking at them, Eric. What am I supposed to see?"

"It's what you don't see!"

Sam studied them a moment, then said to himself, "This is crazy. I'm looking very hard to find what's not there."

"I told you from the beginning that something was wrong, but it just kept eluding this analytically inexperienced mind of mine."

Sam turned to Eric and said, "My, my, what big words you've learned. Eric, you tell me a lot of things that never develop into anything."

"Well, this time it has. We weren't notified that Mrs. Cummings had gone missing until two days after her disappearance. If you recall, we had a lot of melting ice and snow the day we answered that call."

"Yes, and?" Sam prompted.

"Two days prior to that, the day these pictures were taken, we had one of the worst snowstorms we've had in a long time. That Nor'easter came through here like the devil was at its tail! Remember the power outages and closings? It was a terrible day," Eric reminded him.

Sam, still studying the pictures, said, "The snow and ice. That's what's missing, the gall-durn snow and ice."

"Right. Bland lied! Now, why do you suppose he did that?" Eric said, lifting the magazine and looking at Sam.

"Because that fancy-pants son-of-a-bitch didn't take those pictures that day." Sam was on his feet and pacing. He had a rhythm going, smacking his right fist into the palm of his left hand.

"Correct, but why did he feel he had to say he did?" Eric was following him.

"Because he couldn't tell us where he really was. He needed an alibi," Sam said, his thoughts racing in a million different directions.

"And we know why, don't we?" Eric kept baiting Sam.

"Damn straight!" Sam almost shouted.

"Do you think Cummings and Bland worked together to make Mrs. Cummings disappear?" Eric questioned.

Sam stopped abruptly and was almost run over by Eric. He reached for the phone and placed a call to the magazine with the intention of setting up an appointment with Bland. The receptionist informed Sam that Ethan had gone to Mr. Cummings' office, then called in with a headache and reported he was going home and did not wish to be disturbed. Sam, in turn, phoned the mill and asked to speak with Mr. Cummings.

"Hello," Tom answered.

"Detective Robertson here," Sam said in a strong commanding voice.

"Yes, detective?"

"I need to speak with Mr. Bland and I was told he might be with you."

"Not anymore," Tom replied. "He left."

"I see. Would you know where he could be reached? It's important that I speak with him," Sam insisted.

"He left here about fifteen minutes ago. He told me he was going to his office. If he didn't, he failed to make me privy to his plans. I'm not familiar with where he spends his time when away from the office, so I'm afraid I can't help you. However, I'm glad you called. Ethan and I just had an unsettling discussion and I wanted to tell you about it."

"I'm listening," Sam said. He motioned for Eric to pick up the other phone and make notes.

"I have the feeling that Abby is here somewhere and every time I mention it to Ethan, he reacts like I'm a straightjacket candidate. I had another reminder of that this morning."

"What happened?" Sam asked.

"She was in the office sometime last night."

"How do you know that?" Sam asked as Eric looked up at him.

"When I came in this morning, her scent was lingering in my office."

"Perhaps the cleaning lady had plans for the evening," Sam suggested.

"I am very familiar with what my wife wears and she is the only one I know who wears it. She orders it from Paris."

"Could be a guilt-ridden overactive mind!" Sam suggested snidely.

"Yes, I am guilty of causing her distress, but I have not done her any physical harm. As I was saying, there have been other things that have indicated her presence. The attempted break-in at my house, and I know that was her that I saw in Greensboro."

Red flags started to go off for Sam.

"You were discussing all this with Mr. Bland?"

"Yes."

"What was his reaction?"

"He was with me in Greensboro but he didn't see her. He thought I was hallucinating and he considered it farfetched that she could have been involved with the incident at my home. He did, however, hesitate in his disbelief that she was present in this building last night."

"And?" Sam urged him on.

"That was the end of it! He was having lunch here, but suddenly left it unfinished, saying he had to return to his office. If he didn't go there, I don't know where he is. Do you want me to have him call you if I see him?"

"No, but thanks. I guess we'll catch up with him later."

"Very well," Tom said. "But I want you to think about the things I've just told you. Abby is here somewhere. She's torturing me, making me pay for my indiscretions. Maybe she intends to drive me mad."

"I certainly will do that," Sam said.

Eric looked at Sam, who stood staring at the phone he had hung up. "I guess Bland worked alone," he said to Sam.

"Tom Cummings is a lecherous crook, but he was not involved in what happened on that mountain. It was Ethan Bland alone who tried to kill her, and now he suspects she's alive. We've got to find him."

Sam looked at Eric, who was getting quite fidgety.

"Okay, Boss. Tell me. What's next?"

Sam stood, holstered his gun and said, "Let's go."

"Where?" Eric asked as he grabbed his notebook.

"You won't need that book. We're going to the mountains."

Sharon Evans-Rose

CHAPTER
19

THE REPAIRMEN CLEANED up their mess, put their equipment in the truck and promised to return early the next day. It was late afternoon by the time they pulled away.

Abby had shed the sweater after making up the bed and putting a salad together. The kitchen had warmed due to the baking cornbread. Since the repairs had not been completed and the temperature would be dropping, Rafe brought in enough firewood for the night.

Abby sat tucked in the corner of the sofa and after Rafe deposited the wood, he joined her. With legs propped on the table, he relaxed, resting his head on the back cushion. She reached over to run her fingers through his thick black hair.

"It's a good thing the weather will be warming soon or I'd have to start splitting wood again," he said.

"Keeps your biceps fit. Anyway, these cool evenings aren't going to last much longer, then you're going to wish it weren't so hot."

"When we get back, I've got to see where we stand with the air for the cabin," he told her. "It's supposed to be installed this spring."

"Does it get as hot up here as it does in Winston?" Abby asked.

"No. The higher altitude and the shade from all these trees shortens the time we have the dense heat. I like that. Makes it possible to enjoy my hammock."

"I'm looking forward to trying out that hammock and sitting on the porch in the evenings. It's so wonderfully peaceful here." She put her head down on her arm that now stretched along the top of the cushion. "I love it too," she told him.

Rafe turned to smile at her. "I'm glad, because I want you with me when I'm here. I enjoyed the solitude until you came along," he told her.

She leaned into him, wrapping her arms around his neck. "If it weren't for you, I wouldn't be here or anywhere else."

"I love you, Abby," he said.

"And I love you back."

They sat quietly holding hands for a while. Finally Rafe sighed and got to his feet.

"I'm going to have to go down to the store at the base of the mountain. I didn't realize I was out of nails and I need to make a few repairs while we're here," he said. "Do you want to go with me?"

"I think I'll stay here. Why don't we have a bowl of stew first and I'll clean the kitchen while you run your errand?" she suggested.

"Stew! I thought it was going to be hot dogs and potato salad," he reminded her.

"Well, we're still going to have S'mores."

"Do you want to eat this early?" he asked.

"It's not that early," she said, looking at her watch. "Do you mind? Its been a long and trying day and the past twenty-four hours have been very draining. I'm a little tired and looking forward to relaxing."

"Sounds like a good idea," Rafe admitted.

Abby started toward the kitchen. "Come on, everything is ready and it's hot."

Following her, Rafe made an offer. "Why don't you leave the dishes for me? I'll do them when I get back," he said.

"Don't be silly. I'm not that tired and considering that narrow winding road, I'll have them finished by the time you reach the bottom of the mountain."

They dined on salad, stew and cornbread with iced tea.

"That hit the spot!" Rafe said. "You certainly know the way to a man's heart."

"I do, and it's not by way of the stomach," she stated as she cleared the table.

Rafe laughed and followed her to the sink where he planted a big kiss on her forehead.

"It was delicious," he said. "Thank you."

"Be careful on that wiggly little road," she said over her shoulder.

"I won't be gone long but I'll have my cell phone with me. If you think of anything else we need, call me."

"Take your time," she said.

It was a simple cleanup for a one dish meal. She folded the towel and laid it on the counter. Pulling the sweater off the back of the chair, she put it on and buttoned the three bottom buttons. As she picked up her cell phone and dropped it in the pocket, she heard knocking at the front door. Assuming the repairmen must have returned, she moved into the living room.

With a welcoming smile adorning her face, she pulled the door open to find a well-dressed stranger waiting at the threshold. He stood stunned, bringing his hand to his throat.

"Are you ill?" she asked, concerned. "Do you need help?"

"I'm, uh, in a little bit of trouble," he said. "I must have taken a bad turn somewhere and I've come up the wrong mountain." He watched her carefully, wondering if he were standing in shadow and she couldn't see him. "There seems to be something hung under my vehicle and I don't have a flashlight."

"I'll look for one. Would you like to wait inside?" she asked.

"Thank you," he said, stepping through the door with his hand in his pocket. She continued to smile at him as he stepped in the well lit room.

Amnesia! The thought cast a blanket of relief over him. He would be able to accomplish what he failed to do earlier without interference. All he had to do was wait for the right moment. The hand in his pocket grasped the pistol to receive a surge of control from the cold steel. He wanted to ask if she lived alone but was afraid it might scare her into thinking she had made a mistake taking him in.

As Abby turned to close the door, she saw his SUV. "You've left your lights on," she told him.

"They're on a timer. They'll go off," he replied.

She momentarily stiffened, staring at the vehicle as Rafe's voice rang in her head. "The lights were bright and large, double, one atop the other and set high off the road... an SUV." Abby began to tremble. How would she conceal her fear? She must not let him know that she suspected anything.

Instantly, she experienced a mind flash. She saw Ethan at the office and another of him taking her into his vehicle.

Taking a breath and relaxing her face, she turned to face him and smiled. Her hand was in her pocket and on the phone. While trading pleasantries, she located the number two, pressed it, then hit send.

"Please have a seat," she offered.

"Thank you, uh..." he hesitated.

She had given the phone time to ring once or twice and now she pushed end, waited, then repeated the process.

"I'm Kathryn." Abby offered him her hand. She wanted to assure him that her mind was not intact, that she would not know him.

He took it and as they shook, he smiled and said, "I'm Will Conners."

"It's nice to meet you, Will."

Rafe had located a couple of boxes of nails and was looking over the other hardware when his phone rang. He lifted it to see Abby's number listed on the caller I.D. before putting it to his ear to find no one on the other end. He hung up assuming she had accidentally hit his rapid dial number.

He chose a new screwdriver and started to the counter to pay for the items when the phone rang the second time. Getting the same response when answering, he decided to call her.

Abby had just gotten her visitor seated when her phone rang and she pulled it out of her pocket to check the caller I.D.

"Excuse me," she said, as he started to rise from his seat, "It's the furnace repairman. That's why the heavy sweater," she smiled.

Ethan relaxed into the chair.

"Hello."

"Abby, is everything all right?" Rafe sounded uneasy.

"No. No, it isn't, Ralph. Now that's not necessary."

"What?" Rafe said. He wasn't certain he had heard correctly.

"Tomorrow will be fine," she added.

Rafe was trying to assimilate what she was saying. Was she having a relapse? Why was he suddenly Ralph again? Must have been a slip of the tongue. He was glad she hadn't called him Albert! *Wait, did she say no, when I asked if everything was all right?*

Ethan was looking about the room in a pretense of interest, but stayed totally attuned to her words.

"Oh, wait," she continued. "Tell Albert that Belle called and wants him to come home, right away," she emphasized, then paused and smiled over the phone at the man in the chair. Drawing her brows together and raising her hand, she mouthed the words, "I'm sorry." He smiled back nodding.

Finally she said, "Thanks, Ralph, I'll see you tomorrow. Bye now," but Rafe had already hung up.

She put the phone back into her pocket as she explained, "They are such nice men. Albert's wife is in her third trimester and gets very anxious when she's alone. Let me locate that flashlight for you."

Going into the kitchen, she spotted the hammer that Rafe had left on the counter and picked it up.

"Will, would you like a cup of coffee?" she called out, walking directly toward the back door.

"No, thank you," came the reply as she slipped quietly outside.

Moving at almost a run, she headed to the woods. Shifting the hammer to her left hand, she pulled the phone out and hit number two and send.

"Yes?" Rafe said anxiously.

"I'm going into the woods," she whispered.

"Can you speak a little louder, I'm having trouble understanding you," Rafe said. His heart was racing.

"It's Ethan. Ethan is the person who tried to kill me. He's here. Hurry, Rafe," she pleaded.

"I'm coming. Leave your phone on so I can listen but don't talk unless you have to. That would help him to locate you."

It was late dusk and would be dark soon but perhaps not soon enough. She stopped behind a large tree to catch her breath and listen for any sounds indicating he had followed. There were none. With no plan, other than putting distance between them, she started moving again.

Perhaps this would be a good time to catch her off guard. He might even be lucky enough to find her with her back to him. Standing, Ethan slipped his hand back into his pocket.

"Can't you find it?" he called out. "Maybe I can help."

When she made no reply, he quickened his step. He looked cautiously into the kitchen and found it empty. Turning about, he saw two more doorways. One was open, the other closed.

Moving to the closer closed one first, thinking she might be more likely to be in a room with the door closed, he eased it open to find a dark, empty bathroom. Slipping to the next one, he once again asked, "Kathryn, may I help you?"

Still, no answer. He flipped the light on in the bedroom, but knew before he did so that it, too, would be empty.

She knows, he realized. *Well, haven't you become a cunning little actress!* Pulling the gun from his pocket, he went to the back door and stepped outside. He stood there briefly waiting for his eyes to adjust.

Rafe was driving too fast, he knew, but it was imperative he get there before it was too late. He was familiar with the road and he had no worry about meeting another car because there were no other connections to this road between his present location and the cabin.

When roads were laid in up a mountain, they had to wind the edge of the hillside. This always put the cut away wall of rock and dirt on one side of the car and the drop off down the wooded mountain on the other. There were very few places with enough room for a safety shoulder and some areas of the road were so narrow it would be impossible to pass an oncoming car. As he approached the sharpest curve he waited a little too long to brake and the dirt and gravel caused the vehicle to fishtail. Coming to a stop, Rafe found the car positioned crosswise on the road. Jumping out, he ran to the back, knelt on one knee and looked underneath. He had maybe two feet of maneuvering space before the drop off. He stood and ran to the front where he shook his head to find how close he was to the cut away. The side of the front fender had scraped the rock wall as the vehicle had made its sliding turn to stop.

He got back into his car with determination. It wasn't impossible to get out of this mess. If he had to, he would abandon the Land Rover and run up the mountain—if he didn't back over the edge first. Shifting into reverse, he eased slowly as he turned the steering wheel as sharply as possible. When his nerves told him that was far enough, he stopped and turned the wheel completely back, then inched forward. Four more times he did this, until his anxiety had his heart skipping all over his chest.

After backing up once more, he shifted the gears and started to roll to the front at a sharp turn, watching the hillside closely. He hesitated only briefly before deciding he had it cleared. He lightly pressed the accelerator and watched the front fender, hoping to miss the wall. *Very close,* he thought, but his nerves urged him on. A crunching of glass forced him to brake.

Damn, there goes a headlight.

He threw it into reverse, backed up as far as he felt it was safe, then turned the wheel and mashed on the pedal. At that point, he didn't care if he took off a fender, he had to get to Abby. He cleared the mountain side and vanished around a curve.

Sam stopped at the small shop at the base of Pine Knob and rushed inside. He looked at a rather startled young man behind the counter. Two customers in less than half an hour and it was almost dark. For such a late hour, things were really picking up.

"I'm looking for the Adams cabin," Sam told him as he flashed his badge. He chose a roll of antacids and laid it on the counter with two dollars.

"It's at the top of the mountain. About five miles, but it's a small curvy road so you'd better take your time," he said, pointing out the direction.

"I see," Sam said as the clerk turned to make change.

"Dr. Adams was just here, but he got a call and threw his items on the counter and ran out the door. You'd think he had just run across a nest of rattlers," the boy said laughing.

He turned to give Sam the coins but found him gone. The antacids remained there. The sound of the car was already fading.

The young man jumped onto the counter, landing on his knees. Leaning onto his hands he peered very carefully over the edge to the floor.

Abby sprinted a few more yards and stepped behind another tree to listen. This time she heard footfalls coming down the steps. She stiffened and held her breath. He had stopped, probably trying to decide which way to go.

"Where are you, Abby?" he called before descending the last two steps. "Imagine my surprise to find you risen from the dead! I'm most interested in learning how that occurred. You know, I can't let it happen again."

He began a slow walk, looking for hints of her footprints. Seeming to pick up her trail, he increased his pace.

Abby pushed the hammer handle up the sleeve of the sweater and cupped the head in her hand. She moved slightly to the side of the tree and saw him coming her way. It was time to move. She spotted a full pine and headed for it. Ethan sighted a flutter of movement and adjusted his line of direction.

"You may as well wait for me, I'm on my way!" Ethan yelled. The stalking was invigorating to him. She must be so frightened. Good! The bitch thought she was going to ruin him. Knock him down to where she thought he belonged. He laughed—almost a maniacal sound.

Facing away from him in an attempt to disguise the direction of her voice, she shouted, "Ethan, you were my best friend. Why would you do this?"

"Friend? No, I was your charity case."

"What do you mean?" she asked seriously.

"Abby, are you in denial? You and all your rich little buddies shed me as soon as you were old enough to realize your station."

"That's not true, Ethan. As we grew older, we all developed different interests, different friends and new activities, but I made a point of keeping in touch with you."

"Until you got involved with other guys!" Ethan yelled. "Then it was good-bye ol' Eth!" He was coming into the woods now.

She sprinted for the next large tree. Her head was swirling. Why would Ethan have gotten so upset? Life changes.

"Ethan, couples don't usually take a third party with them on dates," she told him.

"If you wanted a date, why didn't you ask me?"

What was he saying? They were friends, that's all. Did he think it had been more? Had he been hurt?

Abby realized suddenly that she was doing what Rafe had cautioned her to refrain from doing and exactly what Ethan was purposely causing her to do. She was speaking. That's why he was keeping up with her. She was bringing him to her.

"Just as I thought. You have no answer to that."

Clinching her teeth together, she stood quiet.

"Abby, did you hear me?"

She did not reply. Standing in fear she waited for his next move. He seemed to be building into a rage.

"Then, when I get my life on track, with a good job and new friends, you call. I shouldn't have joined you, but I did and I was good for you and the magazine." He stopped then screamed, "Wasn't I, Abby?!"

Chills ran up her spine. She dropped her chin onto her chest and with closed eyes, she remembered Ethan shaking her in the vehicle before he started to hit her. He had been totally out of control.

"You needed me. That was nice. And as a bonus, Tom and I developed a profitable little sideline." He was speaking loudly.

Was she hearing him properly? The two most important people in her life were using her. Actually, they were stealing from her. One of them tried to kill her.

"You were going to get rid of Tom, now where would that have left me? A lot less financially secure, I can tell you. I was not going to take it again. Being pushed aside. I was *not* going to let you do that again!" His delivery had now become a shout.

He was getting closer and she knew she had to keep going. She started to run, then tripped over a tree limb that had been felled by the ice and went down to her knees, hitting them on the rocks.

"Ouch, damn those river rocks." She picked up one and gave it a hefty long pitch through the woods. It landed, drawing Ethan's attention away from her and to that spot. Taking advantage of this, she started for cover again.

In that moment, Rafe pulled up behind Ethan's car, jumped out and ran into the house for his hunting knife. The 'rocks' comment told him approximately where to locate her. *Hold on, Abby, I'm on my way.* He stepped on the back doorstep and stood, searching and listening for a clue to Ethan's whereabouts.

"Your reprieve is just about over," Ethan called to her.

Rafe heard Bland's voice, but it was difficult to pinpoint his location. He assumed he must be close to Abby and he knew the direction in which Abby was headed. To move as silently as possible, he would have to take it slow. Surprise could be a weapon in itself. He started traveling in a large semicircle to get to where he thought he would find them.

Abby tried to remember how to reach the wall of brush and pines that she and Rafe had stepped through for privacy that day. If she could get there, she would tell Rafe and maybe she could hide behind them with the hope that he could save her.

Rafe made it down to the spring then started circling upward. He slowed in an effort to move more quietly.

Sam pulled in to join the other two vehicles. He and Eric left the car and crept up the porch stairs. Standing on each side of the open front door, Sam said loudly, "Dr. Adams, are you here?" He paused. "Mrs. Cumm, uh, Abby, it's Detective Robertson," he called out.

With no answer, Sam looked at Eric and tilted his head toward the cabin. Eric responded with a nod. With gun held in two hands in preparation for firing, the older detective lunged onto one foot through the door, looking quickly to the right then left, as Eric, taking his stance in back of Sam, checked the area in front of them. Finding the room empty, they checked the other rooms before discovering the open back door.

"They're in the woods," Eric said.

Moving outside, they approached the woods with caution. They separated to widen their range of search.

"Take your time. We know they're ahead of us so try to keep close to cover when moving," Sam said quietly as he looked in Eric's direction. Eric had taken his gun into his right hand and was pulling out his flashlight.

"Don't turn that flashlight on, you idiot, you'd be a moving target. Give yourself time and your eyes will adjust," Sam cautioned. "Now, listen for clues and don't talk!"

Abby could see the protection she had been hunting but there was nothing to provide cover between where she stood and where she was going. She waited, listening intently. Her heart was beating so loudly, her breathing staggered and heavy, that it seemed she, herself, was drowning out all other sounds.

Looking about, she saw no movement or human form, so she made a quick sprint forward. About halfway to her destination, she halted and stooped down close to the ground in an effort to hide in plain sight. When it appeared no one was following, she stood and ran toward the wall of forest growth. Turning to back up to it and keep a keen eye on what she might be facing, she suddenly felt someone grab her arm as the voice of Ethan said into her ear, "Gotcha!"

With a quick intake of breath, she stiffened. In an effort to let Rafe know where they were, she said loudly, "How did you get in front of me? I couldn't see you against the pine."

"That's quite obvious," he replied. "I seriously doubt that you would have intentionally run into my arms," he laughed.

"I trusted you. Why would you do this?" Abby asked.

Ethan smiled. "Abby, Abby. I know how intelligent you are, so don't play dumb. Tell me, does someone live in that cabin? Is that how you got help?"

"If you thought you had killed me, why did you come back?" She wanted to distract him and at the same time postpone what was about to happen.

"It was that wonderful perfume of yours. You shouldn't have worn it to Tom's office last night."

Rafe's heart dropped at Ethan's words. He had put her in danger again. How would he live with himself if Bland took her life this time? Moving more quickly, he was closing the gap between them. Reaching the heavy growth of pine, he stayed as close to it as possible. This put him out of their peripheral vision. Ethan had his back to Rafe which placed Abby facing him, however, he doubted that she could even see him. This would be a good thing because he didn't want her to give away his position.

Rafe put his phone in his pocket. Since he had them in sight, he wanted to keep one hand free. He didn't know what might happen but he had to be ready to make a quick decision and react on instinct.

A movement far to his right caused him to hesitate. It was getting darker and he had to squint slightly to get a clear view. It was Sam Robertson and Eric Burke creeping through the woods, slipping behind trees for coverage when they could. Both had their guns drawn. This frightened Rafe because their intended target was with Abby. He eased slowly toward the couple, alternating his focus between them and the detectives.

Abby seemed to be purposely involving Ethan in conversation. Rafe knew she was smart and he was proud of her for keeping her head. She was preventing Ethan from noticing what was going on around them, allowing him time to get to them.

Ethan, too, was increasingly involved in the conversation. Bland must have a lot of things he wanted her to hear before she died.

Sam stepped on a dead branch and it snapped loudly. He, Eric and Rafe ceased moving instantly. Rafe held his breath. Ethan and Abby both turned to face the sound. Ethan had pulled a small hand gun out of his pocket. Abby was to his left. She let the hammer slip down just far enough to get a good grip on the handle slightly below the head. Upon spotting Robertson, Ethan stepped behind her, raised his arm over her shoulder and pointed the gun in the direction of the detectives.

"Stop!" he shouted. He remained very calm, evaluating his options.

"You must give yourself up, Mr. Bland," Sam said. "There are three of us and one of you."

"No, you're wrong. There is one of me and two of you. Abby is simply an extension of myself, and in order to get me, you have to go through her."

"Mr. Bland, you're facing a charge of attempted murder or at the least, malicious injury. There's every possibility of making a deal if you give yourself up. Maybe a plea bargain, but if you kill three people, you'll never see the light of day again."

"If they catch me, but you underestimate my abilities, Detective."

"Please, Ethan," Abby begged, "don't hurt anyone."

"Shut up!" Ethan's breathing was heavy in her ear.

He turned the gun to her head and yelled, "I think it's time for the two of you to leave, unless you want to watch this."

Eric jumped into full view and shouted, "No! Don't do it."

Ethan turned the gun in Eric's direction. As he steadied his arm on Abby's shoulder and brought his head down to take proper aim, he began to squeeze the trigger.

Abby lifted her arm forward as Ethan was positioning himself and with all her strength, swung the hammer back into his knee, setting off a domino effect of incidents. They happened so quickly, yet, later explanations would seem to describe a surreal slow motion execution of consecutive actions.

With the blow, Ethan's arm began a downward movement as the hammer connected. The gun fired, sending Eric to the ground and setting Sam into a furious run toward Ethan as he expelled a screaming growl, "You bastard. Damn you, you stinking bastard."

Rafe scrambled toward Abby, who was holding her hand over her ear. She seemed to be stunned.

The blast of pain in Ethan's knee bent him over as he stumbled backward. Still clutching the gun, his movement knocked Abby forward. Two large leaps set Rafe against Abby, allowing him to grab her and take her to the ground beneath him.

Ethan was struggling to gain control of his balance as the searing pain in his knee made it a Herculean effort on his part. With arms flailing about and the loaded gun so critically close, Rafe and Abby were in danger of being shot, if not by design, then by accident.

Rafe pulled the knife from his belt beneath him, rolled quickly away from Abby to free his arm, held the blade and threw strongly toward Ethan's staggering form.

The knife connected with muscle and rib just below Ethan's shoulder. He howled in reaction, hurling himself up and backward through the brush and pine. Still clinging to the gun, he disappeared from their view. Staggering backward and in terrible pain, he worked to keep his balance until suddenly, there was nothing to connect with his footing.

The hideous scream on the other side of the brush brought Sam to an abrupt halt and Abby closed her eyes as Rafe rolled back to hold her as the scream faded, then ceased. Rafe, filled with unbelievable relief, held on to her tightly. With cheeks pressed together, their tears mingled in a mixture of high emotions. Total chaos had ended with a deadly silence.

Sam was standing beside the hospital bed when Abby and Rafe walked in. He turned to see their smiles and welcomed them with handshakes.

"Look at this lazy boy," he said, turning back to Eric, who brightened at seeing them. "Two days, and he's still not out of here."

"How's the leg?" Rafe asked.

"Doing fine," Eric said weakly. "Mrs. Cummings, if it weren't for you, he probably would have gotten me in the chest." Eric batted back tears. "Thank you," he muttered.

"Yes, and if it weren't for you, I may not be here," she said humbly. "So, thank *you*, Eric."

"The bullet broke the bone, but the doc says he'll heal up like new," Sam said, trying to change the mood, before he too, clouded up.

Abby stepped forward with a box of Godiva chocolates. "These are for you, Eric. If you want to share them that would be nice," she said smiling at Sam, then back to Eric she added, "but if you don't choose to, you'd better keep your eye on the big guy."

"I'm so grateful," Rafe said, putting his arm around Abby's shoulders. "I don't know if either one of us would be here if you two hadn't come up that mountain."

228

"I always wanted to return to that beautiful spot, but not like that," Sam told them.

"I'll tell you what, when you have a free weekend and want to get away, give me a call. You can pick up the key to the cabin and take your wife for a good mountain-air-filled rest."

"He's got a hammock that I hear is great for sleeping," Abby added.

"I'll take you up on that Doc," Sam said to Rafe, then turning to Abby he added, "I hope the tide has turned for you, uh, Abby. How's it going?"

"You probably know more than I do," Abby answered, "but as far as the Tom and Abby saga goes, I've filed for divorce and depositions have been set for next week. Anyway, my attorney believes we can settle things in one meeting with Tom and his lawyer."

She hugged Sam, who blushed, and told him again how thankful she was for what they had done. She walked over to Eric and planted a kiss on his cheek. His red face beamed.

The door opened and everyone turned to see the cute nurse walk in with a bouquet of flowers. She smiled and nodded as she walked to the chest where she placed them among two others. Lifting the card and carrying it to Eric, she waited while he read it and passed it to Sam.

Eric looked toward Rafe and Abby. He said, "It's from the guys at the station."

The nurse took the card and returned it to the flowers before she began fluffing Eric's pillows. "I think you need to rest now," she said.

Eric looked over her head and winked at Sam. "But these are my friends, and they just arrived," he protested.

"Well, they can just depart," she stated, walking around the bed to pour a fresh glass of ice water. "You need your rest and they can visit another day."

"That's right," Abby said. "It's important that Eric recover."

The nurse acknowledged them with a nod and added, "Yes, I'm glad you understand."

Sam leaned over Eric and said, "I'll not take another partner. I'm going to wait for you, so you'd better hurry up and get back on your feet."

They shook hands as Eric replied, "Sure thing, Boss."

"If you need anything, you call me," Sam said, turning to leave.

"We'll take care of his needs," the little-lady-in-white told them.

As the visitors were making their way to the elevator, Rafe was the first to speak.

"She certainly is a cute, but sassy, little thing."

"Yes, she acted like his mother," Abby quipped.

"Soon to be wife," Sam said.

It was on a dreary day that Abby chose to return to her home in Prestonburg. She felt that staying with Rafe any longer would not be the proper thing to do and could harm her divorce efforts. She took a cab home after Rafe left for work. Not wanting to face the good-byes, she simply wrote him a truly heartfelt and sincere note of thanks and propped it on the kitchen table.

The house was so terribly quiet and lonely. It seemed to have turned on her while she was away. Tom had moved out at her request. She felt sorry that his life, as he had known it, was over. What a waste. And how did things get so turned around with Ethan? In her mind, she had gone back over her teenage years, time and again, in search of something she may have done to have caused him to feel so much malice toward her, but she always came up empty.

Trying to find a friendly spot, she wandered through the house, touching things, opening drawers and doors, looking at all the framed photographs and sitting in one chair after another. While in the bedroom, she picked up a bottle of *Minuit Etoile,* removed the stopper and passed it beneath her nose. Turning, she carried it into the bathroom and poured it down the drain.

In the great room, she curled up on the sofa where she remained until the sun began its descent. The rain was coming down steadily and hundreds of little rivulets chased each other down the wall of windows.

Abby stood, walked to those windows and watched hypnotically as the water patterns altered rhythmically on the panes. Then a distraction caught her eye. She could see movement among the trees off to the side of the pool area. Adjusting her focus she homed in on the trees, especially the large one that had always been there.

She caught the movement again and squinted for a clearer view. It would come and go, come and go. She opened her mouth with a quick intake of breath. There was a child in the swing that still hung from the strong, faithful limb. Abby could see the little girl better as the swing came forward and she would fade as it moved back into the trees. The vision would come and go until on one backward swing, it didn't return.

Abby cupped her hands around the sides of her eyes and leaned against the window. There, she could see her again. The child was suspended in midair. Abby's focus followed the rope from the child's grasp upward until she saw two strong hands holding the swing still. The small face was laughing heartily.

Slowly, the swing was lowered and the little girl jumped out. She stood there smiling in Abby's direction until a figure stepped from the trees and took her hand.

Abby swallowed hard in an effort to alleviate the pressure from the lump that had formed in her throat. Her father raised his hand in a wave, then turned with the girl and walked back into the depths of darkness. He was gone.

Abby stood there with hand raised and tears rolling down her cheeks and onto the window panes. It was as though the house was crying with her. When she was certain he was not going to return, she spun around and grabbed her cell phone. With shaking hands, she punched the number two.

Abby sat with her attorney, awaiting Tom.

"Are you sure this is what you want?" Robert Hudson asked her.

"Yes, I don't ever want to look at him again."

The door was open and her attorney indicated that he saw her husband coming. She had not talked to Tom since her return to the magazine. The image of *Success* was going to suffer greatly due to Ethan's connection with Tom. The damage could be irreparable. Abby was going to be faced with the decision of whether or not to continue with the publishing.

She had fiercely dreaded this day. It was going to be very difficult to keep her anger in check.

Tom had tried to contact her after the divorce papers had been served, but Abby refused all calls and avoided any personal contact. She was stunned that he had the nerve to even try to get to her. *Desperation can make you do anything*, she decided. The two of them entered the room and Mr. Hudson stood, inviting them to be seated. Abby smiled at Tom's attorney when introduced, but did not acknowledge Tom's presence. Had she given him her attention, she would have seen a thinner, more haggard and defeated man.

Abby's attorney passed two copies of the settlement papers across the table. Everyone was quiet while they scanned through them.

Tom's attorney said, "This leaves Mr. Cummings out in the cold. He worked with Langford Mill for more than six years and ran it without Mrs. Cummings for the last two to three years. He certainly deserves something for that."

Keeping her eyes on the forms, Abby said, "Donald kept everything together while Tom was busy using the company to stuff his own pockets. He's taken much more than he deserved already." Pointing to the papers, she stated sternly, "This is the way it's going to be."

"Then, the home should go to him with a decent monetary settlement," the attorney tried.

At that moment Abby looked up and into Tom's eyes. Speaking to Tom's attorney but keeping her gaze steadily on her husband she suggested, "Perhaps he can stay with his mistress and allow her to support him. That is, if the government doesn't provide him a home."

Without blinking, she now spoke to Tom. "You have two choices. You can sign these papers as they are and do it now to end this sham of a marriage. Also, I don't know where you have hidden the money that you took from the mill, but if you can get to it then I want you to make a donation to the Guardian Inn in Winston-Salem. Nothing less than a hundred thousand, if you have that much left after the Internal Revenue Service finishes with you. You do those two things and it's all over between us with no charges filed by me."

She turned to his attorney now and added, "Or, he can refuse, and I'll bring charges against him for fraud, embezzlement, defamation, alienation of affection and any and all other illegal activities that I can. Then, he definitely won't have to worry about where he'll be living for quite some time because I'll see that he's sent up the river so far, his ass will freeze sitting in an igloo at the North Pole!"

Looking at the attorneys, she added, "Excuse my French."

And now, turning her attention back to Tom, she said, "You don't do this now, and it's not going to be over between us until I see you in court. Between the Feds and me, you may never see the sun set again. What's it going to be?"

SIX YEARS LATER...

TODAY WAS A big day for Rafe. The Guardian Inn was going to be dedicated and Abby was frantic trying to get the family ready. The twins were dressed and that left only sweet two year-old Belle to chase down. It would have been easier if she had hired a sitter and left them at home, but she wanted them to be together as a family on this important day. She moved to the head of the stairs and called to her husband.

"Rafe, would you watch the boys until I get down there? I don't want them all disheveled when we leave."

"Sure thing," he replied. "Ralphie! Al! Where are you?"

THE END